FROST
BURN

ERICA STEVENS

Also from the Author

The Ravening Series

Ravenous (Book 1)

Taken Over (Book 2)

Reclamation (Book 3)

The Survivor Chronicles

Book 1: The Upheaval

Book 2: The Divide

Book 3: The Forsaken

Book 4: The Risen

Books written under the penname Brenda K. Davies

The Vampire Awakenings Series:

Awakened (Book 1)

Destined (Book 2)

Untamed (Book 3)

Enraptured (Book 4)

Undone (Book 5) Coming spring 2016

Historical Romance

A Stolen Heart

Special thanks to my husband
for understanding I can be a little crazy,
my mom for being such a strong force,
my siblings for being awesome,
and to my nieces and nephews.
Thank you

To all the fans who kept asking for Julian, and who kicked my butt into gear on a character I'd originally intended to kill in The Kindred Series but came to love.

I can't wait for everyone to get a chance to meet him and to develop him further. I really hope you like him!

To Leslie Mitchell at G2 Freelance Editing for all her hard work and encouragement. To Christina and Linda for their hard work and skills.

PROLOGUE

Fire and ice licked over her flesh. The fire was due to the pain lancing through her body from the knives driven through the palms of her hands and the one just beneath her sternum. It felt like the fire was consuming her, burying her within its raging depths, devouring her very soul. The ice, well the ice was from the weakness stealing through her and dousing the fire beneath it.

The sensations were so overwhelming and contradictory to each other that they briefly blocked out the shrill screams of those around her. Her *family*. Tears slid down her cheeks. She tugged at her hands, trying her hardest to free them, but the knives had been buried deep into the wood floor beneath her. Blood trickled down from the wound on her right temple and the slice down the center of her chin. Pinned down, she could only lay still as she helplessly listened to the dying cries of those she loved.

Like some kind of ghoulish painter throwing paint at a canvas, blood splashed across the family pictures hanging on the wall, and one of the many screams abruptly went silent. She had to get to her family, had to try and save them somehow. A scream of frustration and agony burned in her throat. The fire licked back over her body as she strained to tear her hands free of the knives. She tried to arch up in an attempt to dislodge the one in her stomach, but a wave of blackness washed over her, threatening to bury her within its depths. Panting heavily, she fell back on the floor. She couldn't pass out; it would be certain death if she did.

A tsking sound coming from her right caused her to turn her head in that direction. She blinked back the bloody tears and sweat clogging her lashes. "Such a shame." She shrank away from the hand brushing over her forehead. "Such a fighter."

A man's face loomed over her. A face she knew she'd remember for the rest of her life, which given her present circumstances might not be long. "Shh child," he murmured as he continued to brush her hair back. "It will all be over soon."

His blue green eyes swirled with malicious glee, his wide nostrils flared as he inhaled the scent of the blood pooling beneath her. The high arch of his cheekbones gave his face a rat-like appearance she found completely appropriate for this horrible monster. A mole at the corner of his left eye had a long, creepy hair curling from it. His thin lips pulled back to reveal his lengthy, razor sharp fangs.

A cry of protest escaped her, but she could do nothing to stop him from driving his fangs into her throat. More fire lanced over her skin as she fought against the monster pulling her blood from her body, even as the heat crept in so did the ice. Weakness slipped into her limbs, up through her belly and toward her chest.

She wasn't ready to die, not when she'd finally started to live, but just as she couldn't escape the knives pinning her body to the floor, she couldn't escape this monster feeding off of her in greedy, slurping pulls. The ice crept further up, dousing the fire beneath its crushing flow. She wasn't ready to give in, but she had no choice in the matter as her heart began to slow. It gave a dull beat before pausing for endless seconds then pumping again.

The monster above her pulled away and wiped the blood away from his mouth. "Delicious," he purred before rising to his feet and walking away.

It was only after he'd gone that she realized how quiet the room had become. *Her family.* She felt the overwhelming need to cry, but she didn't have the energy to muster a single tear. She could only stare at the blood-coated photos across from her as her breathing became shallower and her heartbeats further apart. The distant murmur of voices drifted to her, she couldn't make out their words as the ice slid up to her neck. The click of the door closing sounded abnormally loud in the hush, she realized the monsters had left but it didn't matter now. Nothing mattered anymore as the ice encompassed her, her heart finally stopped beating, and the world went black.

CHAPTER 1

"Has anyone ever told you how beautiful you are?"

Julian cocked an eyebrow at the question, he kept his eyes closed and his arms folded across his chest. He pretended not to be eavesdropping on the conversation going on near the back of the RV, but his ears were acutely attuned to it. Melissa *had* to see through that line, any woman with an ounce of commonsense would, but her small chuckle following the cliché question made him frown. It hadn't sounded like a condescending chuckle or even one trying to placate the ass who had uttered the line to begin with.

"Come on, let's look at that cut," Melissa said.

"Whatever you say darling," the ass drawled. His accent hinted at a Texas origin but they'd discovered him in southern California.

Julian's eyes rolled behind his lids when she giggled. His eyes flew open when he heard the door to the back bedroom close. Chris sat at the table across the way from him. His fingers shuffled with rapid grace through the deck of cards in his hands. Lou who was sitting opposite of Chris turned sideways in his seat to stare at the closed door Melissa and their newest recruit, Zach, had vanished behind.

Lou glanced over at him; a blush stained his fair cheeks when he caught Julian staring at him. He hastily turned back around and picked up the cards Chris had dealt him. "Sounds like Zach has some moves," Chris said as he gathered his cards from the table.

"Hopefully they move him out of this RV soon," Julian muttered.

Chris gave a small *hmm* sound. "I don't know, he might decide to stay on the road with us. I don't get any bad vibes off of him."

"It's cramped enough in this thing without adding wonder boy to the mix," Julian retorted, but he had to admit he'd seen nothing menacing in the guy when they'd shaken hands. His ability of psychometry had allowed him to flip through some of the images in Zach's mind. He'd been flooded with pictures of surfing, sand, drinking and women, but nothing hostile, at least nothing hostile committed by Zach's own hand. The vampires who had been trying to kill Zach when they'd stumbled across him were an entirely different ballgame and had been at the forefront of Zach's mind when they'd touched. "Never mind having Romeo waxing poetic every chance he gets. I might open the curtains up and let the sun beat on me if I have to listen to that from now on."

Chris grinned as he tossed down three cards and pulled three more from the deck. "There was a time I would have offered to do it for you."

There had been, and Julian bet there were times Chris would still like to do it, but over the past two years of traveling on the road together they'd developed a friendship most would consider odd. Just two years ago, they'd been mortal enemies and trying to kill each other, but then Hunters like Chris, Melissa, and lover boy out back had been trying to eliminate vampires like himself for centuries.

There were still times he'd like to drain Chris of every ounce of his blood, but those times had become fewer and farther between recently. It was no longer the promise he'd made to Cassie not to eat his roomies that kept him from killing Chris, but he'd actually come to like the guy enough to admit he'd miss him if he were dead. There weren't many people he could say that about and most of them were on this RV, minus smooth talking Zach in the back.

"It would be nice if at least one of us could have some kind of a dating life," Chris said. "This nomad lifestyle is seriously killing my sex life."

"What sex life?" Lou retorted.

"Exactly," Chris replied with a laugh. Throwing his cards on the table, he happily gathered his junk food winnings from the center of the table. Lou scowled at him as Chris popped a pretzel into his mouth and chewed on it. "Delicious."

Lou's thin lips pursed, his tawny brown eyes focused on the next cards Chris dealt him. The shaggy brown hair curling at the collar of his shirt had made more than a few teen girls swoon. Lou's growth spurt a year ago had caused him to become ganglier than when they'd first met, but his six-foot frame had finally begun to fill out when he'd turned eighteen last month.

Julian rose to his feet and stretched his back when Melissa's flirty giggle drifted from the back. Great, they'd moved on from chuckles to *that* girly sound. Chris leaned toward the aisle and stared at the closed door with a pursed mouth as he tried to stifle his laughter. "I don't think I've ever heard her flirt so openly before," Chris said.

"I definitely haven't." Lou placed a handful of Hershey Kisses into the center of the table.

Julian walked the five feet to the front of the RV. Leaning over the passenger seat, he pulled the curtain next to the window closed all the way around to block out part of the front windshield. Stepping around the seat he sat next to Luther, who was in the driver's seat, and propped his long legs up on the dash before him.

"Save me from the teenage angst," he muttered.

Luther shook his head. "You might have to save us all now that you've obstructed part of my view of the road with your curtain."

Julian cracked his knuckles. "Just stay in this lane."

"Thank you for the driving advice."

"You're welcome." As Luther eyed the curtains suspiciously, Julian knew now was one of those times when someone would like to pull the curtains open on him and watch him burn. A little giggle from the back set his teeth on edge. "Freaking Romeo and Juliet."

"You know they both died, right?" Luther inquired.

"I'm nearly six hundred years old; I've read some Shakespeare in my day." Luther gave him a doubtful look over top of his Lennon style glasses that had slid down to the middle of his hawkish nose. Over the past two years, Luther's salt and pepper hair had become more salt than pepper. The lines around his mouth and eyes hadn't been there when they'd first met, but his grey eyes were as astute as ever.

"I read the play, centuries before you were born." Julian dipped into the cooler between the seats and pulled a bag of blood out. He grabbed a straw from the top of the cooler, jabbed it into the bag and took a lengthy pull before lowering it to his lap. "I just prefer those newfangled motion picture thingies you humans went and invented, to books nowadays. Sometimes the human race is useful for something other than blood."

"Good to know," Lou commented dryly. He folded his arms over his chest as Chris happily confiscated the last of his chocolate kisses.

"If not Romeo and Juliet then maybe it's West Side Story back there," Julian said as he pulled at his straw. "Hopefully without all the singing."

"I know you're aware Tony died in that one," Luther said as he switched lanes on his side.

"It was a good ending," Julian replied and licked the blood from his lips.

"If I didn't know better I'd think you were jealous."

Julian laughed and dropped his feet down. "Only tired of horny men climbing onto this RV."

"You don't mind when it's a woman," Chris said.

"Of course not, but we haven't found one of those in a couple of months." They'd been traveling the country, through Mexico, South America, and Canada in search of more misplaced Hunters and Guardians, but they'd only found a dozen of them over the past couple of years. "Maybe it's time to stay in a town or motel for a couple of nights," he said with a pointed look at Luther. The man may be straighter than an arrow, but he had to have his own needs too and he *had* to let them blow off some steam sometimes. "We don't have any new leads and we're days away from home."

Home, the word still felt unbelievably strange to him, but he had one now. For the first time, in as long as he could remember, he actually had a home, even if he only saw it a combined month total out of the year. Every time they returned, they were greeted with open arms and warm smiles. If he ever decided he didn't want to search for the remaining Hunters and Guardians, he would be welcomed at the compound and allowed to build a life there.

He wasn't ready to settle down somewhere permanently yet, and not because Cassie and Devon were there, together, but because he still had a life to live and things yet to do. Cassie and Devon were content to be settled in together, and they deserved every bit of happiness they'd finally been afforded, but he wasn't ready to be in a place with little to no risk. He needed excitement; he *thrived* on it.

First things first though, he *had* to get out of this rolling house on wheels for a few nights to blow off some steam. They spent at least four nights a week in a hotel instead of the RV, but it had been at least three months since they'd taken any time off from searching for Hunters and Guardians. Right now they were returning to the compound to drop off the lothario in the back. A break for a few days wasn't out of the question.

"Good idea," Chris said. "I could definitely stretch my legs, have a couple of drinks…"

"You're not old enough," Luther cut in.

Chris shrugged. "Hasn't stopped me before."

Luther shot Julian a look. Julian smiled innocently back at him. "I don't see why he can't have a few when he could die any day now."

"Hey!" Chris protested.

"It's true, human," Julian replied.

9

"All it takes is one little accidental pull of the curtain."

"Won't kill me right away, not in this light."

Chris unwrapped another piece of candy and popped it into his mouth. "A stake would."

"You'd better be faster than you are now." Julian looked away before Chris could respond and focused on Luther. "You know you wouldn't mind a couple of days out of this thing too."

Luther's hands twisted on the wheel as he considered Julian's words. "I wouldn't," he admitted.

"We're all in agreement then!" Julian declared. "Now to stop somewhere with some excitement."

"And maybe a strip club," Chris suggested around a mouthful of chocolate.

Julian shook his head at the suggestion. He appreciated a naked woman just as much, if not more than the next guy, but he wasn't willing to pay to see it. "I'm going to stop at the next exit with a hotel and a place to eat," Luther said. "If there's something in the area then so be it, if not you still get three days to explore the desert."

"Every vampire's dream vacation," Julian muttered.

"We could keep driving," Luther replied.

Julian stared at him hard, even Chris gave him a venomous look. "No one has ever accused you of being the life of the party have they, Luther?" Julian inquired.

"At one time I was a lot of fun," Luther said.

Chris snorted. "Were dinosaurs still alive?"

Luther shot him a look in the rearview mirror, but Chris only continued to chew on his chocolate. Returning his attention to Julian, Luther jerked his head toward the back. "You're going to have to move if I'm going to take an exit."

Julian glanced at the darkening sky before tugging the curtain open. The faint rays of the fading sun fell across his skin. The heat burned into his flesh, but thankfully there was no smoke and his skin didn't blister. Over the past two years, he'd been exposing himself to the sun more and more with the hopes of one day being able to walk outside during the daylight hours like Devon could. It was a lengthy, excruciatingly painful process, but his tolerance to the sun's rays had begun to build. He could take the setting sun with no ill effect, and stand within full daylight for almost a minute before being forced to retreat.

Patience and his name had never been synonymous with each other, but being able to feel the heat of the sun against his skin again, without bursting into flames, made it all worthwhile. A smile tugged at the corners of his mouth as he turned his hand over before him. "You're getting better with that," Luther said as he took the next exit.

Julian nodded; it was difficult for him to take his eyes off the shafts of sun dancing in golden rays across his flesh. If he spent another six hundred years looking at this he still didn't think he'd ever get enough of it.

The heat of the sun vanished when it dipped behind the dunes of the sandy desert they drove through. He finally tore his attention away from his arm to the narrow roadway they were on. Wooden buildings and homes, most with chipped paint, lined both sides of the roadway. A handful of stucco and brick facades were tucked in amongst the wood; they added splashes of red, yellow and orange color to the roadside. The houses in this section of the town appeared as alive as King Tut right now. Upon closer inspection, he saw signs of life in the potted plants on the porches, the curtains lining the windows, and the vehicles in the driveways.

At a set of stoplights, Luther made a right and entered a livelier section of town. Lights spilled onto the roadway from a scattering of restaurants and stores lining the main thoroughfare. The side streets were mostly dark with a few lights shining from the windows of the homes. Behind the storefronts, he could see more of the reddish brown desert broken only by the cactuses, straggling grass cropping's and rock formations rising high into the air.

"What state are we in?" Julian inquired.

"Arizona," Luther answered.

Chris rose from the table and knelt on the sofa Julian had been sitting on. He pulled back the curtain behind the sofa to peer out at the night. "Tombstone?" he inquired.

"No," Luther answered.

"It would have been fitting." Chris dropped the curtain back into place and returned to his spot at the table.

Julian had to agree, but right now, he would take this town any day over staying in this vehicle. Luther drove past a larger bar with a grouping of motorcycles, pickups and cars filling its dirt parking lot. It looked like a promising place to start, Julian decided as Luther pulled into the motel only ten buildings away.

CHAPTER 2

Julian was still in the shower when he heard the door between the rooms open. There was a time when he would have killed anyone who dared to enter his room, but over the past two years he'd come to realize Chris didn't have many boundaries. If he'd locked the door, Chris would have stood outside, persistently knocking until Julian got out of the shower and flung it open with threats of ripping Chris's head off and playing beer pong with his eyes. Threats that would only make Chris smile in return and breeze into the room with the maddening confidence of someone who knew idle words when they heard them.

So in order to get in a relaxing shower, Julian had simply started unlocking the door between the rooms. The two of them always ended up bunking beside each other. Over the pounding water, he could clearly hear the click of the lock on the main door when Chris let

Lou in. He made out a few words of their murmured conversation before someone turned on the TV.

He scrubbed at his skin with the soap, rinsed the shampoo from his hair, and climbed out of the shower. Toweling off, he dressed hastily before exiting the steamy room. Chris and Lou barely glanced at him as they were both focused on a rerun of The League. The show was amusing but Julian walked over and hit the off button on the older model tube TV.

"I didn't escape the RV just to be stuck in this room with you two. Let's go Beavis and Butthead." Chris mumbled something unintelligible. He gave Julian the finger, but they both climbed to their feet. "Where's Melissa?"

"Taking a shower," Chris answered. "She said she'd meet us here."

"Is Romeo coming?"

"I don't know; I haven't seen him since the RV."

Julian nodded and led the way out of the room and into the cooling night. Even this far south, the edge of winter could still be felt in the air flowing over his exposed skin and wet hair. Tilting his head back, he stared at the stars in the seemingly endless sky. The full moon hung heavily above them; its glow illuminated the buildings and desert more than the few streetlights lining the roadway did.

"So glad we're not in Canada right now," he muttered and shoved his hands into his pockets to ward off the chill of the breeze.

"You are really cold blooded, dead boy," Chris said.

Julian's eyes narrowed on him. "I stopped being a boy long before I was turned into a vampire. Plus, I don't have a pulse to warm my body."

Chris's sapphire eyes focused on him. "True."

He may only be nineteen, but Chris had most certainly stopped being a boy already too. Julian wasn't sure exactly when it had happened but sometime between their final battle with The Elders and their search now for more Hunters and Guardians, Chris had matured far beyond his years.

The final battle with The Elders had aged them all, and decimated the hierarchy that had ruled the vampire race for most of the time he'd been one of the undead. The only two Elders still alive were he and Devon. Three years ago, he'd been more evil and twisted than most vampires. Now, he was the second oldest vampire in existence, one of the most powerful on earth, and he was working side by side with people he'd once considered his sworn enemies.

If someone had told him three years ago this is where he would be, and the company he'd be keeping, he would have laughed in their faces before ripping their throats out. He could clearly recall the vampire he'd been before meeting Cassie and her friends, but he felt no connection to his past self anymore. *That* vampire had died when he'd been held prisoner by The Commission with Cassie in that godforsaken basement beneath the school. The vampire who had emerged from there wasn't an angel, but he also wasn't a bloodthirsty monster determined to destroy Devon, the Hunters and Guardians, and any other unsuspecting soul who managed to piss him off. Over the years, he'd come to realize that if his kill ratio was any indication, he found many who walked this earth to be extremely irritating.

It had been two years since he'd consumed blood from a live human. A small part of him still believed he would return to it one day, but he knew he would never take an innocent life again. He didn't kill anymore because he was tormented by the atrocities he'd committed in his past, those deaths didn't haunt him. He'd quit because he'd finally figured out he didn't have to be a monster just because he was a vampire. When he'd first been turned, and throughout most of his lengthy existence, he hadn't understood he could be something other than a murderer. If he had, then he never would have snuffed out all of the countless lives he had over the years.

There were far too many years ahead of him to be weighed down by regret and sorrow for his past transgressions. He'd spent five hundred and seventy-four years as a killer after being turned into a vampire, and two years doing good. Since he planned to live at least another six hundred years, he figured he'd eventually even out his bad/good ratio and that was enough for him.

They reached the bar with the packed parking lot. Julian glanced at the large glass window in the front with the name, *Clint's Bar,* painted in white on it. Stepping back, he pulled open the door for Chris and Lou. The sour smell of stale alcohol, peanuts, pretzels, smoke, and body odor filled his nose; the sound of clanking pool balls echoed in his ears. He looked around for the pool tables, but the noise came from a room he couldn't see through the talking and laughing crowd.

Julian began to make his way through the people. Without knowing why, humans instinctively stepped out of his way when he approached them. He found most people to be about as sharp as a marble, however their instincts still recognized when a predator was near, and he wasn't the only one they stepped away from.

Chris may not have his murderous nature, but the power emanating from the boy caused humans to move away from him when he walked past. The vampire blood used to create the Hunter line Chris was a part of, was evident in the way he carried himself with an assurance and grace that pronounced him as more than human. Oddly enough, the power that initially pushed people away also drew them in like a bee to honey.

As a Guardian in training, Lou instructed future Hunters in fighting techniques and the history of the Hunter line. A Guardian was an integral part of the system. Unlike the Hunters, they were entirely human which allowed Lou to blend in seamlessly with the people in the bar.

Julian studied the people pressed close together. A third of the bar was dressed in leather and wearing vests with a motorcycle driving through flames stitched on the back of them, a third were wearing cowboy hats and boots, and the final third were dressed in plain clothes. More than a few of the patrons had the darker skin, brown eyes, and broad cheekbones inherent in some-one with a Mexican or Native American heritage.

The ages in the bar ranged from barely legal, if they were even legal to begin with, to some in their sixties and possibly seventies and eighties. The oddly diverse crowd mingled together with ease, apparently they were used to being together in here. His gaze scanned the women within as he hunted his prey for the night. He may not taste their blood anymore, but humans did serve other purposes. Beside him, Chris was doing the same thing as he rose onto his toes.

"Drinks," Julian said and gestured toward the bar.

Chris followed him, Lou tagged along behind with his hands shoved into his pockets and his shoulders hunched up against the bodies around them. He looked even thinner in the mass of middle-aged beer bellies and twenty-something biceps. Julian stopped walking and waited for Lou to catch up so he could let him walk ahead before he got lost in the crush.

Arriving at the bar, Julian leaned over the top and flashed his smile at the young redhead pouring beer. Her mouth dropped open when her eyes landed on him; the beer flowing from the tap overfilled the glass. She jumped when the cool liquid poured over her fingers. Hastily she grabbed hold of the beer tap and turned it off.

Julian couldn't help but grin when the eyes of the men gathered around the bar swung toward him. He didn't acknowledge them as he gave the redhead their order. She hurriedly filled it and came back with their drinks. Handing the beer out to him, her fingers slid invitingly over the back of his hand when he took it from her. The wink he gave her caused her cheeks to become the color of her hair. She was pretty enough to be an option for later, he decided, but there were a lot of other options in this bar as well, too many for him to be tied down already.

He handed Chris and Lou their beers. If he ordered their drinks for them, it was rare either of them got carded, no matter how young Lou looked. They risked their lives on a daily basis to protect the human race without people knowing they did it. For that, Julian figured human law didn't apply to them.

Turning away, he pointed toward the back room where the pool tables were located. They were almost there when he spotted Melissa gliding across the floor toward them. Last month she'd cut her shiny black hair into a sleek bob beneath her ears. The shortened haircut enhanced her high cheekbones and made her appear at least five years older than her nineteen years. Her smooth olive skin and onyx eyes were due to her half Egyptian heritage, but her grace and poise came from her Hunter legacy. The pretty young girl he'd met two years ago had been replaced by a beautiful woman who caused heads to turn as she walked by.

"Beer?" he inquired when she stopped before them. He held out the bottle he'd yet to take a sip from.

Her black eyebrows drew together; she pursed her full mouth before shaking her head. "I feel like something girly tonight."

"That's a first."

She flashed a smile before lifting a shoulder. "Sometimes I like to mix it up."

"So I've noticed. You need me to get it for you?" In response, she gestured toward the bar. Julian spotted Zach leaning over the counter talking with the redhead who nodded before turning away. "Ah, Romeo," he drawled.

Melissa rolled her eyes and grabbed the bottle of beer from his hand. She took a long swallow before handing it back. Julian scowled at his half-empty beer while she spoke. "He heard you call him that."

"And?"

"He didn't like it." She was trying to sound disapproving, but her lips twitched as she had a difficult time hiding her smile.

"That makes a whole world of difference."

"You're going to torment him aren't you?"

"It is what I do best."

"Very true," Chris agreed.

"What ability does he have?" Julian inquired. He drank the rest of his beer and handed it to a passing waitress with an order for another one.

"He can control air," Melissa answered.

"Air?" Lou inquired. "Haven't heard of that one before."

"You should hit the books more," Julian said and took his fresh beer from the brunette waitress. "All of the elements can be manipulated by certain vampires and Hunters; we just haven't come across a Current yet."

Chris looked questioningly at him. "Current?"

"As in air current," Julian said. "It's what those who can control air are called."

"I see."

"It's an interesting and useful ability to have. How strong is he?" Julian turned his attention back to Melissa.

"He said he can create hurricane-like conditions for short bursts of time and once made a five foot high tornado," she answered. "But he may have been exaggerating."

Julian chuckled as his gaze ran over Melissa's striking face and lithe figure. Romeo had been telling the truth when he'd said she was beautiful. Beautiful enough to make a man exaggerate many things in order to impress her. "I'm sure he was, but we'll find out eventually."

"A new power for Cassie's growing collection of abilities at least," Lou said.

Julian shifted his feet as his gaze slid back to Zach. Yes, it was a power they hadn't come across before, but then there weren't many Hunters and Guardians left. The Slaughter that The Elder vampires had unleashed upon the Hunters and Guardians eighteen years ago had left their numbers decimated and scattered.

Zach turned and easily wound his way through the crowd with two pink drinks in hand. Julian stepped away from Melissa and continued toward the poolroom. Walking through the door of the poolroom, an interesting scent caused his eyes to shoot to a woman in the back of the room. She had a notepad in hand while she took the order of a group of men in their thirties wearing cowboy hats. She never glanced their way, but he knew she was aware of their presence, or at least *his*, by the subtle stiffening of her shoulders.

Julian's nostrils flared, the scent emanating from the woman filled his senses. Stepping away from one of the men, she tucked her pad away before turning toward him and his friends. Across the fifty feet separating them his gaze locked onto a set of eyes the color of honey. Unlike the food they resembled, there was nothing sweet in these eyes as they glittered with menace.

"Is that..." Zach started.

"Yes," Julian grated from between his clamped teeth.

The woman thrust out her pointed chin before making her way through the crowd toward them. Hair the color of chocolate glimmered in the neon signs on the walls and the fluorescent lights hanging over the two pool tables in the room. The end of her hair hung to the middle of her back and swayed with every step she took toward them. He couldn't tear his eyes away from the fire in her slanted eyes and the high slope of her elegant cheekbones. A faint, reddish scar ran from the middle of her full bottom lip to under her chin. Another scar ran from the end of her right eyebrow toward her right temple where it disappeared beneath her thick hair. The hair on her eyebrow, where the scar cut across, no longer grew in. They were injuries that must have been sustained when she'd still been human if they hadn't completely healed.

Her gaze darted briefly around the room before coming back to him. The doorway they stood in was the only escape from this room, unless she planned to go straight through the wall, but judging by the apron tied around her waist and the cheerful greetings directed toward her, he didn't think she'd be running anywhere. She'd established a life and an identity here that allowed her to blend in with the humans. Something she most certainly was not.

Her lithe, athletic body flowed effortlessly across the ground. She wasn't an Elder and he didn't get the impression she was all that old, but he did get the impression of extraordinary power. So much so that it caused his skin to crackle. She was young, he knew it, but the closer she got the more his skin felt electrified by the waves of power radiating from her.

She was a disconcerting puzzle, one he meant to figure out. However, if he knew one thing about his kind, it was that they weren't much for talking, especially when their lives were on the line. As she neared, he moved to stand protectively in front of Chris and Melissa. They were perfectly capable of taking care of themselves, but something about this vampire threw him off.

Distrust shone in her eyes, her shoulders were set in such a way as to indicate she was prepared to launch at him if he made a move toward her. It wasn't something he planned on doing, but when she stepped equal with him, he found his hand irresistibly drawn to her arm.

Heat sizzled through him when his fingers connected with her bare flesh. But even as his body heated and reacted to her, a strange sucking sensation gripped him. It felt as if the energy, the very *life* drained from him as all of his cells seemed to crash into his hand before being pulled from him and into *her*. Held immobile by the grip she had over him, he could only stand

and stare at her as their supernatural abilities mingled together.

Blood, death and brutality flooded his mind as images of her life bombarded him. Screams of agony and terror resonated within his skull. Faces of people he didn't know flashed like picture cards through his mind. Their expressions were twisted in suffering; blood streamed from their torn throats and splattered the pictures hanging on the walls. Those pictures contained a beautiful, smiling family, the same family who was dying before him in his mind.

There had been a time when he would have savored memories such as these, gotten off on them and craved more, however that time had passed. Now he would have pulled away from someone before he saw this much, but he was entangled in whatever hold she had over him and couldn't break free.

A jolt of something hit him so forcefully it knocked him back a good three feet. Coming up against the wall, he inhaled a deep breath before recalling he hadn't needed air to breathe in centuries. Across from him, her honeyed eyes were hooded as she stared at him. She'd adjusted her stance, prepared to defend herself if he should attack her.

He remained against the wall as he watched her. If he'd been human the jolt would have killed him, but she hadn't been the cause of the violent images that had flooded his mind. No, she'd been one of the children in the smiling family photo hanging on the wall.

Julian grabbed hold of Chris's arm when he took a step toward her. "No," he cautioned in a low voice.

The girl across from them took a step away and turned on her heel. Julian watched as she walked to the bar and placed her order.

"What did she do to you?" Melissa bit on her bottom lip as her eyes rapidly scanned over him.

"I'm not sure," Julian murmured. "But we're going to have a talk with her."

"Is she a threat to us?" Chris asked.

"She's definitely lethal."

CHAPTER 3

Quinn tried to keep her hands steady as she loaded the drinks onto the tray, but she couldn't stop the shaking. Her gaze was irresistibly drawn toward the strange group gathered near the doorway of the pool-room. *What is a vampire doing with a bunch of humans?* She pondered as she dropped a bowl of pretzels onto the tray.

Humans who knew exactly what she was and what *he* was. She'd heard their whispered words to each other and could feel their inquisitive gazes burning into her flesh. Staring at them, she began to wonder if they were something more than human?

But it was impossible. No vampire would be with a group of Hunters, and no Hunters would be with a vampire. They'd be fighting to the death if they ever encountered each other, not standing in the doorway of a bar sharing drinks as if it were just a night out with friends. Unless they planned on breaking their bottles and going to war in the next few seconds, but she didn't get that vibe from them. They were all extremely at ease as they stood close to one another.

Her gaze went back to the stunning vampire with them. Other than her, most of the vampires she knew were vicious, murdering bastards, however he stood amongst a group of humans as easily as if he were one. The distinct lack of a heartbeat, and the vibe of power radiating from him, was more than enough to indicate he was anything but human. He was also far more powerful than she was. The small blast she had given him would have been enough to knock out a weaker vampire, it seemed to have barely fazed him.

What was she going to do?

This was her home; she'd established a base here. She'd blended in with the humans and made a few friends. When she'd first arrived in this town, she'd been determined to keep her distance from the locals. She'd lost enough people she'd cared about over the years and wasn't willing to have her heart crushed again by losing even more.

She hadn't planned to stay here for more than a month or two. That had been her standard amount of time in any one place over the last three years, but once here, she'd found it impossible to resist some of the friendly people she'd met. They'd been determined to get to know her better, to wedge their way into her life. No one, no matter how close she'd gotten to them, knew the most pertinent details of her life, but they were her friends.

This town had become the home she'd believed forever stolen from her. She could hide here while she searched for and trained to fight the monsters who had destroyed her and her family. She'd only run into a dozen vampires in the three years since she'd moved here, but they'd all been weaker and younger than her, and easily dispatched.

One of them had even been like her and had only been looking to pass through without incident. She'd spoken with the woman before they'd gone their separate ways.

Aside from that woman, those other vampires had been the complete opposite of the man standing across from her now. She didn't know who or what they all were, but she was certain their presence here was about to turn her orderly life completely upside down.

Get it together, she told herself as she lifted the tray from the bar. She had to walk back by them to deliver her order. Inside she felt like a mass of loose live wires tossed in a storm, but she kept her shoulders back, her chin out and her eyes on the dominant vamp. His presence seemed to take up the entire eight foot wide doorway as he leaned against the frame with his muscular arms folded over his chest.

"Don't touch her," he said in a low whisper to the others.

It eased her a little to realize he wouldn't try to pounce on her, however she wasn't fooled into thinking he couldn't kill her. She recognized a vampire who was older and stronger than her when she came across one. She may be young, but she wasn't a fool.

Those icy blue eyes followed her every step as she approached him, the white band encircling his pupil expanded as she neared. The waves of power emanating from him made her fingers tingle with the urge to touch him and taste a little bit of his power again. Most of the time she could keep her ability under control, but he was a temptation the likes of which she'd never come across before.

Setting her jaw, she fought back the urge to reach out and absorb some of him again; she'd be wading into extremely dangerous territories by doing so though. Out of control, her ability was lethal, and it would swallow her whole if she allowed herself to become lost to it. She feared the dark, sucking lure of her ability more than she feared her thirst for blood.

He shifted protectively closer to the humans around him. He was the most magnificent man she'd ever seen with his vivid eyes, chiseled face, and large, well-muscled body. Cut short, his white blond hair emphasized the angles of his broad cheekbones and square jaw. The nearly white of his hair was a startling contrast to his black eyebrows and the shadow creeping across his jawline and over his cheeks.

If she hadn't been so thrown off by his presence here, she might have actually been a little dazzled by his looks. Now all she wanted to do was tug her stake free of her boot and whip it at his heart. She had no doubt he could avoid the stake, but it would give her a chance to rush him before he knew what she planned.

Such an action would also put everyone else in this place in peril, and alert everyone to the reality that their nightmares actually walked the earth. Her fingers itched to grab her stake, she kept moving forward to deliver her drinks. Her stride remained steady when she moved past them and on toward the cowboys in the back corner.

When one of them grabbed her ass, she smacked his hand away and forced a flirtatious smile, he smiled back at her before she made her way out of the room. What she really would have liked to do was drive her fist into his hooked nose. That would be a big mistake though, she may not have to be concerned about aging and death, but she did have to pay her bills and her meager tips were the only thing helping her do that. Punching the customers was a sure fire way to end up living on the street.

Throughout the rest of the night, she watched the new group in the poolroom with the same intensity as they watched her. She had no idea what would happen when the bar closed, she didn't see this group walking away from her though. Her body tingled with the adrenaline coursing through her and the realization this night could end up in a battle to the death. One she might not walk away from but was more than prepared to wage.

"That guy is hot." Angie rested her hands on the bar and leaned over the top of it to announce this to her. Angie's feet kicked in the air as she spoke, her hazel eyes twinkled mischievously; Quinn detected the elevated beat of her heart as her gaze turned toward the poolroom. Quinn didn't have to look up to know whom she was talking about. "Like I'd take him out back and do him right now, kinda hot."

Quinn had no doubt Angie would do just that, but she bit her tongue to keep from retorting that it wouldn't be the first time. Three years ago, Angie had been in a relationship with the love of her life, Seanix. The two of them had been together since they were toddlers. When Quinn first met them they'd been inseparable and even finished each other's sentences. It had been an annoying trait, but one she'd found cute and endearing. Their wedding date had been set for the following year.

Then Seanix had lost his job at the factory in the neighboring town and decided to get his license to drive trucks. Two years ago, he'd gone out on a run to Atlanta and never returned. He'd texted once since he'd left to tell Angie he'd met someone else and Angie should move on.

For the first year after, Angie walked around in a stupor, cried more than she spoke, and looked as if she'd just rolled out of bed and grabbed whatever clothes she found lying around. Most days she'd smelled and looked like she hadn't taken a shower. Clint, the owner of the bar, had at first been understanding of Angie's plight, but when the customers started to complain about the poor service, the weeping over their beers, and her unfortunate odor, he'd stepped in to put a stop to it.

Quinn had gone with him to Angie's small apartment. They'd discovered Angie living in a room full of empty food containers, scattered clothes, and discarded tissues. After giving the apartment a good scrubbing, Clint sat down to tell Angie she had to pull it together or he would have to let her go. He hadn't been cruel when he'd said it, but none of them knew what to do to help get her through her misery. Her job and her friends from the bar were all Angie had left, and Clint had hoped the threat of losing them too would get through to her. It hadn't happened over night, but over the following weeks, Angie's smell improved, her hair began to shine again, and she started to smile once more.

Then, she'd done a complete one-eighty and become a vivacious woman who was always on the prowl for a party, and a man. Quinn knew Angie was still heartbroken and trying to figure out a way to ease her suffering, but she worried about Angie getting mixed up with the wrong guy. The prime example of that would be the vampire Angie was eyeing up right now. She'd tried to talk to Angie about her grief multiple times, but Angie refused to speak about Seanix any more.

If Angie tried to get entangled with this guy, Quinn would tie her friend to a chair until she realized Seanix was a jerk that was better off forgotten and she was better off without him. She would do what she needed to do until she knew her friend would be safe from the vamp while this crew remained in town.

Quinn poured a couple of beers from the tap and slid them onto the tray. "Seriously Quinn…"

"I know, he's hot," Quinn agreed before Angie went into a full on tirade about the vampire's many attributes.

"With the way he's been watching you all night, you should go for him," Angie said excitedly. A rosy hue began to creep into Angie's round cheeks; her eyes sparkled in a way that made Quinn shift her feet uncomfortably. It wasn't often Angie tried to play matchmaker; she was too busy making her own matches to worry about Quinn's lack of boyfriends, but when she did she was like a pesky mosquito at a bar-b-que.

"He's not my type," Quinn said and grabbed a bottled beer from the cooler.

"*No* one is your type."

"Not all of us can like them all." Quinn smiled at her friend in order to ease her harsh words. She shouldn't have said that to her, she knew what Angie had gone through, but his presence here had made her edgy and short tempered. She supposed she had a right to be edgy; there was a chance she might die tonight, for good this time. But she didn't have a right to be rude to her friend. "Sorry."

Angie dismissively waved her hand. "I can't help it if my type is breathing." Angie grinned at her before hopping off the bar.

Quinn's gaze slid back toward the imposing stranger holding a pool stick and talking with the beautiful black haired woman at his side. Perhaps he actually wouldn't be Angie's type, as he most certainly wasn't breathing anymore.

"I'm definitely breathing, honey," the middle-aged biker next to Angie said. He slapped Angie on her ass when she shook it at him.

Angie laughed and tossed her hair over her shoulder. "You might not be by the time I'm done with you."

The biker and his friends laughed loudly, Angie bounced away into the crowd. Quinn finished filling her order and carried the tray into the poolroom. The clanking of the pool balls grated on her hypersensitive hearing. She tuned them out as she handed the drinks over to a group of younger guys who commuted to college over in Yuma. None of them looked old enough to be drinking, but she knew they were all of age as they'd become regulars here last year when they'd turned twenty-one.

"You looking for some company tonight?" one of them asked her.

"Not tonight handsome," she replied.

The response was so automatic she was already turning away when she answered him. One thing that completely sucked about being a vampire in a bar was the never-ending stream of sexual propositions she had to fend off. The only good thing was she could kick the ass of any guy who got a little out of hand and had already done so on one occasion.

She wasn't expecting it when the kid grabbed hold of her arm and spun her around. One of the bottles on the tray slid to the side. It almost flew off but her hand shot out, she snagged it out of the air before it could smash to the ground. A ripple of anger slid down her spine. She struggled to keep her fangs leashed and her eyes from changing.

Turning back to the kid, she directed the power within her to the place on her arm where his hand held her tight. He yelped and with the speediness of a cat landing on a hot stove, jerked his hand away. He shook his hand before raising it in front of him and then looking toward her. "Winter. Static electricity," she said with a smile. "It sucks."

His forehead remained furrowed in confusion; he shook his hand again. "Yeah, it does," he muttered.

Feeling more than a little pleased with herself, she turned away and came up against a broad chest. She almost stomped her foot in frustration; she'd just gotten rid of one pest to come face to face with another. Except this one wouldn't be thrown off by a little jolt.

Her eyes slid up his solid chest, a chest alluringly enhanced by the fitted black t-shirt he wore. On the etched muscle of his right bicep was the tattoo of a weeping angel. Done entirely in black ink, the angel's wings were hidden beneath the sleeve of his shirt but appeared to stretch to his shoulder. She'd bet anything this man could easily make the angels weep and probably had more than a few times in his life.

She should be concerned about her safety around this man; vampires had been her enemy since birth. However, this one did strange things to her. He completely threw her off her game, but more than that, he was the first one she'd ever encountered who made her feel as if her heart were actually beating again. It was one of the things she missed the most about being human, the simple reassuring thump of the vital organ filling her with life.

He was also the first one she'd encountered who could probably kill her and most likely would when he found out what she really was. With that reminder digging its way into her brain, she forgot all about those spectacular eyes burning into hers.

"Excuse me," she said in a clipped tone.

The corner of his mouth quirked in what could have been amusement, but it was too fleeting to tell for sure. He stepped away from her, and she hurried from the room. She hated the eyes she felt burning into her back with every step she took. It was going to be an endless night.

CHAPTER 4

Quinn polished another glass and slid it onto the rack over her head. "Come on Quinn, no one has done that in fifteen years," Angie complained as she dropped a case of beer on top of the bar.

"All the more reason to do it now," Quinn said and slid the next glass into place.

It was a ridiculous thing to do, no matter how much time she took, she would have to leave here eventually, and she suspected the strange group would still be lurking outside, waiting for her. She didn't like the idea of fighting with them, she didn't harm humans, and she sure didn't want to tangle with *that* man. She hadn't given him the full force of her power earlier, but unlike the other vampires she'd killed with it, she had a feeling he would still be standing if she did completely latch onto him.

Ugh, she'd never been a chicken before; however, there was something entirely off putting about him. She hated this cowardice, but even as she cursed it, she began to polish another glass while Angie restocked the cooler.

"This is what happens when you never get laid," Angie muttered.

Quinn shot her a look, but she didn't offer up a witty retort. Angie didn't know anything about her history, they were friends, but Quinn would never reveal that to anyone. They'd run screaming from her if they ever knew the truth. She slid another glass onto the rack over her head as a knock sounded on the front door.

"We're closed!" she called out. "Did you remember to lock it?"

Angie paused with two bottles of beer in her hand. "I don't remember."

"Angie," she moaned.

"Hey, if you hadn't decided to turn into Mrs. Clean we could have been out of here by now."

Angie's point was good enough to suppress any further complaints from Quinn. "I'll make sure it's locked," she said as she dropped her rag on the bar and walked around the end of it toward the door.

Through the window of glass on the front door, she could see the hulking figure of someone huddled within their jacket. Her hands went to her apron pocket; she tugged her keys free as she caught a whiff of something more than human outside the door. Power wafted from whoever stood out there. The scent of it reminded her of cayenne peppers, potent yet almost pleasant. It had the strange effect of pricking her hunger and causing her fangs to tingle.

She fought constantly against her volatile and lethal nature, but she couldn't deny that the power right outside the doors was nearly as enticing to her ability as the human blood she denied herself every day. It wasn't as potent as it had been from the vampire who had been here earlier. She may be able to take this one in a fight, but not in front of Angie.

The doorknob began to rattle when she was half-way across the bar. "We're closed!" she called out again but she knew, before she took another step, it didn't matter.

She slid her keys back into her pocket and rested her hand on the small wooden stake she kept tucked into a holder against her waist. The black shorts she wore were part of her uniform but they hid her weapons well, as did the nearly knee high black boots she wore.

She hoped to avoid having to stake the vampire in front of Angie, but she might not have a choice. The knob on the door turned, then it thrust open forcefully. Her gaze locked onto a pair of surprisingly beautiful turquoise eyes; however, all attractiveness about the man standing across from her ended there. His hawkish nose was over large and crooked to the side, his eyebrows so bushy they had become a solid unibrow. His thin lips pressed into a disapproving frown she suspected might be permanent.

His lips pulled back to reveal his glistening fangs, eliminating any doubt she might have had as to why he was here. Judging by the power radiating from him, he was older than her. She had no idea what ability he had, but then he was just as clueless about what she could do too. He'd come here thinking he would win an easy battle with a younger vamp, but he'd encountered a war.

"We're closed mister," Angie said from behind the bar.

His gaze didn't even flicker toward her. The glass bottles Angie placed into the cooler clattered together, it was the only sound in the hushed room. Quinn's fingers tingled, she had to keep this guy away from her friend, and keep Angie from witnessing something that would alter her life forever and thrust her existence into jeopardy.

"It's ok, Ang. This is an, ah, old friend of mine," she lied and badly.

Angie gave a small snort but all noise behind Quinn ceased when Angie stopped moving. In the three years Quinn had been working here, she'd never once said she knew a person or mentioned a friend. The only thing she'd revealed about her past was to say her family had been killed in a car accident and she liked to move around.

One revelation was a lie, and the other one a half-truth. Before coming here, she'd moved around a lot but because she had to, not because she liked it. She'd hated living out of a box from one town to the next and one crappy apartment to the next, but there were no other options, not for her.

"You can take off, Angie. I'll finish up here," she said. She tugged the stake free of its holder and palmed it as she continued to smile at unibrow. "We have some ah… catching up to do."

"Are you sure?" She'd expected Angie to bolt out of here like an Olympic runner off the line, but she heard the concern in her friend's voice.

"Yeah it's fine." She didn't dare tear her gaze away from the vamp across from her to look at Angie. "I'll see you tomorrow."

A small huff of laughter escaped the vampire as his gaze traveled to Angie. His deep brown hair glimmered in the few lights left on in the bar. Tall and thin, he didn't look like much; she knew how deceptive appearances could be when it came to the vampire world though. "You could always join us." His tone of voice made her skin crawl.

"We have far too much catching up to do," Quinn replied.

"Are you sure you're going to be ok, Quinn?" Angie inquired.

"I'll be fine." *And if not I simply won't see you tomorrow*, she thought but kept the forced smile on her face.

"Ok then, have a good night."

The material of Angie's apron whispered when she dropped it on the bar. Her friend fluffed her hair as she walked toward them. "Maybe I can find the after party," she said brightly.

"I'm sure you can," Quinn assured her.

Angie flashed her a smile as she made her way out the door and closed it behind her. In the hush that descended over the bar, Quinn could hear the hum of the motors in the coolers behind the bar and the distant tick of the clock in the poolroom. The ticks of the seconds continued onward until the hush stretched into a full minute.

"You're young," he finally said. It was faint but she detected the hint of an Irish brogue in his tone.

Quinn gave a brief bow of her head as she gripped the stake tighter and braced her legs apart. She'd been knocked on her ass once before by a vampire who could wield electricity, but she was prepared for that now. If he was capable of wielding electricity he might give her a shock, but it wouldn't launch her across the room like last time.

Quinn had no words for him. He tried to lift one eyebrow, because they were attached both of them went up. "But you're powerful. Where does so much power come from I wonder?" The question was about her, but it hadn't been directed at her. She could practically see the wheels turning in his mind as he tried to figure out what she was. That would never happen. No vampire could ever predict or think it possible to come across the likes of her. "How many people have you killed in your short life?"

"I'm not a killer," she growled.

He held his hands out before him. "We're all killers, child."

"Not all of us," she murmured.

"Is that what you tell yourself to sleep at night? You *are* a killer."

An unsettling feeling began to twist inside her stomach. Vampires spouted lies; she knew. By nature, every vampire was a liar, including herself. They were forced to hide from the day, forced to fit into a human world where they would be killed if people ever knew what they were. Every day she pretended she wasn't a monster, but no matter how much she pretended, she knew the truth. She drank blood, the sun had shunned her when she'd died, and if any human ever learned the truth about her they would leave a person-sized hole in the wall when they fled from her.

She may not sustain her existence by the senseless murdering of random humans, but she *was* a monster. She awoke with that realization every day and went to sleep with it every night.

"I don't kill innocents," she told him.

"Who are you to judge what others do?"

Quinn put more of her weight into her toes so she could react faster. "I don't judge; I simply know the difference between right and wrong."

"Ah such a foolish child," he murmured. "You will learn. Passing by, we sensed you from outside." *We?*

The word caused the hair on her neck to rise. "I'm here because you would be better off with a group of vampires than on your own, especially now that we've all been left so vulnerable by the death of The Elders. Something that also left *you* vulnerable."

"I don't give a rat's ass about vampire politics."

"You should," he purred as he folded his hands into the sleeves of the loose fitting shirt he wore. It was a gesture meant to make him appear less intimidating; she wasn't fooled by it. He would be on her in a heartbeat if she let her guard down. "The oldest of the remaining vampires are beginning to regroup. We're trying to regain the power stripped from us by The Commission, Hunters and Guardians so we can protect ourselves from them."

"The Commission is also on the run," she murmured. "I've heard the rumors."

"What is left of them is, but those maniacs were never our biggest concern. They were humans playing God, but the Hunters and Guardians are creating a new force. One bent on destroying every vampire they come across."

"That's always been their mission," she couldn't help but say, despite her determination not to believe one word this man uttered.

"But they've grown stronger and more hostile now."

Quinn pondered his words before responding. "I'm sure they are but I can't help you. I only have six vampire years on me; nowhere near enough to be considered an Elder. Sorry you wasted your time coming in here."

"You could never be a waste of my time, child. Every vampire is special, and they should all be brought into the fold."

He sounded like the leader of a cult, one she wanted nothing to do with. "I'm not a *fold* kind of girl."

That irritating smile curved his mouth again to reveal his fangs. "You think you have some kind of choice in this. Your power drew me here, others may not pick up on it, but I did."

"I guess I'm just special." She took a step away from him in order to get as much distance between them as possible in case he tried to electrocute her.

"Yes." The way he purred the word made it one of the creepiest things she'd ever heard. "Yes, you are."

Over the tick of the clock and the hum of the cooler, she heard a board squeak in the kitchen. She stiffened as she realized the '*we*' he spoke of a moment ago had arrived through the backdoor. One of the kitchen doors swung open and the first of five more vamps stepped into the main barroom.

They wanted her alive, but what they wanted her alive for, and what they might force her to do, was more than enough for her to decide she'd prefer to be dead. Jerking her arm back, she let her stake fly with deadly accuracy at the first vamp who had walked through the swinging door.

She had no shot of hitting the one she'd been speaking with, but these five weren't completely prepared for her. They would be now as the stake found its intended target and the vampire let out a howl. The stricken vamp fell back, his fingers grasped frantically at the stake embedded deep within his heart. Even if he pulled it free, it was too late for him; his life was over.

Without missing a step, she bent low and tugged the two remaining stakes from her boots. She wouldn't be able to throw these, but if they got close enough to her she would make them rethink ever trying to touch her again. She rose back to her full height just as one of the others tossed aside their dead friend and hefted a barstool over his head. Quinn spun away from the chair hurtled at her with so much speed it was mostly a blur even to her enhanced vision.

Her deft movement kept her from taking a direct hit, but she was unable to avoid the stool completely. It felt as if the leg of the stool had actually crashed straight into her bone instead of a layer of her muscle, fat and skin first. A small grunt escaped her; the force of the stool caused her to stagger forward a few steps.

She regained her balance quickly, but not quick enough to escape the grabbing hands of a burly vampire. What would have been considered a beer gut if he were human hung over his belt, but this was most likely a blood gut.

He jerked her toward him with one, harsh tug. Adrenaline and her instinctual need to survive caused her ability to kick in of its own volition, with far more deadly ferocity than she was used to. The sensation of tentacles, or perhaps suckers, shooting from her body to grab hold of his hand filled her. She didn't actually grow tentacles, but she'd always pictured her power like an octopus grabbing hold of someone while the suction cups drained them of their life force.

His chipmunk cheeks shrank, his ruddy skin took on a grayish hue, and all of the color leached from his face. A startled cry of agony escaped him. She could feel him trying to jerk his hand away, but once the tentacles took hold they were impossible to break free from until she released them.

Blood Gut's brown eyes bulged, his mouth hung open in disbelief as he continued to shrink in size. The whites of his eyes were yellow when they rolled back into his head. His now ninety-pound, saggy body dropped to the floor like a crumpled skeleton. It had been six years since she'd required air to breathe, but she still found herself gasping for breath when he finally fell away from her.

She bent over, shaking as she fought the influx of power surging through her body. Her ability had been weakened by the interaction, but his life force kicked around in her body like a ghost in a haunted house. This unsettled and jumpy feeling inside of her was one of the many reasons she tried not to completely drain the life force from someone.

A little snap to get them to let go, or to ensnare them for a few seconds within her trap was usually enough time for her to be able to stake them or warn them off. But she was outnumbered now with only two stakes left on her. Her best option had been to show them what she could do, hope they stayed back afterward, and that they didn't suspect her power had been drained by the interaction. If they were looking to kill her this would have been an entirely different scenario, but thankfully this group meant to keep her alive, for now.

She had enough power left in her to give one more of them a good blast, but from the looks on their faces, she didn't think they were going to take one step closer to her. They stared at her with gaping mouths and bugged out eyes. The only one who didn't look about to turn and run was the first one who had entered. The smile on his face brought to mind a praying mantis hunched over its prey.

"It's *you*." Out of everything she'd expected to come from his mouth, those words were the farthest from her mind. "We've been looking all over for you. This worked out much better than I'd ever anticipated."

Her head spun as she tried to process his words. "Who's been looking all over for me?"

He didn't get a chance to respond as another sound drew her attention around the corner of the poolroom and to the kitchen doors. The blond vampire from earlier and the humans gathered around him stood behind the other vampires. The human's gazes were riveted upon the sack of skin and bones lying at her feet. The blond vampire and an older man with glasses were the only ones looking at *her*. The human looked completely fascinated as his gaze ran over her.

It didn't matter what they thought of her; her eyes remained locked upon the assessing ice blue eyes of the vampire she'd interacted with earlier. He knew what she could do now, knew a little of what she'd done to him earlier, but instead of looking infuriated, fascinated or even slightly terrified, a smile began to curve the corner of his full mouth.

CHAPTER 5

Julian stared at the emaciated remains of the vampire lying on the ground in front of her. He'd never seen anything like it, never known a power like that existed, but it had been one of the most amazing and disconcerting things he'd ever witnessed. He couldn't help but smile as he met her dilated golden eyes. He didn't know what to make of her, but she seemed more on their side than most of the vampires they came across.

She most likely wouldn't be able to drain the life force from him. However, he knew what it was like to be ensnared within her trap and realized now she could have chosen to do a lot more damage to him than she actually had. Figuring out exactly where she stood was something to figure out later; there was someone else who had to be dealt with first.

His gaze traveled to the ugly little man standing by the front door. The look on his face reminded Julian of a vampire in the first throes of bloodlust as he eyed the girl eagerly. He couldn't believe there actually wasn't drool running down the side of his face. He'd hoped to never encounter this particular vampire again, but unfortunately fate had other plans. The only good thing was Scully wouldn't be walking out of here alive.

Scully's eyes were a fiery red color when he looked toward him. "Julian," he greeted in a flat tone.

Julian held his gaze, "Scully."

"This doesn't concern you."

"If you think I'm going to walk out of here and let you take this girl, you're dumber than you look."

Scully's upper lip curled into a sneer. "Don't make me have to kill you."

Julian released a harsh bark of laughter. "It's good to see you're still such a joker, Scully."

A muscle twitched in Scully's cheek, but he made the wise choice to remain where he stood. "Bring her to me!" he commanded brusquely. The remaining four vamps he'd brought with him enthusiastically shook their heads no. They took an abrupt step away from the girl who'd just killed their associate with only a touch.

They're not fools, Julian decided.

"You idiots!" Scully barked. "She's burned herself out, bring her to me!"

"Stay away from her," Julian hissed to the people gathered around him before stepping away from them.

"For once I'm not going to argue with you," Chris muttered but he and Melissa spread out as they moved into the barroom behind him.

"No one is bringing anyone anywhere," Julian said in a low voice as he tried to keep his eyes on the girl near the poolroom and Scully by the front door.

The four men standing in between him and the girl all took an abrupt step toward her before taking two more back toward him. Julian would have laughed at the torn looks on their faces if they weren't a danger, no matter how small. The fact they were frightened made them a bigger threat, but the biggest menace remained standing by the front door.

Julian braced his feet apart and dropped his hands to his side, Scully wasn't foolish enough to attack him, but he stood in between the other vampires and the door. Those vamps were going to do everything in their power to get out of here, something he wasn't going to allow after their attack on the girl. This group was up to something, and he was going to find out what.

"I didn't think I'd ever see your ugly mug again, Scully," Julian said.

"I'd hoped to never see yours again," Scully grated from between his teeth.

"This," Julian said and waved his hand in front of his face. "Is far from ugly." Scully sneered at him; Chris and Melissa made a disgusted sound. "What are you doing here?"

"Anything pertaining to vampire business stopped having anything to do with you when you turned your back on us."

"I did no such thing."

"You helped to destroy The Elders."

"Zane and his cohorts got what they deserved and you know it," Julian retorted.

"You're killing us off one by one."

He shifted his feet, his gaze slid toward the girl when she took a step back and adjusted her hold on the two stakes in her hand. His attention returned to Scully when the other vampires moved further away from her. "Only the ones who deserve it."

"Who are you to judge? You were one of the worst of us."

"I still am." Julian gave him a smile that revealed his elongated canines. "I just play by a different set of rules now. A moral code of conduct, you could say."

Scully's upper lip began to twitch. His buddies looked as if they were actually contemplating plowing through the wall in order to get out of here, but no one moved. "You're a pussy," Scully spat.

"I can still kick your ass all over this bar," Julian assured him.

For the first time fear flickered over Scully's face. Julian knew he was going to make a move before he did. He rushed forward as Scully spun to the side. Scully grabbed one of the high top tables, lifted it over his head and heaved it at him. It flew through the air with the deadly trajectory of a missile.

Julian flung his arm up to knock the table aside. The fifty-pound wood and metal table slammed off of his forearm. One of the wooden legs shattered on impact and the rest of the table spun away into the wall with a loud crash. A snarl tore from Julian as pain lanced down his arm; his hand flipped over to catch the broken leg of the chair before it could fall to the floor.

Pulling his arm back, he flung the leg sidearm at Scully. The vampire flung himself toward the ground, but the broken end of the leg still drove into his arm with enough force to bury itself halfway into his flesh and bone. Scully let out a yelp; he tried to roll away as Julian leapt at him.

Shoving his foot into Scully's back, he pushed him so hard into the ground that the piercing crack of one of his ribs breaking resonated through the barroom. Squealing like a trapped rodent, Scully's arms and legs flailed at the floor. He tried to get his hands under him, but Julian forced him down again.

With Scully firmly pinned to the ground, Julian lifted his head to take in the others. Melissa had one of the vampires pinned against the wall; the girl had two cornered in the poolroom. Julian almost laughed at the spectacle of the men cowering against the wall in an attempt to stay away from the woman who had killed their friend. Luther and Zach closed in on her right and left; they were giving her the same look they would a hungry anaconda.

Chris stood over the body of the other one, a stake protruded from the center of the vamp's chest. Julian turned away from them, he bent down to get a better look at Scully. Rabid dogs would have been afraid of the look on Scully's face; Julian simply smiled at him. "What were you and your friends planning here, Scully?"

Scully spat at him, but in his position, the liquid didn't get very far. "Not smart." Julian pressed his foot into Scully's back hard enough to crack more of his ribs. Scully let out a low moan, his fingers left scratch marks as they dug into the dark wood beneath him. "Now why were you looking for this girl?"

This time when Scully tried to spit at him all that gurgled up from his mouth was a stream of blood. He could pull the answers from Scully by touching him, but he found this a much more preferable way to extract the information he sought. If Scully didn't spill what he knew, then Julian would dive in and tear the answers from him.

"Give me a stake," Julian commanded and held his hand out to Lou. The color had drained from Lou's face as he approached, but his hand remained steady when he handed the stake over. "I'm not going to ask you again, Scully."

He removed his foot from Scully's back. Before the vampire could leap to his feet, Julian drove the stake halfway through his back. Scully howled, his hands flattened against the floor. He went completely still as the stake brushed against his heart.

"One more centimeter," Julian murmured. "And I'll be dragging your body out for the sunrise tomorrow. Now tell me what you meant by, *"we've been looking all over for you,"* and just who is looking?"

"You're going to kill me anyway," Scully retorted.

Julian twisted the stake a little. The sides of it scraped against bone and caused Scully to jerk reflexively. "But I can make it fast or I can make you squirm for days. You know me; you know what I'm capable of." A low moan escaped Scully, his whole body convulsed again when Julian twisted the stake once more. "You know how much joy I find in the pain of others. Now what are you doing here?"

"You saw what she can do!" Scully blurted. "A Seer had a vision about what she can do too. We've been hunting for her."

"How did you know she is the vampire of this Seers vision?"

"I didn't know it was her when we came in here."

Julian glanced up at the girl. Her eyes were focused on Scully. "Do they know what she looks like?"

"No. Her face hasn't been revealed yet."

The *yet* didn't sit well with him. There was a chance another vision could reveal her face to them, it might be a slim one, but he didn't like it. "What do the vampires want with her?" Julian inquired.

Scully started to shake his head. When Julian turned the stake so it dug sideways into his flesh he began to rattle off words so fast Julian had a difficult time following them. "For protection against you and yours! To rebuild our future. To be the leaders The Elders once were, but to be stronger and faster. Her ability and…"

Scully's words broke off as a round of coughing caused blood and spittle to fly from his lips. "And what?" Julian inquired when the coughing stopped.

"It's like nothing we've ever seen before. We need her against *your* kind!" Scully blurted.

"Oh, *my* kind," Julian purred. "You could be one of my kind."

"A whipped puppy? I'd rather die!" he spat.

Scully cringed away from him when Julian rested his hand on his cheek, but Scully would never escape him. His time with Scully was coming to an end; however, he had to make sure they'd learned everything they could before he finished the job. He enjoyed a good bit of torture, just not in front of these people, and not in front of *her*. He didn't know why but the idea of her seeing that side of him unsettled him.

"And you will," Julian promised.

Julian drove the stake the rest of the way through, piercing his heart. Scully jerked, his hands beat against the floor; his feet kicked in the air. Strangled sounds escaped him, blood spilled from his lips, the muscles in his neck stood sharply out. His face turned completely red before he finally went still.

"Kill them," he said to the others and tossed the stake back to Lou.

"What if there's more they can tell us?" Chris protested.

"There's nothing more, at least not anything truthful."

"I'll tell you anything!" The one with Melissa protested instantly.

"You don't know anything," Julian told him. Melissa looked questioningly at him when the man began to spew denials. "Do it."

She gave Julian a grim smile before plunging the stake into the vampire's heart. The last few vampires were rapidly dispatched by the girl and Chris, their undead yet lifeless bodies thumped loudly as they fell to the floor. They would have to deal with the remains soon, but there was something far more important to deal with now as his gaze fell upon the only other vampire in the bar.

Her chin jutted out, she braced her legs apart as she relentlessly held his gaze. He had to admire her fire, but he'd kill her if it became necessary.

**

"Now, what do we do with you?" the exceedingly deadly vampire across from her inquired.

Quinn's teeth grated together. She had no idea how she was going to get out of this mess with her life still intact. She had enough power to take out at least two of the humans but she hoped she wouldn't be forced to do that. Besides, after watching this group she knew they were more than human, or at least some of them were. She should still be able to drain one and at least jolt another in order to escape the bar, but she doubted she'd be able to outrun *him*. Not after what she'd just witnessed.

He was ruthless, he was brutal, but more than that, he was *fast*. Even if she could shock him enough to knock him off of her, she'd never be able to outrun him. "You're not going to do anything with me," she retorted with far more bravado than she felt.

She held her hands up before her and looked pointedly at the two humans standing closest to her.

Their eyebrows shot up, they took an abrupt step away from her. "She has to touch you," the man with the glasses said, drawing her attention back to him. "She's powerful." She didn't like the inquisitive, excited gleam in his eyes one little bit. "But she has to touch you in order to drain you."

"Drain us?" the beautiful black haired woman inquired.

"She's a Soul Master; it's an exceptionally rare gift…"

"Gift," Quinn snorted. "We have different ideas on what constitutes a present."

The man gave her a small smile. "It's a gift if you know how to use it."

"I *know* how to use it, and I *know* what it can do."

"I'm sure you do." He took a step away from her and walked over to sit on the edge of the pool table in a gesture meant to put her at ease. It failed to make her feel any more relaxed. "I just witnessed the damage you can do, but you can also breathe life back into things. Humans, animals, plants, you can give them all life again."

Her mouth parted as she gazed at the people gathered within the room. She'd suspected they were more than human when she'd seen them move, his words only solidified it in her mind.

But none of it made any sense, what would a group of Hunters be doing with a vampire? Her gaze drifted back to the imposing figure standing near the front door. Julian folded his arms over his chest while he held her gaze.

She turned her attention back to the man on the pool table. "You're a Guardian."

He smiled as he waved his hand toward the lanky youth on her other side. "We are."

She glanced between the other girl and two boys. The ones who had been faster and more lethal while killing the vampires. "And you're Hunters."

"We are," the boy with sandy blond hair confirmed.

A strange tug pulled at the area of her heart but she shoved it aside. The past was the past, and she definitely didn't have time to get caught up in her memories right now. "I'd heard most of you were dead." She kept her face completely impassive when she uttered the words, but she felt like she had a big sign over her head screaming *liar*. She'd never reveal she'd done more than heard to this group of strangers.

"We took a big hit during The Slaughter, but we're working to find more survivors and rebuild our numbers," the man on the pool table answered.

"Have you heard what happened to The Elders?" the vamp inquired as he stepped forward.

She lifted one shoulder in a shrug. "I have, but I don't do a whole lot of talking with vampires."

His gaze slid over her once more. "You run into our kind often?"

"I try to avoid it at all costs."

"And why is that?"

"I don't exactly have a good track record with them," she replied with a wave at the dead bodies. "They certainly didn't seem pleased to see you either."

His eyes actually sparkled as he flashed her a smile that revealed his perfectly even, white teeth. She imagined his smile had disarmed many women around the world; she scowled back at him. His grin only widened. He dropped his arms to his side and came at her with a mesmerizing grace. She shifted defensively and gripped her stake tighter.

"There are reasons for that," he told her.

"I'm sure there are," she retorted.

Julian didn't look amused by her now as his face hardened. "You've attracted attention to yourself. After seeing what you can do, and hearing about this vision, I can guarantee they're going to keep coming for you."

"They don't know where I am or who I am."

"If someone has had a vision of what you can do, they could also see where you are and possibly your face."

"You can't know that," she protested.

"I can and I do. There are more of them, *many* more out there looking for you."

She folded her arms over her chest as she looked him up and down. "Is that your super power? You can tell when people are lying."

"I'm not a comic book character. I don't have super powers."

No, he most certainly wasn't fictional, but she didn't know how else to describe it. "Whatever you want to call it then."

"Not that," the boy with the sandy blond hair said. "But Julian is right, the man wasn't lying."

Julian's eyes remained pinned on hers as he took another step forward. "They want you, and they'll do everything they can to find you."

"Thanks for letting me know," she replied with a casual air she didn't entirely feel. "I'll make sure to stay on the lookout."

"You're not a killer," Julian said.

She waved her hand toward the shrunken body near his feet. "I think that guy would disagree with you."

"You know what I mean." His gravelly voice sent a shiver down her spine. "Do you kill humans?"

"No." *Or at least not in six years*, she added silently.

"And that's why we haven't killed you yet."

Her hands clenched. "I'm not easy to take down."

"No, you're not," he agreed. "But we both know it can be done."

Her upper lip curled back, she was half-tempted to give him a blast he would never forget. The only problem was she didn't know how much it would actually affect him, and she still wasn't up to full power. "Try it."

His smile, no matter how dazzling, grated on her nerves. "If I planned to try it, I already would have. We're all on the same side here."

"Your side is a freak show," she muttered.

"Been called worse," the sandy blond said. His sapphire colored eyes held hers as he extended his hand toward her.

Quinn's gaze fell to his hand before shooting back up to him. "You want to touch *me*?"

"I understand you jolting Julian earlier. Believe me, I know how much he deserves it, and so did that other vampire. I'm trusting you." There were few who had ever known about her ability and been willing to touch her. They were all gone now, but she'd never expected a stranger to say those words to her. Especially after what he'd just witnessed. She cautiously took hold of his hand. "I'm Chris."

"Quinn."

"It's a pleasure to meet you, Quinn."

The slender, raven-haired girl stepped forward next and enfolded both of Quinn's hands within hers. "Melissa."

The others introduced themselves to her, Julian came last. A daring sparkle lit his eyes as he extended his hand to her. "Julian, but you already know that." The tempting urge to give him a zap still ran through her, but when his hand enfolded hers she ended up being the one to experience a shock. Her hand instinctively tightened around his. Heat sizzled over her skin, up her arm, and into her chest. His eyes flickered as they ran over her face before she pulled her hand away. "There is a lot of power in you," he murmured.

"In you too."

His smile wasn't nearly as one thousand watt or as careless as it had been before. "I've got some age on me, but I'd guess you're no older than twenty in vampire years. You feel at least a hundred if not more though."

There was no way she would ever tell him the truth about her. She already felt too exposed around him and his merry group. "I guess some of us are just different."

He leaned closer to her and though neither of them breathed, the minty scent of his breath washed over her. "That we are. Some of us can even see things others desire to keep hidden."

Unable to suppress a shudder, she stared defiantly back at him. "And you are one of those vampires I take it."

"I am." Before she could question him further about his ability, he turned on his heel and walked away from her. "We have to get rid of these bodies before daybreak."

Questions spun through her mind as he bent and tossed the body of the one he'd staked over his shoulder.

CHAPTER 6

Quinn had never realized how small her apartment was, until now. The group gathered within it took up almost all of the space in her living room. She slid around the back of the couch she'd picked up from the side of the road a couple of months ago. Yellow bits of stuffing poked through the gray striped fabric on the arms. One of the cushions bowed in the middle, but she avoided that side and the material didn't smell like piss or have stains all over it, which was a noticeable upgrade from her last couch. To her, it had been the find of the decade.

After what had happened in the bar, and having to hide the bodies somewhere they wouldn't be discovered before the sun could hit them this morning, all she wanted to do was curl up on the couch right now and relax. That wasn't to be as she had a pack of watchdogs nipping at her heels.

"Would you like something to drink?" She dropped her coat on the couch and made her way toward the galley style kitchen. It didn't bother her some closets were bigger than her kitchen; the only thing she cared about was that the fridge kept her Mountain Dew and peanut butter cups cold. They were her left over addictions from her human years; she didn't get any nourishment from them but she still loved them.

"You have something other than blood?" Chris inquired.

"Mountain Dew and tap water."

"Poison," Melissa muttered.

Quinn stopped walking to stare at the young woman in confusion. "She doesn't mean you poisoned them," Chris hastily explained. "She's a health freak so soda's not really her thing, but I'll take one."

"So will I," Lou said but the others shook their heads no in response to her questioning look.

She grabbed three sodas from the fridge and walked back into the living room to give the other two to Chris and Lou. Popping the top on her can, she took a swig before placing it on her milk crate coffee table. She didn't know what to say or what they were all doing here, but her eyes were irresistibly drawn toward Julian as he stared around the room.

She didn't have many things in here; she couldn't when she might have to leave at a moment's notice. There was nothing that would tell anyone where she came from in this room, or anywhere else in this apartment. The only things that meant anything to her, she always kept on her. Instinctively her hand fluttered to the heart locket with two pictures inside. It had belonged to her cousin, Betsy. The coolness of the gold against her flesh was a constant reminder of those she'd lost.

Her fingers fell away when Julian's eyes slid to her. "Don't spend much time here?"

"Only my days," she responded. "But the TV works…"

"It does?" Lou asked in disbelief.

She glanced at the old, fifteen-inch tube TV. It wasn't anything fancy and had to be turned on and off by hand, but it worked well enough that she was able to watch the News and Netflix. "Yes, it does," she informed him. "Since you've all insisted upon following me here, and you know what I can do, it's only fair you tell me what you're capable of."

There hadn't been much time to talk while they'd been carrying the bodies out of the bar and cleaning up the mess. She didn't consider this group her enemies, but she wasn't about to let her guard down around them either. The furniture in the apartment was sparse, but she stood within a foot of the nearest hidden stake and within three feet of five more of them. It wouldn't take her more than a second to retrieve each one and start flinging them at people.

She also knew she could leap from this third story apartment and be out of here in less time than it would take them to blink. Granted the window had always been open when she'd practiced her escape before, she did pay for the a/c and heat here, she wasn't about to have plastic over the window twelve months a year. The glass would slow her but not by much, and she knew this town better than Julian. He may be more powerful than her, but he wouldn't expect her to leap out the window, she hoped. Once free of here, she could lose herself amongst the stores and homes if it became necessary. It was an escape route she'd practiced weekly over the past three years to keep herself honed and prepared if it became necessary.

She'd been caught with her guard down once already, it would never happen again. Inadvertently, her fingers slid up to the scar running from her eyebrow to her hairline. Her hand hastily fell away when Julian's eyes latched upon her. She threw back her shoulders and held his gaze.

"Well," she prompted.

Melissa perched on the arm of the couch. "I have visions, or I suppose you could call me a Seer."

Quinn didn't know how to take that revelation. "Have you seen anything about me?"

Melissa shook her head. "Whatever was seen about you has been an entirely vampire revelation, so far."

She didn't want them to know how much Melissa's words had just unsettled her. Acting far more nonchalant than she felt, she turned to Zach. "How about you?"

"I can control the air," he replied.

"I can tell things about people, sense their emotions, read them," Chris said. "I know when they're lying, when they're evil or hiding something."

An uneasy feeling settled into Quinn's stomach. Her whole existence was built on nothing but secrets and lies. Secrets she'd never let *any*one know. Secrets two members of this group might eventually uncover if she wasn't extremely careful around them. She kept her face impassive as she held Chris's gaze. Questions about her past would be best avoided in his presence.

"As Guardians, Lou and I are mere mortals," Luther said with a laugh.

She'd never considered the Guardians mere mortals, though she supposed they technically were. They had none of the abilities of the Hunters or vampires.

She wouldn't require a stake to take them down but her fingers itched for a weapon. They would have attacked her by now, if that had been their objective, and they most certainly wouldn't be standing here, with *him*. No, there was far more to this group than met the eye, and her morbid curiosity kept her standing there.

"You're more than mortals," she murmured.

"You have knowledge of the Hunter and Guardian line?" This question was from *him*.

"Doesn't every vampire have at least some knowledge of those who hunt us?"

"Most, yes. Your sire filled you in on the details?"

It probably normally happened that way, but her transformation had been anything but normal. *Chris can detect a lie,* she reminded herself. "Sort of." It wasn't technically a lie; it was more a hedge.

"Sort of?" he inquired.

"If you're going to reveal *every* detail of your life, then feel free, but I'd prefer to keep my private life *private* from people I don't know."

His head tilted to the side before he gave her a brief nod. "Fair enough."

"What do you know about them?" Luther inquired.

"I know Guardians train Hunters and keep the knowledge of their history. I know The Hunter line was created from vampire blood, through experimentation by The Commission as a way to fight against vampires. I know The Commission was the leading body of The Hunters and Guardians." She didn't miss the muscle twitch in Julian's cheek when she mentioned The Commission.

Wonder what that's all about? She pondered but didn't ask. She was going to keep her secrets, so she wasn't about to start asking him to divulge his.

"You know a lot then," Luther muttered. "You said you've heard what had happened to The Elders but have you heard about The Commission?"

"I've heard the rumors they've both been decimated," she confirmed.

"They were."

"And I suppose you had something to do with it?" She took a small step closer to her escape window as she asked the question.

"They were monsters who had to be stopped. *All* of them." Julian's low, gravelly tone caused the hair on her nape to rise.

Quinn's gaze slid over the Hunters and Guardians standing with him right now. "I never had any interaction with either group." Again that revelation wasn't a total lie, but not the whole truth either. If she kept this up maybe she could continue to fly below Chris's lie-dar.

"How did you hear the rumors?" Julian inquired.

"I've been a vampire for six years now; I've run into more than a few of our kind since my creation. Thankfully, one of them didn't start spouting nonsense about Seers and try to capture me until tonight."

His eyes narrowed on her, causing hers to do the same as she stared at him. "And the others?"

"They were monsters who had to be stopped. *All* of them." She tossed his words back at him.

His mouth pursed. "Yes, there are some of those."

"The others have told me what they're capable of, but what about you?" she inquired of him.

"Psychometry."

She did a double take at the word. "What in the world is that?"

"It's the ability to learn about a person by touching them or an object they've touched."

The floor didn't lurch out from under her, oh no, the whole freaking thing exploded under her feet. She was certain her knees were going to give out on her; her willpower somehow managed to keep her standing. *What had he seen of her when they'd touched? What did he know?* The questions clogged in her throat. She needed the answers, but what if he hadn't seen much of her and her questions only caused him to dig further?

"Interesting," she forced herself to say.

"It can be," he drawled.

The urge to scream filled her; it took all she had not to stomp her foot like a two year old. He wasn't going to reveal anything he may have seen when he'd touched her. She was determined not to ask if all of her secrets had been laid bare to a man she barely knew and who could crush her skull with a flick of his wrist.

She didn't think he'd seen much of her, no matter how much he was trying to hint that he had. This conversation would be going in a completely different way if he had. "How old are you?" Lou inquired.

Her attention was drawn to the lanky young human standing by her kitchen doorway. "I was turned into a vampire six years ago, at eighteen."

She couldn't resist the pull of the ice colored eyes burning into the side of her head. Julian's arms were folded over his chest; his legs stretched out before him as he leaned against the wall by her bedroom door. The fact he appeared so nonplussed, while she felt as twitchy as a murderer on death row, only put her more on edge.

"What about you?" she demanded of him. Her tone came out far more hostile than she'd intended, but he'd just tossed her well-ordered life into the crapper.

"I was changed when I was twenty-two, that was five hundred and seventy-six years ago."

Quinn was extremely proud she managed to keep her mouth from dropping. "You're an Elder?"

"One of the only two left."

Oh this whole situation kept getting better and better. Any vampire over five hundred years old moved into the Elder category and held a whole new level of supremacy over all the younger vampires. It definitely explained the power sizzling off of him and causing her skin to tingle. She had no chance of escaping him by jumping out of the window, she realized.

"And some of The Commission may still be out there too. If they are, they will be taken care of," Julian continued.

"Bad experience with them?" she inquired.

"You could say that." Her curiosity was piqued by his clipped tone, but she didn't press him further.

She wistfully eyed the couch again; she didn't even have the energy to haul her ass into her bedroom right now. A few hours to try and collect her thoughts would be awesome, instead she settled for finishing off her soda. She walked into the kitchen to grab another soda and a package of Reese's.

"You do know you're a vampire right?" Chris asked her.

"So I've been told," she replied around a mouthful of melting peanut butter and chocolate that somehow failed to make her feel any better.

"It would be best if we left this town," Julian said. "If the ones looking for you realize vampires died here, they may come here to search for the source of the disappearance."

"This is my home." It didn't matter if she'd have to leave eventually, she wasn't going anywhere with an Elder vampire who could learn about her by touching her, or the things she'd touched. She wondered if he could see into her life from touching the wall right now. His flesh wasn't in contact with it, but then she didn't know if that kind of contact would be required. "I'm not leaving."

Hopefully you will, she thought as she popped the second chocolate cup into her mouth.

"Well now, Dewdrop, we're going to have ourselves a problem then." Quinn stopped chewing on her candy, her jaw locked as she glowered at Julian. "Because we're not leaving you alone in this town. Not with *that* ability, and not with them searching for you."

The peanut butter went down like mud when she swallowed. "I can take care of myself."

"Against one or two, sure. Against a dozen or two dozen, you'll end up as free as the birdman of Alcatraz."

There were a thousand responses running through her mind. Instead of speaking, she found herself simply staring at him as she tried to figure him out. She was beginning to think it might be impossible to do so. "I don't need your help."

"But you do; you're just unwilling to admit it," he replied.

"I don't *want* your help," she insisted.

"And I don't want to be stuck in this Podunk town, but I'm not leaving here until I'm sure you're safe. We've all been through hell to make sure The Hunter line stays intact; I'm not about to let it all fall apart because of you."

Her hands fisted as she fought the urge to claw his infuriating eyes out. The pressure on her jaw caused her teeth to ache as she ground them together. "I have friends in this town. I'm not going to leave them behind to be destroyed by a bunch of vampires because you're too scared to stand against them."

A strange flash of red blazed around the white band circling his pupil while the rest of his eye remained blue. It was the oddest thing she'd ever seen and yet strangely captivating. "I'm afraid of nothing and no one," he growled. "But I don't like putting my friends in danger unnecessarily."

This time she was unable to stop her mouth from parting as his aura of power rose to a whole new level. It pulsed against her in vibrant waves that caused her skin to ripple and her mouth to go dry. His obvious care for the people standing around him caused his more lethal air to break through his steel exterior. Yep, there would never be any figuring this man out, she decided.

She would like to trust this group gathered around her, but she didn't know them and she wasn't going to bet her life on them. She'd made it this far by staying to herself; that wouldn't change now.

"Then go," she whispered.

He shook his head no. "Not an option."

He was the most infuriatingly stubborn man she'd ever encountered, but as she looked around the room, she saw the same resolve on all of the faces surrounding her. They weren't going to leave, and she wasn't going to go with them. Her shoulders slumped as she glanced toward her bedroom.

"Your choice, but I'd like to get some rest now, if you don't mind," she grated out.

"Not at all." Julian walked over to her front door and pulled it open. He made a sweeping gesture with his arm to the others. "I'll stay here."

"You're not staying here!" Quinn blurted.

That smile, no matter how adorable, really should be wiped off his face for a few hours. She could feel her right eye beginning to twitch when he closed the door behind his friends. "I'm not walking into the sun and bursting into ash either Dewdrop, so you're stuck with me for the day."

Now not only was her eye twitching, but she could feel a muscle in her cheek beginning to jump. *Control your temper*, she told herself. She couldn't afford to lose control around this man. Too much would be revealed if she did.

"You can't stay in my apartment." It took everything she had to keep the panic from her voice, but she couldn't have him in here touching her things, learning about *her*.

"And why not?" he inquired.

"I'm not going to have a man I don't know staying in my apartment." She kept her tone reasonable but she hadn't been able to keep an edge out of it.

"I didn't take you as someone to be frightened of things."

"I'm not, but that doesn't mean I'm going to let a stranger in my apartment while I'm sleeping."

"Fair enough."

Stunned by the lack of a fight, Quinn stared at his back as he opened the door and stepped into the hallway. She remained unmoving for a few minutes before walking over and sliding the deadbolt into place. She didn't know where he'd gone, but she had a feeling it hadn't gone far.

CHAPTER 7

Julian lifted his head at the sound of footsteps in the hallway. He winced at the discomfort the movement caused his twisted neck. He'd managed to fall asleep for a couple of hours, but sitting on the faded, dirty blue rug, with his neck down, hadn't been the best sleeping conditions. His body reminded him of that now.

Luther fought back a grin as he stared down at him with his hand resting against the wall and a bag in his hand. "Sweet dreams?"

"Bite me," Julian muttered.

Luther chuckled before sliding down the wall to sit beside him. He dropped the bag in between them. "Chris assumed you'd appreciate some clean clothes."

"Thanks."

"Our newest friend didn't like the idea of having you in her place?" Luther asked.

"Apparently strange men aren't welcome in her home."

"At least she's not stupid."

Julian leaned his head against the wall and draped his arm over his knees. He stared at the popcorn ceiling over his head. "No, she's most certainly not stupid, but she is a rarity. She has far more power than any vampire of her tender years should."

"Cassie level power?" Luther inquired.

"No one has that level of power. However, Cassie was an empty vessel waiting to be filled. Quinn *is* stronger than she should be for her age. Maybe she was a Hunter before she was changed, it might explain why she's so strong."

Luther shook his head and lifted his glasses up to rub at the bridge of his nose. "I spent all night pouring over books. I've called the only other Guardian I trust. Neither of us were able to locate a Hunter named Quinn who would fit her age parameters. Even if she'd lied about her age by a couple of years there is no record of a Quinn ever having existed amongst the Hunter line. She's more powerful, but it's not because she was a Hunter before being turned."

Julian pondered this as he continued to stare at the ceiling. "If she's lying about her age, it's not by much. She's a fledgling vampire; I can feel it. Is there any chance her family could have kept her hidden from The Commission and other Hunters?"

"There's a chance, but I don't see why they would. She would have been born before The Elders unleashed The Slaughter on The Hunters and Guardians. Born before we realized what bastards the members of The Commission were. There would have been no reason to keep her hidden."

"So we're back to square one." It felt like a woodpecker had mistaken his head for a tree. He rubbed at his temples as he tried to ease the throbbing there.

Luther dropped his glasses back into place. "Perhaps she was turned by an extremely powerful vampire and that's why she's so strong."

Julian shook his head. "It doesn't work that way."

"I didn't think so, but it's the only other guess I have." Julian turned to look at the man beside him. Luther was the smartest guy Julian knew, if he was out of guesses then they were in trouble. "Chris thinks she's trustworthy. She's fearful of our intentions, and he thinks she's had it rough, but she's not malicious."

"She's not," Julian confirmed.

"What did you see when you touched her?"

"A lot of death, blood, pain and screams, but she didn't create it. She's definitely experienced a traumatic and brutal past event."

"You didn't see anything to explain her existence?" Luther asked.

"No."

"Do you plan to try and look deeper?"

Julian bowed his head and ran his hand through his disheveled hair as Luther asked him the question he'd been contemplating all night. "No. She's not a threat. If it becomes necessary for me to search deeper, I will, but she should be allowed to keep her life her own, for now."

"Maybe if you tell her that you'll get the couch tonight," Luther replied with a laugh.

"You could always keep watch tonight."

"I think I'd get the couch, she seems to like me more."

"I think you always get the couch when it comes to women," Julian retorted.

Luther slapped him on the back. "Not always my friend. You're just not used to being kicked out of a woman's place."

Julian shook his head at him, but after two years, he couldn't deny he still found pleasure in moments of friendship like this. "I'm not," he agreed with a smile.

Whatever Luther's next words were going to be, they were cut off by the deadbolt being released. A second later the door to Quinn's apartment opened, and she poked her head into the hallway. Her eyebrows shot up when she spotted them sitting there.

"Did you stay out here all night?" she demanded.

"I did. This old bag of bones wouldn't have been able to handle it." Julian waved his hand at Luther before rising to his feet.

Delicate lines etched her forehead as she shook her head. "Are you going to stay out here for the rest of the day?"

"You may prefer it if I did, but I'm not walking into the sunlight anytime soon," he replied.

She glanced at the other closed doors lining the hall before looking at him again. "You're going to freak out my neighbors."

"Sweet old lady across the hall, we exchanged pleasantries this morning." His smile only earned him a scowl. He'd known many women in his lifetime, but she'd glared at him more in one day than any of the others.

Her attention turned to Luther before she took a step back. "You might as well come in again."

"I have to get back to the motel," Luther said and rose to his feet. "I need some sleep."

Julian's attention was drawn to her right hand on the doorknob and the faded red scar marking it. The scar ran across almost the entire back of her hand in a straight slit. Judging by how faded it was, it was about the same age as the scars marring her face. His gaze slid to her left hand. The palm was turned toward him to reveal a nearly identical scar running across it.

What has she been through? He thought as his eyes darted back to hers. Her skin had become paler, her face drawn as she held his gaze. "Try not to ruin anything," she told him briskly and stepped aside.

A lot of cracks about what he was sure was junkyard furniture ran through his mind, but he held his tongue. She'd kick him back out faster than she'd let him in. The command had also been her way of saying, *don't come in and snoop around by touching my things.* His interest in her grew stronger with each passing second; he would find out about her, but she would be the one to tell him.

"I'll see you tonight," he said to Luther and stepped into her apartment.

Quinn stared at Luther before shutting the door and sliding the lock back into place. She gave him a large side step as she walked toward the kitchen. He contemplated telling her he could turn his ability off, but he figured as long as she kept her secrets he could keep a few of his own too.

***

Quinn had been hoping she'd be wrong, and he wouldn't be sitting in her hallway. However, it hadn't surprised her to see him there. She felt his eyes burning into her as she walked around him. She resented that he'd inserted himself into her life, but she had to admit he looked more delicious than any peanut butter cup right now.

His hair was tussled; a shadow lined his square jaw. The predatory glint in his eyes made her body quicken in response. She was supposed to be staying as far from this man as possible, not admiring him.

"Is your hair dyed?" she blurted. It was the most inane question, but it had been meant as a way to distract herself from the urge to jump him.

He ran a hand through his platinum blond hair. "Do I look like the kind of guy who would dye his hair?"

"You look like the kind of guy who would rip off someone's head and use it as a soccer ball, so I imagine you'd be up for anything."

A smirk curved his luscious mouth. "I can assure you Dewdrop, I'm not much for soccer, but I am one hundred percent natural. I was simply blessed with these abnormally striking looks." No one could ever accuse him of having no self-confidence or being shy, she realized. "I can always prove I'm a natural blond if you'd like me to," he added with a suggestive waggle of his eyebrows.

There wasn't one drop of saliva left in her mouth. As enticing as the proposition was, and she wasn't above admitting it was *extremely* enticing, it could never happen. "Thanks, but no," she responded with more composure than she felt.

"Your mouth says no, but your eyes say yes."

Her skin felt like it crackled as fury slithered over her. How he'd managed to survive for as long as he had without someone killing him completely mystified her. She may be the one to remedy that by the time she was able to free herself from him. "Believe me that's not what my eyes are saying," she bit out.

"Murder and passion are a fine line, no?"

"Ugh!" she shouted.

She threw her hands up, turned on her heel and stormed into the kitchen. Peanut butter cups and Mountain Dew weren't going to be enough to take the edge off, but she didn't have to look at the windows to know the sun was still out. What she needed was blood and not animal blood, *his* blood. She shot him a scathing glance over her shoulder as she grabbed a soda from the fridge.

"I'll take that as a yes." He leaned in the doorway of the kitchen to watch as she walked over to sit on the edge of the garden window. It was the one place in the apartment she truly loved. Even if she couldn't stand in the sun's rays without suffering excruciating pain, she could feel their warmth through the blinds on the window.

"How has someone not killed you yet?" she asked.

"Many have tried, all have failed."

"I believe you."

"You'll learn that I never lie." She didn't have his or Chris's ability, but she didn't doubt him for a second. He rubbed at his neck as he studied her. Dropping his hand down, he gestured to the bag at his feet. "Do you mind?"

"Do I mind what?" she inquired.

"If I change my shirt."

"No, the bathroom's through..."

Her instructions died on her lips when he grabbed hold of the end of his shirt and pulled it off. Whatever she'd been about to say became lost in the rapid circuit fire of her brain as she strained not to gawk at him. His adorable sleep disheveled appearance became the least of her problems when presented with his broad, muscular chest. Those pecs were enough to make any woman drool, and forget about a quarter, those abs would bounce a brick!

The compulsion to start whistling and stare at the ceiling grabbed her. She would *not* back down from this man though, no matter how much she yearned to run her fingers over his pale, silken skin. The wings of his angel tattoo touched against his shoulder, the muscles it was etched onto flexed as he bent to tug another shirt free from the bag. He slid the maroon colored shirt over his head and tugged it down over the muscles she was doing everything in her power not to lick. He finally covered the body she'd found so unsettling, but she knew if she closed her eyes she would vividly recall every chiseled detail of that torso.

"Where did you get that couch, the dump?" he asked.

And nothing like his insults to douse the heat he'd stoked within her. "The roadside."

He gave a small snort. "Dewdrop come on, you're a vampire."

"So?" she retorted.

"So you can still get things without having to kill people. Steal if you must, but living in squalor is below any of our kind."

"I'm not living in squalor!" she snapped. Her gaze slid over her apartment, it wasn't a mansion, but it was far from an alleyway. She had everything she needed. "I've worked for everything I have. I didn't steal it, hustle anyone for it, or use my abilities to get it. Maybe you should try being a decent person sometime."

"But we're not people, Dewdrop."

Frustration got the best of her. "Why do you keep calling me that?" she demanded.

He gestured toward the can of soda in her hand. "You're still trying to be human; the rest of us have accepted our fates."

Her fingers curled around the can as she briefly contemplated heaving it at him. The aluminum crinkled inward with a crunching noise that made him grin. "I accepted my fate years ago."

"Not completely."

"That's awfully freaking funny coming from someone hanging around with a group of Guardians and Hunters. If you've accepted your fate what are you doing with them? Shouldn't you be hanging out with your own kind?"

"*Our* own kind." Quinn's nostrils flared; before she could heave the can at him, he continued speaking. "It's a long and complicated story, one I'm not much in the mood for telling."

"And I'm not much in the mood for your outstanding insights, but I'm still forced to hear them."

He'd stopped smiling as he studied her. "Maybe one day I'll tell you, but not today. I'm going to take a shower."

"Oh, sure, make yourself at home," she muttered when he turned away.

She couldn't complain too much, at least he remained dressed while he walked through her living room toward her bedroom. The idea of him in her bedroom bothered her. At least she'd remembered to make her bed and toss all her dirty clothes in the hamper before opening the front door.

"I plan to as long as you insist upon staying here," he called over his shoulder.

Quinn seethed as she heard the water of the shower turn on, but even as her fingers crushed the can further within her grasp, she couldn't help but picture water running over his sculpted flesh. *Ah shit*, she thought and tossed the can into the sink. She was so screwed right now, she didn't know how to begin to dig her way out of it.

She briefly contemplated digging the punching bag out from her closet and taking some of her frustration out on it, but she decided against it. She might forget all about the bag when he got out of the shower and punch him instead. The same with the dummy she used to practice her stake and knife throwing on. It definitely wasn't a good idea to have stakes and knives in her hands while he was walking around.

CHAPTER 8

Julian kept the pool stick in his hand and watched Quinn as she made her way around the room to wait on the people gathered within. There would be more vampires coming for her. He knew that, but if she refused to leave town then he was going to make damn certain she stayed safe. Her ability in the wrong hands would be disastrous, and if the vampires succeeded in taking her, they would destroy her.

There were few who came through the transformation from human into a vampire with the ability to withstand their malicious, driving impulses. Impulses that turned them into murderers and made them believe they had no other choice but to kill. He wasn't about to let her be destroyed by the corrupting ability and cruelty of many in the vampire race. Destroying someone, bending and warping them was something he knew could be done; he'd done it more than a few times himself over the years.

The idea of throwing her over his shoulder and forcing her onto the RV was entirely tempting. With her insistence she stay here, there was no way he could drag her onto the RV. She could kill the Guardians and possibly Melissa, Chris, and Zach if she got her hands on them. He wasn't about to put their lives at risk if she felt cornered enough to turn on them.

He didn't like the idea of staying here, but right now he didn't have much of a choice. He'd gotten as much information as he could from Scully when he'd touched him. Most of what he'd gleaned, Scully had already revealed to him.

"Your turn," Chris said to him.

Julian walked around the table to set up his next shot. The balls hit each other with a high-pitched clinking sound. The eight ball rolled across the table and fell into the pocket. The ball traveled through the mechanisms of the table and clanked against the others when it finally reached its destination. He tossed his stick to the pouting human he'd been playing against and collected the hundred dollars from the table. Quinn gave him a look of disdain when he shoved the money into his pocket.

"Fleecing the humans?" she inquired.

He grabbed a shot of whiskey from her tray and downed it in one swallow. The liquid burned its way down his throat, but he'd long since become accustomed to the way it tasted. "At least I have the money to pay for that drink now." He tossed a ten onto her tray.

"Jerk."

"You've only scratched the surface, love. I can promise you'll be calling me a lot worse once you get to know me better."

He didn't know what it was about her, but he enjoyed needling her, getting her face to flush, and her honeyed eyes to gleam with ire. He had the urge to tug on her ponytail, he sensed she might punch him if he did though. It was a pity too, as her shimmering chocolate hair was as enticing to him as her peanut butter cups were to her. His fingers itched to know if it was as soft to the touch as it appeared.

"I already have," she retorted and snatched the shot glass from his hand. Spinning away from him, he heard her mutter a string of curses while she walked away. Julian grinned as he handed his pool stick out to Zach. "Take this for me, Zachary."

"It's just Zach," the kid muttered.

Zach brushed aside a wisp of his dark blond hair to reveal the tree of life tattoo on the inside of his right wrist. His brown eyes narrowed upon Julian. Julian pretended not to notice his glare as he smiled in return. The angles of Zach's high cheekbones were prominent beneath his tanned skin, his pointed chin jutted out. He was slightly taller than Julian at about six-foot-three, but Julian had a good thirty pounds of muscle on Zach's lean frame. The twenty-two year old Hunter had been beneath the pier on Imperial Beach in California. Zach had been using his surfboard to fend off the three vampires encircling him. He'd been holding up against the vamps, but it had only been a matter of time before their numbers tired him out and allowed them to take him over.

"Sure," Julian replied dismissively.

He walked toward the doorway of the poolroom to survey the crowd gathered within the bar. The mix of the group was much the same as it had been last night. However, because it was Friday there were at least fifty more of them. Quinn stood behind the bar, pouring new drinks as the men all leaned closer to her. Even without the natural pull of her vampire allure, she was enticing. Especially with her hair pulled into a ponytail to emphasize her pert nose, striking eyes, and full lips.

From here, he could see the scars marring her face. Some may have considered them a flaw in her pretty features, but he found they added to her appeal. Her scars were a sign that she'd been molded by her past but not broken by it. It would take him a while to get her to open up to him about it, but he would do it.

"She's not a bad person," Chris said as he stepped beside him.

"She's not a person," Julian reminded him.

"No, but there's nothing evil inside of her. She's one of the few of you who didn't go all wonky and become murderers after being turned."

"Wonky?" Julian inquired. "Is that the technical term for it?"

"It's better than brutal, uncaring, homicidal monster."

Julian gave him a dark look, but there was little he could say to that, it was true. Of course, there were those who did know they had a choice about killing and didn't care. He'd never believed he had a choice until he'd met Cassie. She'd made him understand there was true good in the world and real love. Even if Cassie could never be his, he knew he could be a better man because of her.

Approaching the bar, he gave a young kid with a Mohawk a scathing look when he bent low to try and see down Quinn's loose fitting, black button up shirt. The kid nearly tripped over his own feet as he backtracked away from him.

"Don't scare away my customers, not all of us are thieves," Quinn admonished. "I have bills to pay."

He rested his elbows on the bar and leaned toward her. "I'm only a thief of hearts." He knew she was trying not to, but eventually she lost the battle and a small smile tugged at the corner of her upper lip. "A smile, at me?" he teased. "Now was that so tough?"

"Yes." The smile faded as she placed her drinks onto her tray. She lifted the tray from the bar and walked away from him.

He rested his elbow on the bar as he turned to watch her go. "Can I get you something to drink?" the small brunette waitress he recognized from the previous evening asked him. He glanced around, but didn't see the redheaded bartender from last night anywhere.

"I'm good," he told her.

"You just ask for me the next time you need something."

"Thank you…?"

"Angie," she supplied.

"Thank you, Angie." She fluttered her lashes as she smiled up at him. It was nice to finally have someone smiling admiringly at him again. Even as he thought it, his eyes were drifting away from her and back toward Quinn. He couldn't help but admire the sway of her hips as she vanished into the poolroom again. Tuning out the noise of the pool games, he focused on the drunken conversations going on in the room.

A loud shout caught his attention; he stepped away from the bar as what sounded like a chair breaking drifted to him. Chris lurched forward and disappeared into the room when more shouts resonated. People in the barroom turned toward the sounds; none of them moved as the distinct thwack of a fist connecting with cheekbone echoed throughout. The crack of splintering wood drew him more rapidly forward. It was followed by the loud bang of someone being thrown into a wall.

Some humans shouldn't drink whiskey, he thought as he approached the backroom, but then he had always enjoyed a good fight himself.

Stepping into the doorway, he shook his head when he spotted a group of younger kids fighting with a group of cowboys. He was tempted to let them kill each other but Quinn, Chris, Zach and Melissa were in the middle of it, trying to break up the brawl. The dozen or so men fighting threw punches over the top of their heads and around the sides of them. One of the men let out a squeal that sounded more like a little girl than a grown man in his thirties. The squealing man held his arm; he reeled away from the group and fell into the wall.

Julian smiled grimly as he realized Quinn had given him a good zap. Melissa grabbed hold of another guy and shoved him away, nearly knocking him on his ass. A punch to Zach's jaw caused him to stagger back a step. He countered it with an uppercut that caused the man's eyes to roll back in his head before he slumped lifelessly to the ground. The kid was new to the group but he had moves, Julian decided. He strode forward to put an end to the fight before someone got injured.

Quinn ducked a punch thrown at the man to her right, but it had been so off the mark it nearly caught her in the jaw instead. Anger slid over Julian's skin as another man yelped and jumped away from her. Chris punched a young man in the stomach, the man's arms pin-wheeled as he fell backwards over a table. Bottles and mugs of beer slid over with the man when the table flipped over on him. His legs kicked in the air, as he tried to right himself from the tangled mess of the table and drinks. Julian would have laughed, but he'd stopped finding anything amusing about this situation when Quinn had almost been hit.

Reaching the fray, Julian seized hold of a man's fist and shoved him carelessly back. The guy bounced off of the jukebox before hitting the floor. Another one jumped onto his back and grabbed hold of his neck in a chokehold that might have affected his breathing, if he'd required air. Instead, he laughed at the man clinging to him before seizing the man's arm and pulling him forward. Julian jerked him over top of his head before ducking a punch aimed at his eye.

He bit back a bout of laughter at the young kid trying to hit him. Leaning back, he easily dodged the blow and drove his fist into the kid's stomach. He barely hit him, he would have killed him if he'd hit him with his full force, but the blow lifted him off his feet and threw him into a table. The table broke beneath the force of his weight when he crashed down on top of it.

"Enough!" Quinn yelled as more men from the bar jumped into the melee.

Out of the corner of his eye, he spotted a chair swinging toward him. He swung his hand up and grabbed hold of the chair before it could crash down on his back. Jerking it from the man's grasp, Julian placed the legs against the man's chest and shoved him backward. Humans were idiots, he realized as Quinn shattered a younger guy's nose before kicking another so hard in the nuts that even Julian winced for him. The kid grabbed hold of his crotch, his eyes rolled up in his head before he slumped over backwards.

"Hey, stop!" the high-pitched command came from Angie as she tried to separate two men double her size.

Quinn leapt forward to help Angie but the two men continued to swing at each other over top of Angie's head. Quinn let loose with a rapid fire of right elbows to the man's face that would have crushed his cheekbone if she'd decided not to hold back. He was certain she'd still cracked the bone.

"Enough!" Quinn shouted again. "If you all don't stop, I'm going to ban every single last one of you!"

Julian sidestepped another man, but a big group of humans were shoved up against him by a large man wielding a table as a weapon. When he'd entered this fight, he'd shut off his ability in order to keep himself protected from images he didn't want to see from everyone involved. It wasn't always the best thing to know who was cheating on who, what went on in a person's bedroom, all of the little neurotic thoughts about looks and weight, or who was stealing from their family for drugs. He had enough weight on his shoulders trying to keep his more malevolent impulses in check, without having the added weight of knowing a bunch of things he cared nothing about.

This time, the images inside of one of the people who were shoved against him broke through his walls and played out before his eyes in a macabre dance of the doomed. Something volatile and evil slithered over his skin as blood and death came to life within the synapses of his mind. He'd been and seen many things, *done* many things over his lengthy life, but what broke through his defenses now was something worse than he'd ever been, and these images came from a *human*.

The screaming of women and children echoed in his ears with enough force to stagger him forward a few steps. Stars exploded behind his eyelids; it felt as if his head were splintering apart from the barrage. His attention was drawn away from the fight enough that a punch landed on his jaw, knocking his already pounding head to the side. His vision blurred as his fangs extended. The blow didn't have him teetering on the edge of murder, but rather it was the horrific images flooding his mind. Blood, so much blood, it brought out the part of him that had once thrived on brutality and death.

Maybe not this kind of tortuous twisted death, but death nonetheless.

Struggling to regain control of himself, his shoulders hunched up as his head bowed down. There were at least ten humans scrambling over him. So many of them he couldn't begin to pinpoint who emitted the visions in waves. His muscles bunched as strength surged through them. With a snarl, he rolled his shoulders and flung his arms backward, throwing all of his pig pile companions onto the floor. He spun toward the group that had been pressing against him. Apparently, he'd knocked them over too as he spotted Quinn, Angie and Chris amongst the mass of those he'd tossed aside.

His eyes were riveted upon the men scrambling to get to their feet. It was one of *them* that had caused what he'd seen in his mind, one of *them* was a cold-blooded killer. He took a step toward them in order to find out exactly which one had to be put down.

Before he could grab the first one, a short man with a thick gray beard and shaggy gray hair standing out around his head like Einstein's stepped into the doorway. The man braced his legs apart as he glared into the room. The leather belt at his waist appeared to be losing the battle against the belly hanging over top of his jeans. He lifted a gun into the air and fired a shot; the bullet slammed into the ceiling above him. Bits of wooden debris and dust rained down around the man. He didn't move as he lowered the weapon and pointed it into the room.

"Everybody out, now!" he barked.

Julian stepped forward to try and stop the men from leaving the room. The man in the doorway leveled the revolver at his chest. The shot wouldn't kill him, but it would hurt like hell, and he really didn't have the time to explain why he wouldn't require an ambulance afterward.

"I'll shoot you, Billy Joel. I swear I will," the older man told him in a voice made gravelly from years of cigarette smoke.

Julian shot Chris, Lou and Melissa a look when they began to laugh; Zach snickered beside him. "I've killed people for less," he growled at the newcomer to their group from the corner of his mouth. Zach's smile slipped away, he took an abrupt step away from Julian's side.

The group of fighters scrambled to gather their unconscious friends and escape the poolroom. Julian took another step forward; a wave of the gun still aimed at his chest stopped him from going any further. He raised his hands in the air as he memorized the faces of every man scurrying past the guy with the gun. He wished Luther had decided to come out tonight instead of trying to do more research; he'd have been able to diffuse this situation far better than Julian could.

"Oh for crying out loud, Clint," Quinn muttered as she stalked forward. "Put the gun down."

"How do I know he didn't start it; he looks like trouble," Clint retorted.

"He didn't start it," Quinn told him. "And you're thinking of Billy Idol. Not Billy Joel."

"What's the difference?"

"One is an eighties rocker that his look is definitely based on…"

"I told you this is all natural," Julian retorted.

"The other sang Piano Man," Quinn continued as if he'd never spoken.

"Oh." Clint dropped his arms down and slid his gun into the holster at his side. "I like that song."

"Most people do," Quinn replied.

"Are you girls ok?" he demanded.

"We're fine," Quinn assured him.

His gaze went past her to Angie. "Fine," she replied with a small smile.

"What happened here?" Clint inquired and pulled a piece of gum from his pocket. He shoved the gum into his mouth as his gaze traveled over Julian, Melissa, Chris, Lou, and Zach.

"Some townie kids trying to prove their might, pissed off some cowboys," Quinn told him. "These guys were trying to help us break it up."

Clint's brown eyes searched over them before he gave a brisk nod. "Thanks for the help. You've earned yourselves a free drink. Can you clean this up, Quinn?"

"On it," she assured him.

She rested her hands on Clint's small shoulders and turned him toward the main room. The people out there hastily became preoccupied with their alcohol and friends again when Clint's eyes fell upon them. Julian stalked across the room as the last of the people involved in the fight scrambled out the door.

Pickup trucks, cars, and motorcycles were firing up as he pounded down the steps and into the dirt parking lot. His gaze ran over all the people jumping into their vehicles. Taking five giant strides forward, he grabbed the arm of a man trying to climb into a jacked up Jeep.

"Hey." The kid's voice was slurred due to his swollen jaw and missing front tooth, but Julian was already turning away from the flashes of beer helmets, girls and football the kid emitted.

He grabbed hold of a man with a cowboy hat next but swiftly turned away from the cubicle and computer that filled his mind. Dust kicked up around him as more vehicles fled the parking lot, he managed to grab hold of another kid, but all he saw were images of textbooks. He spun to try and find someone else only to discover he was now alone. The last pickup kicked up rocks and dust with a squeal of tires. One of the kids in the back of the truck swore at him before tossing a beer bottle his way. He jumped back as glass shattered around his feet and liquid splashed over the bottom of his jeans.

There were times he really wished he were still a killer, he realized as he stepped away from the broken shards of glass.

Chris jogged up to his side. "What are you doing?"

Julian stared down the deserted road as the red tail-lights of the pickup faded into the distance. "One of the men involved in the fight is a killer."

"So are you," Zach said.

The look he gave the kid caused Zach to blanch. "They were nothing like me," he said. "They have to be stopped."

CHAPTER 9

"Do you know everyone who was involved in the fight?"

Quinn barely paid Julian any attention as she kicked her shoes off and walked toward the kitchen. Her feet ached, her jaw was sore from a punch she'd taken. The only thing she wanted to do was lie down and sleep until sunset tomorrow. Instead, she had an extremely angry, large vampire hovering in her doorway. She grabbed a can of soda and the whole bag of peanut butter cups before slumping into one of her wobbly kitchen chairs.

She opened her soda, before peeling the wrappers from ten peanut butter cups and placing them on the table. She methodically began to eat each one as she tried to ignore Julian's nearby presence. Maybe if she ignored him for enough time he would simply go away. She knew it would never happen, but she was going to enjoy her snack before she had to deal with him.

She popped the last candy into her mouth and lifted her right foot into her lap. She rubbed at her foot and braced herself. He'd left her alone for this long, she knew it wouldn't continue, and she was right. He pulled out the chipped white chair across from her and plopped into it. Quinn bit on her bottom lip as she waited for the chair to break apart beneath him.

"So do you know everyone who was involved?"

"I know most of them," she admitted. "I'm sure there were a few I missed or don't know. Clint and Angie would probably know the ones I don't. I can always ask them."

"Good, we have to find the people involved."

"Most of them will be back to the bar, eventually. Whenever there's a fight some of the people involved go to Hawtie's for a week or two to give Clint a chance to calm down. The rest either go to the bonfire usually held a couple of times a month, or they go to the Mitchum's."

"What are Hawtie's and the Mitchum's?"

"Hawtie's is the strip club on the other side of town. Mitchum's is an old movie theatre the couple bought and renovated."

He folded his arms over his chest and leaned back in his chair. It groaned beneath him but still somehow held his weight. "What goes on there?"

Quinn dropped her foot down to lift her left one up. A groan escaped her as she rubbed at the sore extremity. "I don't know. They have parties every weekend there. I always assumed it was normal party stuff, but I've never been."

"Maybe it's a key party?" he suggested with a wink.

She frowned at him. "What's a key party?"

"It was something that was popular in the seventies with the swinger crowd."

"Do I want to know what they did with those keys?"

He gave a small laugh. "The men put their keys into a bowl and the women picked them out later. Whoever's key they picked was who they spent the night with."

Quinn's eyebrows rose. "Seriously?"

"Yep."

"That sounds… awful. I don't think that's what goes on over there. I hope," she added in a mutter. "But way to date yourself with that reference."

"Dewdrop, I was already old in the seventies."

She shook her head at him and lifted her soda. She held his eyes over top of the can as she took a swallow and dropped her drink back down. "You do emit an ancient aroma."

"And what is an ancient aroma exactly?"

"Kind of musty with a hint of mushrooms, and…" she paused to scent the air. "Vinegary." It was a complete lie, he smelled delicious enough to eat or at the very least lick. The fresh scent of soap and the peppery scent of power emitted from every one of his pores.

He smiled at her as he dropped his arms and leaned toward her. "I may smell like an ancient vinegary mushroom, but I can assure you I don't taste like one, if you ever decide you'd like to take a bite."

Despite her best intentions, her mouth dropped and her body flushed at his words. "I… uh… *never*," she sputtered in protest.

"Again your mouth is saying no, but your eyes are saying yes."

She almost threw her can at him, but she thought he might enjoy that too much. "You're an ass," she muttered.

"I'm an ass who you're tempted to kiss."

Her hand fisted on the table. "Stop."

"As you wish Dewdrop, but for future reference I've never turned down a kiss before."

"Oh, I'm sure you haven't," she retorted. "I bet there have been thousands."

"Not thousands, but I like that you have so much faith in my prowess with women."

"Ugh! Seriously, how are you still alive?" she demanded.

"Luck, plus I've got skills. You'll take me to those places tonight."

A friction of resentment slid over her skin, goose bumps broke out across her arms. Her teeth clamped together and she hissed her words at him. "I'll do what?"

He must have realized what he'd sounded like as he shook his head. "Sorry," he muttered and ran a hand through his hair. "I need you to take me to find those men, and if they're not at any of those places, then you'll have to let me know where to find them."

"What do I look like the town yellow pages?" she retorted.

The smile slid away from his face, he stared at her for a minute before leaning toward her. "You look like a highly pissed off vampire right now. You have to understand, what I felt from that person wasn't good, and they're going to kill again. *Soon.* They're hunting women and *children.*" Her stomach twisted sickly at the idea, her blood ran cold as she gawked at him. "Children are the *main* thing they're hunting, and what they take the most pleasure in torturing and killing."

All right, she had to admit that was far more important than the fact that he was an arrogant, exasperating ass. "I'll help you find as many of them as I can."

"Thank you."

"We can't really do anything now anyway." She gestured toward the blinds covering her window and the rays of sun beginning to peek around them.

"No, but at sundown. You'll have to call out of work."

"I have the night off." She rose to her feet, snatched up her wrappers and walked over to toss them in the trash. "I don't suppose I'll get lucky enough to get you to stay out of my hallway today?"

He grinned at her and shook his head. "Hate to disappoint. You're stuck with me for the day again. Even if vampires can't move about in the day, I'm not leaving you unprotected."

Uneasiness slid through her, she glanced around her small apartment. She couldn't have him spending another night in her hallway. The neighbors hadn't complained last night, they would if he continued to sit out there though. They may call the cops, which could become ugly if one of them tried to drag Julian outside into the day. But if he came in here, he could learn everything about her.

He was already sitting in her chair, at her table, she reminded herself. Touching her things and yet he'd mentioned nothing of her past. There would be no keeping silent about it if he knew the truth, he would confront her on it, she was certain of that.

Had he lied about his ability in an attempt to get her to spill her guts? Or was he keeping silent on the things he'd learned and just waiting for his chance to pounce on her? Or maybe touching her things didn't give him detailed images and memories from her but only glimpses?

Either way, the damage had already been done. She'd make sure not to touch him again, but she didn't see the harm in allowing him to crash on her couch. It was the far better option to having the cops storming her hallway or her neighbors calling the landlord to complain. She didn't have much money, this was the only decent place in town she could afford, and she couldn't lose it.

"You can stay on the couch," she muttered.

He did an exaggerated double take and lifted his right hand to his ear to pull it toward her. "I'm not sure I heard you right."

She made a disgusted noise and shook her head. "I'd prefer not to lose my place or see you dragged out by the cops. As much as I don't like it, you've left me no choice."

"Let's get this straight Dewdrop, I'm going to make sure you stay safe, but you always have a choice."

"My neighbors..."

"I'll stay in the supply closet at the end of the hall."

"With the plungers and whatever else the landlord keeps in there?"

"Tools, I've already snooped through. Believe me, I've slept with worse."

"Oh I bet the plunger probably beats out a few of the things you've slept with," she replied with a smile.

"You do have some claws; I like it."

"I'm thrilled," she deadpanned. "There's an extra blanket and pillow in the closet." Before he could say anything else, she turned on her heel and walked out of the kitchen. It took everything she had not to look back at him as she hurried into her room.

***

"Hello, Dewdrop."

Quinn barely heard Julian's words. Her attention was solely focused on the brand new, tan couch sitting in her living room. It hadn't been there when she'd gone to the bar to grab the stub for her paycheck. She had automatic deposit; banker's hours didn't exactly work for her, but she'd decided to check with Clint and Angie and make sure she hadn't missed anyone from the fight last night. They hadn't mentioned anyone she didn't already known was there.

She hadn't been gone an hour, but he'd been extremely busy. "What is that?" she demanded.

"It's a couch."

Her eyes shot toward him. "I *know* it's a couch. What's it doing in *my* living room?"

"I wasn't spending one more night on that death trap you scavenged." He rubbed at his neck to emphasize his point. "I texted Chris earlier to find me something comfy to sleep on. The delivery guys dropped it off while you were out."

"How convenient. Did my couch break your neck?"

"No."

"Then I don't see the problem."

"It was hideous and less comfortable than a board of nails. By the way you could have warned me that I was literally sleeping on a death trap." He gestured to the three stakes sitting on top of the milk crate. She'd placed them strategically through the couch. One had been under a cushion, another on the floor beneath the couch, and the third in the springs under it. "One of them kept poking me."

"Not hard enough," she retorted.

He chuckled as he ran a hand through his tussled hair. "I think it left a bruise."

"What are you, the freaking Princess and the Pea?"

"No, I'm definitely all man, but I do enjoy sleeping."

Her teeth grated together, it took everything she had not to start swearing at him. "Who said you were going to stay here again tonight?"

He folded his arms over his broad chest, crossed his legs and leaned against her wall. "I just assumed you would continue to be an inviting ball of sunshine."

There were angels who would have gladly jumped on him and beaten him to death. She most certainly wasn't an angel. "Where is *my* couch?"

An irritated sound escaped him, but there was no way he was more aggravated than her. "I had Chris put it where it belongs."

"If it's in the dump…"

"It is."

"Damn you!" she snapped. "I don't care what you say, or what you think. I want you out of my life!"

His body uncoiled, he closed the distance between them in three lengthy strides. The thunderous look on his face almost made her retreat a few steps, but she refused to give him any more than he'd already taken from her. She tilted her head back to look up at him, and defiantly met his icy stare as he rested his hand on the wall beside her head and leaned closer.

The inside of her body came alive, her ability itched to taste the waves of power he emanated and feast on him. *Stay under control*, she told herself, but the tempting vibrations of his body against hers were almost more than she could stand.

"You can curse me, damn me, do whatever you want to me, but I'm not leaving until there is no more threat to you. It could be a very long time before I walk out that door and out of your life, but we can fight about it later; we have something far more important to deal with first. Now, tell me you know for sure all the people who were involved last night."

She folded her arms over her chest. "I do," she reluctantly admitted.

His face eased. "Good."

"I'm going to help you with this, but don't get rid of my things or try to take control of my life like this again."

"Whatever you say."

"Don't patronize me!"

Her body relaxed when he dropped his hands down and stepped away from her. "I'm not patronizing you." He ran a hand over his face, pulling at the dark stubble lining his cheeks.

A tired air surrounded him. For the first time she realized what he'd seen from the killer was wearing on him. "What you saw last night was really bad, wasn't it?"

"It was," he confirmed. "You should get ready to go."

"Yeah," she murmured.

Despite her persistent urge to yell at him, a part of her would like nothing more than to console him in some way. Shaking her head at the ridiculous thought, she walked into her room and closed the door behind her.

***

Her hair hung in wet tendrils when she cracked open her door and poked her head out. She'd spent the past hour trying to get herself ready to deal with him again. When his head emerged around the doorway of the kitchen, she knew there was no way she could ever be prepared for him. Not with that face and the attitude that came with it.

His icy eyes skimmed over her, a smile quirked the corners of his mouth as he leaned against the doorframe. "Little over dressed for a strip club," he remarked.

Her eyes skimmed over her gray, *Killers* t-shirt barely visible beneath her zip-up black hoodie, blue jeans, and calf high black boots hiding her stakes. The hoodie helped to keep the stake and knife strapped to her waist hidden. They might not be hunting vamps tonight, but she never left home without being fully prepared to kill something.

"I'm not a stripper," she replied.

"Still, you should try to blend in."

She scowled at him as she pulled at the sleeves of her hoodie. "This is as undressed as I'm getting."

The twinkle that came into his eyes made her stomach do little flip-flops as his gaze leisurely perused her body. She was tempted to try and cover herself; he didn't have x-ray vision though and the only bare parts of her were her face and hands. It didn't matter, she felt as exposed as if she were completely naked before him when he looked at her like that. A lazy grin spread across his mouth as he met her gaze again.

"Let's hope not."

It took all she had to keep her mouth from dropping over those words. Somehow, miraculously, she kept her face impassive and her mouth closed. She'd never met anyone who made her as unsettled as this man did. The sooner she could get him out of her home, and her life, the better off she would be.

"Let's get this over with," she muttered.

"Can I shower first?"

"Oh, ah, yeah." She stepped out of the doorway to her bedroom so he could use the bathroom.

"Chris and Melissa will be here soon," he told her.

"What about the others?"

"Luther is going to take Lou and Zach back to the bar to keep watch for vampires who might be searching for you."

Her mouth pursed. "Almost forgot about that fun little nugget of detail."

"Lou and Zach will also let us know if any of the fighters return to Clint's tonight."

"They won't. Clint's temper is legendary, but they know he'll forgive anything after a week or two. They'll wait."

"I'd still prefer to have them there," he said before vanishing into the small bathroom off of her bedroom.

The apartment seemed emptier without his large frame taking up so much space. She stared at her faded blue comforter and the small bureau sitting beside her bed. For the first time she realized how sad and lonely it all looked, but then she'd been alone for years now. She rubbed at her chest as a sharp pang stabbed her heart.

The sound of the water turning on brought her attention back to the bathroom. Her eyes widened when she realized he hadn't completely shut the door. Through the mist filling the room, she spotted his reflection in the mirror, with*out* his shirt on. The blood rushed out of her head as she was confronted with his very broad, chiseled chest. She couldn't tear her gaze away from him when he turned away to present her with his corded back. There was no saliva left in her mouth as he reached out, grabbed hold of the shower curtain, and stepped out of view.

Once he was out of her sight, the strange trance holding her finally broke. She closed her bedroom door and retreated from it hastily. Her mind spun, she tried to process the hated feelings of desire blazing to life within her as his image lingered in her mind. With nothing better to do, and looking to distract herself, she turned on the News before walking over to the sofa and perching on the edge of one of the cushions. No matter how inviting the plump cushions were, she refused to get comfortable on it.

She really hoped they found whoever this killer was tonight. She was in the mood for a fight, and even if they were human, she'd enjoy kicking the crap out of someone who had murdered and tortured innocent women and children. It would be a good way to let out some pent up, excess energy.

She had no idea what Julian planned to do when they found the guy; she highly doubted he would call the police. He couldn't plan to kill the man. She didn't know much about him, but if he traveled with a group of Hunters and Guardians, there was no way they would allow him to kill someone. Or maybe they would, what did she really know of them?

A knock on the door pulled her attention away from her thoughts. The fresh scent of soap and the pounding of human hearts told her Chris and Melissa had arrived. She walked over to open the door for them. Stepping aside, she gestured for Chris and Melissa to enter the apartment. She wondered if Julian would have something to say about Melissa's outfit as her gaze ran over Melissa's jeans and blue turtleneck.

"Hey," Melissa greeted. "I hear we're going to a strip club."

"We are, and apparently Julian would prefer it if we dressed like strippers too," Quinn told her.

Melissa chuckled as she settled herself onto the couch and fell back against the cushions Quinn had been resisting. "Of course he would."

"Has he always been so... ah... annoying?"

Chris laughed. "This is his good side. He was a lot less fun when he was trying to kill us."

This time she was unable to stop herself from gaping. "He tried to kill you?"

"A few times," Melissa said as she draped her arm around the back of the couch. "Well, mostly Cassie and Devon."

"Who are Cassie and Devon?"

"Cassie's our best friend," Melissa answered. "And Devon is our friend and Cassie's mate."

Quinn had no idea how to process this information or what a mate was. "How can you be friends with someone who tried to kill your best friend?"

"Life's funny like that," Chris said. "Sometimes what starts out as one thing becomes something entirely different."

"How did you go from being enemies to friends?" She glanced toward her bedroom door. She didn't think he'd be able to hear her over the running water, through the closed door and the noise from the TV. She didn't know why, but she felt like she was prying in some strange way, and she didn't want him to know she had any interest in his life.

"Cassie and Julian were kidnapped and imprisoned together by a bunch of insane men playing God. You would have heard of them as The Commission," Chris replied. "They were trying to create a new line of Hunters using Cassie and Julian's blood. All they created were monsters. It's why they had to be taken out."

"Really?" Quinn blurted.

She'd never thought about why The Commission had been decimated, and she hadn't cared. She'd been hiding from them from the moment she'd been born;

the loss of them had been a relief to her. It had been the same with The Elders.

"Cassie and Julian were both different when they came out of there. They were friends, they cared for each other, and they had formed a bond. Julian was…"

"He fell in love with her," Melissa supplied when Chris's voice trailed off.

Quinn didn't know why, but those words caused her deadened heart to twist in a strange way. He drove her completely nuts, what did she care who he loved? "I see. Where is Cassie now?"

"She and Devon are living with some other friends of ours. They're taking care of, and training, the Hunters and Guardians we bring to them," Chris answered.

She wondered if Julian was still in love with this woman who had established a life with another man.

"He changed a lot after their imprisonment," Melissa said. "He stopped trying to kill us which made us like him a little more. Though there are times when I'd still like to stake him."

"I can completely understand," Quinn said.

Melissa laughed. "He has that way about him."

"He does," Chris agreed.

"He's ok knowing the woman he loves is with another man?" She'd been trying not to ask the question, but it popped out before she could stop herself.

"He didn't have a choice," Melissa said. "There is no separating Cassie and Devon. Julian knew that before he fell in love with her. But you can't help who you come to love."

Quinn's attention was drawn toward her bedroom door when she heard the shower turn off. Despite her every intention not to let it happen, the image of his carved chest reflected in the mirror filled her mind as she listened to him moving around the bathroom. She hated the heat creeping up her cheeks. With nothing else to do, she walked over and turned off the TV. Standing before the set, she tried to figure out how she was ever going to get through a whole night with Julian, and no customers to distract her.

He was dangerous. He could learn everything she'd been hiding about herself her whole life. More than that, he could make her forget she had to be on guard around him. No matter how infuriating she found him, or how much she knew she had to stay away, she couldn't help but listen to the rustle of the clothes sliding over a body she desperately longed to touch.

CHAPTER 10

There were many things in her life she'd never considered doing; walking into Hawtie's was one of them. It was everything she'd assumed it would be, and more. In fact, there was *more* everywhere she looked, or perhaps it was less. She wasn't bashful, she didn't embarrass easily, but she was fighting a burning blush right now as she gazed around the dimly lit room. The only real lighting in the place was focused solely on the stage and the three poles set up there. Poles that were all occupied by women wearing less clothing than she wore to sleep in at night, and just barely more than she wore in the shower.

Her eyes darted away from them and to the numerous men crammed within the building. A good chunk of the patrons had gathered in the chairs and tables clustered around the stage, but a number of them stood at the bar and moved through the room. There were more women than she'd expected, and not all of them worked here.

The odors assaulting her highly attuned sense of smell caused her nose to wrinkle. She had to fight the urge to pinch her nostrils closed against the body odor, lust and stale alcohol smell permeating the room, but she didn't think it would help her blend into the crowd. The beat of the club music resonated in her ears, her head was already pounding, and they hadn't made it more than five feet past the door.

"Are you sure they're going to come here?" Melissa asked with a wrinkled nose and a look on her face Quinn was sure mirrored her own.

"I see five of them already," she said and waved toward one of the booths on the far wall.

The large booth was crowded with a group of townie kids. They leaned over the table in front of them as they waved money in the air. One of the kids in the booth sported a black eye and his nose had doubled in size. It was a nose she clearly recalled decking after he'd grabbed her boob last night. He didn't look overly upset about his nose as he shook his money more insistently at a woman bending in ways Quinn hadn't considered possible until now.

She scanned the crowd, picking out three more men from last night. They were all wearing their cowboy hats and leaning against the bar. The two groups may have been trying to kill each other last night, but none of them paid attention to each other now. By the time they dragged themselves back into Clint's, she knew they'd all be friends again.

"I'll be back." Julian had spoken the words in a low voice, but Quinn heard them clearly over the noise.

"We'll be at the bar," Chris said and turned away from him. "Checking out Jesse James and his gang."

"Their names are Ross, Ernie, and Jeb," she whispered to Chris. "Some of my best tippers, so be nice."

"Then you can do the talking, and I'll do the reading of them," Chris told her with a smile.

Quinn nodded as she approached the group of men. Jeb's grin split his weathered face and revealed his teeth. His hazel eyes twinkled as he tipped the front of his hat to her. He was a handsome man with curly blond hair and an easygoing charm, but she'd always brushed off his advances. She seriously doubted the, 'hey, I'm one of the living dead,' approach to starting a relationship went over great with anyone.

"Quinn what brings you to this place?" Jeb greeted.

"I thought I'd stop by and say hi to Hawtie, haven't seen her in over a week," she replied, though she'd never come in here to hunt down her friend before. "And show my friends around."

Jeb's eyes slid past her to the others before rapidly coming back to her. "Hawtie and Clint are on the outs again? That explains his actually shooting the gun last night."

Quinn chuckled. "It does." Clint and Hawtie had been on and off since they'd been out of diapers. Despite their tumultuous relationship, they always found their way back together.

"How mad is Clint?" Ross asked.

"You know Clint, by next week it will all be forgotten," she replied with a smile.

"And at eight dollars a beer we'll all be broke," Ernie said and lifted his bottle of beer into the air.

"You know what happens when you get in a fight in his bar," Quinn admonished.

Ernie ducked his head sheepishly. "Yeah, we know, but sometimes the alcohol gets the best of us."

"Not at eight dollars a pop," she replied with a laugh.

Ernie chuckled, finished off his beer and dropped it on the bar. She turned toward the young bartender with shockingly bright red hair. The woman had more piercings in her eyebrow than hair and eyes the color of a pumpkin due to contacts. Her clothes were skimpy, but her breasts were completely covered.

"What can I get you?" the woman inquired.

"I'll take a rum and coke," Quinn answered and looked questioningly toward the others.

"Water," Melissa said.

"Crown on the rocks," Chris replied.

Chris wasn't looking at the three men, but she could feel his attention tuned into them while he watched the stage. His eyes briefly met hers; he shook his head. Quinn's shoulders slumped in relief; she happily snatched up her drink and took a swallow of the cool, sweet concoction.

She knew all of the men who had been in the bar last night, but she knew some of them better than others. She really hadn't wanted it to be one of these guys. They were a good group, normally easy going, fun to talk with, and they didn't constantly try to grab her ass. She couldn't imagine any of them getting any sort of pleasure out of killing women and children, but she knew how well people could keep their secrets hidden from the world.

She took another sip of her drink as Hawtie emerged from a side room. For a woman in her fifties, Hawtie was still one the most stunning women Quinn had ever seen. Her deep auburn hair, piled on top of her head, shone in the dim light. She had high cheekbones and porcelain skin just beginning to crinkle around her warm brown eyes and full mouth.

If Hawtie's face didn't catch someone's attention, her body often stopped them dead in their tracks. Her ample breasts had been thrust upward by a curve-hugging corset. Her round hips were enhanced by the form-fitting black pants she'd poured herself into. It wasn't until Hawtie had reached her teens, or so Quinn had been told, that she'd been given, and still embraced, the fitting nickname of Hawtie the body.

Hawtie's gaze skimmed over her establishment before coming to rest on Quinn. Her painted red mouth broke into a welcoming grin and her eyes sparkled. Hawtie sashayed toward her with a sway of her hips that turned the heads in the tables closest to her.

Her arms opened to embrace Quinn in a hug that crushed her against the warm body. If Quinn had been human, she may have suffocated in the voluptuous breasts she found her face practically smooshed into. She smiled as Hawtie's heat enveloped her and the familiar scent of lavender filled her nostrils.

Hawtie smoothed back Quinn's hair when she pulled away to smile down at her. At five nine, Quinn didn't often feel small around women, but Hawtie had a good three inches on her. "What are you doing in here?" Hawtie demanded.

"Looking for you." Quinn felt bad for lying to her; however, she wasn't about to admit they were here looking for a serial killer. "Haven't seen you in over a week."

"Aw honey, you shouldn't have come in here." Hawtie grabbed both sides of the bottom of Quinn's hair and pulled it forward. It was such a strange yet oddly calming gesture Hawtie did to her often.

"I wasn't sure when you'd be returning to Clint's."

"Pfft, that man," Hawtie said and waved her red tipped fingers through the air.

"Hawtie…"

"You know how it is." Hawtie tugged on her hair before releasing it. "He's a stubborn old coot."

"And you're just as stubborn," Quinn replied. "You should just agree to marry the man already. You've been together long enough."

"And give up this last name?"

"That's not necessary anymore," Quinn said with a laugh.

"I know, but I'm not the marrying type."

"True, but you're also not the dating anyone besides Clint type."

Hawtie's deep, belly-rumbling laughter rolled from her, causing everyone nearby to smile. She slugged down the shot of tequila the bartender placed on the bar before turning back to Quinn. "That I'm not. You know the two of us, by next week we'll be all lovey-dovey again."

"I hope so," Quinn said honestly.

She missed Hawtie when she wasn't at the bar, and Clint became even more of a bear to deal with after the second week they were apart. There had been a time the two had fought for a whole month, by the end of the month Clint had been on one side of the bar and everyone else on the other.

"You could have called, we would have done dinner," Hawtie told her. "Instead of you coming in."

"It's about time I check out your place."

"Sugar, this place isn't for you."

"Hawtie, I'm a big girl. Plus I had some friends who wanted to come in," Quinn told her. *Friends* was an extremely loose term, but she didn't know how else to describe them.

Hawtie's eyes lit with curiosity. "What friends?"

It was a legitimate question, the few friends she had in town Hawtie already knew. Quinn turned and gestured Chris and Melissa forward. "This is Chris and Melissa."

Hawtie grinned and extended her hand to them. Her hand lingered within Chris's as her grin became saucy and she stuck out a hip. "Aren't you just too cute." She gave Quinn a suggestive waggle of her eyebrows before focusing on Chris and Melissa again. "And how do you know Quinn?"

"We met the other night at Clint's," Quinn answered. "They're traveling through the area."

"Isn't that wonderful!" Hawtie declared. "It's great to finally see Quinn making some friends."

If she'd been a thirteen year old girl she would have been mortified, instead she brushed the comment off. "You know my friends," Quinn replied with a false laugh.

"Yeah because they're from this town. So secretive this one." Hawtie pinched her cheek before turning toward Chris and Melissa. "Where are you from?"

"Massachusetts," Melissa answered.

"I'm not much for the cold; I like the heat," Hawtie said and bumped Quinn's hip playfully.

Hawtie's eyes slid past her, but even before they widened in admiration, Quinn knew Julian had returned. The aura of power he radiated caused her skin to ripple with awareness and her body to warm unexpectedly.

"Hell-ooo sugar," Hawtie purred. She released Quinn and adjusted her ample breasts before turning her thousand-watt smile on Julian.

Quinn shook her head, but Julian smiled back at her and propped an elbow on the bar. "Hello yourself there, Red."

It took everything she had to bite her tongue as Hawtie thrust her hand out to him. "Chelsea Hawtie, but you can call me Hawtie, everyone else does."

"I can see why," Julian replied as he took hold of her hand.

Quinn had never experienced jealousy before, but she was fairly certain that was the emotion churning in her belly right now. "Aren't you a smooth one," Hawtie said with a flutter of her sweeping lashes.

"Smooth as ice, but much more fun to play on."

Quinn choked on her drink; her hand flew up to her mouth as liquid sprayed out of it. Her eyes watered as soda surged up to burn her nose. Hawtie laughed flirtatiously, Melissa and Chris rolled their eyes and turned away from them. Quinn swore her blood began to boil when Julian started thumping her on the back, and Hawtie fixed her with assessing eyes.

Moving quickly away from his hand, she gave Hawtie a tight smile before slipping around her to stand beside Jeb and Ernie. She'd hoped having Hawtie in between her and Julian would help to calm her, it didn't. She kept her attention focused on the bottles of liquor lined up in front of the mirror behind the bar. Chugging down the rest of her drink, she pushed her empty glass toward the bartender.

"Refill?" the woman asked.

She was about to tell her to just hand over the bottle of rum when a large hand, with strong pale fingers enclosed the top of her empty glass. Julian's chiseled bicep didn't touch her, but she could feel the heat of his flesh so near to hers. If she moved so much as an inch, they would be touching each other. She knew she couldn't let it happen, but the irresistible urge to feel his flesh pressed against hers, slithered through her.

Instead, she glared daggers at the offending fingers covering her glass.

"People have lost a hand for less," she muttered grumpily.

"I know they have, but unfortunately we have to go." His affable tone caused her teeth to clench.

"I thought we were staying for a bit."

"Change of plans."

Quinn forced a cheery smile to her face when she turned to face him. She felt anything but chipper though as she met his strangely colored, yet captivating eyes. All she felt was completely overwhelmed and more than a little out of her depth. He seemed to realize this too as the corner of his mouth quirked into that aggravating little smile.

"Fine." Looking to escape him, she turned to Hawtie. Her smile was no longer forced as she embraced her friend.

"Be careful of that one," Hawtie murmured in her ear.

"I'd prefer to choke him."

Hawtie laughed, but her eyes were troubled when she stepped away.

CHAPTER 11

"It wasn't any of those guys, but I found out where there's a party tonight from the kid whose nose you permanently rearranged," Julian told Quinn when they stepped outside of the club. He scented the fresh air, glad to be free of the noise and smells permeating the strip club.

Quinn's gaze had been focused on the parking lot, but she finally looked at him. "Bonfire?"

"Yeah."

She shoved her hands into her pockets. "I know where it is."

"You've been before?"

"No." The word was blunt but she didn't expound on it. "We're going to have to borrow Clint's Jeep."

They followed her down to Clint's Bar and waited while she went inside before returning with the keys. She gestured to the back of the building. Julian walked beside her around the bar to the wooden garage set up behind it. He slid the garage door open and stepped back to admire the red Jeep parked inside. The roof and doors had been taken off the Wrangler. The jacked up tires, roll bar running across the top, and the winch on the front made it clear this was more than just a vehicle to get from point a to point b.

"Want me to drive?" he asked.

Quinn shook her head; her face remained impassive, but there was an eager glimmer in her eyes. She climbed onto the high step and swung into the driver's seat. Julian climbed up beside her; Chris and Melissa slid into the back.

Quinn shifted into first, popped the e-brake and pulled out of the garage with a lurch of the massive tires. They didn't head for the road but drove behind the garage and into the desert. The headlights bounced off of a road consisting only of sand packed down beneath the weight of the countless vehicles that had traveled over it.

The sky spread out before them with a vast array of twinkling stars. The full moon hanging heavily in the midnight sky lit the night. Quinn shifted into fourth; her smile grew as they sped across the sand. The cool wind felt refreshing against Julian's skin as it whipped through his hair and tugged at his clothes.

Sand kicked up around them and dinged off the undercarriage of the Jeep when Quinn pressed down harder on the gas. Julian grabbed hold of the roll bar over his head as the Jeep left the earth and briefly caught flight over a dune. Chris's knees pressed into the back of his seat as he braced himself more firmly. Julian heard the clicks of Melissa and Chris's seat belts sliding into place seconds before the tires crashed back to earth. They all bounced in their seats; the struts and springs squeaked and groaned, but the sounds were drowned out by Quinn's vivacious laughter.

The force of the landing was nothing compared to the amazement cascading through him at the sound of her laughing. He'd never heard her laugh before, he found it refreshing and enticing as he turned to look at her. Her honey hued eyes were aglow with pleasure; the smile curling her full mouth lit up her face as she hit the gas even harder. The illumination of the moon and the joy she radiated made her appear softer, and more approachable. She actually looked like a young woman acting her age for a change, something he didn't think she did often.

Her laughter continued as they flew over top of another dune. They crashed back to earth with enough force that he would have been launched from his seat if he didn't already have his hand braced against the roll bar. Quinn let out a whoop of joy; her hair whipped behind her as the Jeep left the earth again.

Julian couldn't stop himself from smiling at the pleasure she took in the speed and power of the vehicle. Flying over top of another dune, Julian spotted a glow in the distance and the scent of burning wood drifted into his nostrils. He wasn't ready for Quinn's laughter to stop, but he realized he didn't have a choice as she eased off the gas and sat back in her seat.

Coming over top of the next dune, the large bon-fire and nearly fifty people gathered around it came into view. Jeeps, dirt bikes, ATV's, and other assorted off road vehicles encircled the bonfire. Quinn parked the Jeep and turned the vehicle off.

"Crazy freaking vampires," Chris said. "You know, *we* can die."

Quinn chuckled as she pulled the keys from the ignition. "You're a Hunter, you heal fast."

"I still like my bones intact."

"We all do," Melissa agreed as she climbed out of the Jeep. "And we can't heal from death."

"I wouldn't have killed you," Quinn promised.

Julian ran a hand through his tussled hair as Quinn hopped out of the vehicle in one easy bound. He studied her as she moved around the Jeep with the flowing grace of a ballerina. He couldn't tear his eyes away from her as he climbed down.

"You're driving back," Chris muttered to him as he walked past.

Julian nodded but his mind was replaying Quinn's words. "How did you know about Hunters?" he inquired as he walked around to meet Quinn in front of the Jeep.

"Huh?" she asked absently, her gaze focused on the bonfire and the people gathered around it.

"How did you know that Hunters heal fast?"

She didn't look at him, but he felt a subtle change in her as she shrugged. "I already told you I knew about Hunters and how they were created."

"Yes, but it took me *years* to find out about all of their capabilities. I learned something new, and somewhat surprising, from another Hunter we're friends with two years ago." He wasn't going to go into detail about what Cassie could do, that was something they all kept secret. "Hunters aren't exactly open about what they can and can't do, especially not around vampires."

She finally looked at him. "I guess I figure things out quicker than you. They were created from us. It would only make sense they would inherit our healing abilities, since they receive an extrasensory ability from our blood too."

Maybe that was true, but he wasn't buying her explanation. Before he could question her further, and maybe uncover a little of what she was hiding from him, a loud squeal sounded and a rolling ball of energy flung herself into Quinn's arms, knocking her back a step.

"I can't believe you came!" It took Julian a second to recognize the human cannonball as Angie. "Finally! You're going to have so much fun!" She hooked her arm through Quinn's and pulled her forward. "Come on!"

Julian watched as Angie dragged Quinn toward the fire and a group of men gathered around a keg. One of the men lifted his hands into the air, and stepped forward to hug Quinn. Julian stiffened; his eyes narrowed upon the man as Quinn remained rigid in his grasp and slapped him awkwardly on the back.

Stepping away from the man, she took hold of the red plastic cup shoved into her hand. "Are we going to walk around and see if we can find the guy?" Chris asked.

Realizing his teeth were clamped together, Julian forced himself to relax his jaw. "Yeah, let's go."

The heat of the bonfire beat against his skin as he walked across the slipping sand. Quinn glanced over at them, said something to Angie, and broke away from the group. She jogged toward them without spilling a drop of her beer onto the sand.

"There's a group of people that were at Clint's on the other side of the fire," she said as she stopped before them. "Angie said there had been another group of fighters here, but they took off when they saw the guys they'd been fighting with last night. This way."

She gulped down her beer as she took the lead. Finishing off the drink, she wiped away the layer of foam on her upper lip and tossed the cup into a trash bag set off to the side. The orange glow of the fire caught her eyes, causing them to gleam like a citrine. She bee-lined through some more people, but began to slow as they advanced on a group of five men and three women gathered around another keg. Three of the men barely looked old enough to drive, never mind drink, and the other two would have been questionable to vote.

"Those five guys were there last night," Quinn informed them in a conspiring whisper. He doubted anyone would have heard her over the competing music coming from the radios of the vehicles parked around the fire, and the crackling of the ten-foot high flames.

"Do you know them?" he inquired.

"Not really, they just started coming into Clint's."

"Ok. Come with me." Her lips compressed into a flat line as she stared at him disapprovingly. He wasn't used to having to play nice with strangers, even after two years he was barely used to playing nice with Chris and Melissa. "It will be weird for me to walk over and start talking with a group of people I don't know."

She glanced at Chris, but to Julian's amazement she didn't protest further. Turning away, Quinn walked beside him toward the group of men and women. The overwhelming scent of alcohol drifted to him, but he also caught the sweeter scent of lust and the mustier scent of sex upon the man and woman holding hands and leaning close to each other.

"Hey," Quinn greeted as she stepped up to the keg. "How's it going?"

Their gazes slid over her, two of them broke into smiles, threw back their shoulders, and grinned at her. The other two were busy filling their cups at the keg. "Ya work at Clint's," one of them said in a voice already slightly slurred.

"I do," she replied with a smile. Then the boy's eyes flickered to him and Julian saw a lot of their interest fade away. They looked past her toward a group of girls who were giggling near a Ford Explorer. Sensing their waning attention, Quinn turned toward him; the smile on her face should have warned him. "You see that guy over there?" They all nodded when she pointed to Chris, who gave them a brief wave. "That's Chris, and this is his boyfriend, Julian."

Julian managed to keep his mouth closed as she continued to smile at him sweetly. He didn't know how to respond, but he was spared from having to by the eagerness of the two guys who had been ogling her before. One of them stepped forward and handed her a drink while the other began to enthusiastically offer up Dorito's and Twinkies.

Julian remained by Quinn's side, as the girls by the Ford gave him a disappointed look. He barely spared them another glance as Quinn laughed with the men. They didn't hear it, but he caught the falseness of her tone. While she kept them occupied, he managed to find a subtle way to touch three of them. It wasn't until Chris and Melissa joined them that he was able to confirm none of these guys were who they were looking for.

"I think it's time to go," Julian said and gave Quinn a pointed look.

"Sorry boys but party pooper here is my ride," Quinn told them.

"Aw," one of them protested. "We can give you a ride."

"Not tonight," she replied.

Their faces fell, Julian's teeth ground together when Dorito boy "accidentally" touched her ass for the third time. It took all he had not to break one of the orange, cheese coated fingers that were far too grabby for his liking.

"Will we see you at Clint's?" Dorito asked eagerly.

"I'll be there," Quinn replied airily. It wasn't until they were out of view of the guys that she shuddered and wiped at her ass. "Do I have cheese on my butt?" she demanded.

"No," Melissa assured her.

"Please tell me one of them was who we're looking for. I don't think I can take anymore skeasy drunk guys, parties, or strip clubs tonight."

"No, they weren't," Julian informed her. "If you hadn't told them I was gay, I would have stepped in and stopped it."

Chris and Melissa choked on their laughter as they swung admiring eyes toward her. "I never told them you were gay," Quinn replied flippantly.

"Yes, you did," he said to her before turning to glare at Chris. "If I were you, I wouldn't laugh so much, you're my partner."

Chris's laughter died down, but he continued to grin like an idiot. "No." Quinn halted and turned to face him. "I told them you were Chris's boyfriend." Julian shot Chris a look when he began to laugh again. "Angie could be considered my girlfriend, but I'm not a lesbian. They jumped to the conclusion you were gay, and apparently, so did you. Is there something you would like to tell us about yourself?"

For the first time in years, Julian found himself completely speechless as she turned on her heel and walked away. Chris lifted his finger and pointed it at Quinn when she stopped to talk with Angie again. "I like her," Chris managed to get out in between grating bursts of laughter. "I *really* like her."

Chris didn't acknowledge Julian's glower at him. "I agree," Melissa replied with a chuckle.

"Yeah, she's a ball of sunshine and fun," Julian muttered. "Or more like a thistle."

Chris and Melissa almost tripped over themselves from laughing so hard when they started to walk with him toward Quinn and Angie. "She knows how to put you in your place," Chris said.

"It's about time someone did," Melissa added.

"What did I ever do to you?" Julian protested. "After I stopped trying to kill you, of course."

"I do remember something about someone being called Romeo," she replied with a smile.

"I stand by my earlier assessment of Zachariah."

"Zach," she replied automatically.

"I've noticed you've backed off the poet too."

"He's a good guy, and he's not really mushy like that, he was just teasing."

"But?" Chris prodded.

"But nothing. I've known him for three days, can I know him a week before you two start questioning me on it."

"Ok," Chris agreed. "We'll give you a week."

"Thanks," she muttered sarcastically.

"Anything for you," Chris assured her as he draped his arm around her shoulders.

Quinn barely glanced at Julian when they stopped before her and her friends. Angie bit on her bottom lip; her admiring gaze raked him from head to toe. Julian instantly looked away from her when Quinn began to speak. "Angie says the four men who took off from here earlier were heading to the Mitchum's place."

"Then we should get going," Julian said.

"It's at someone's house, they might not let you in," Angie interjected.

Julian flashed her a smile. "There's nothing I can't get into."

Angie giggled, "I believe it." Quinn's nose wrinkled, her upper lip curled before she pressed her lips flat in disapproval. "Why are you looking for those guys anyway?"

"One of them stole Chris's wallet during the fight," Julian answered.

"That's awful!" Angie gushed. "But you can always find them some other time, maybe tomorrow."

"Need my license," Chris said. "And credit cards."

Angie's face fell. "Oh yeah." She turned to Quinn. "You finally come out and you're going to leave already." Her gaze scanned over him again; she gave a little shrug. "I guess I can see why."

"It's not like that, Ang," Quinn murmured. "I'm only trying to help out, and I know where the Mitchum's place is."

Angie's head tilted to the side as she studied them all. "What happened to your friend from the other night?" she inquired.

Julian frowned questioningly as he turned toward Quinn. "Oh, Scully was just passing through town and could only stay for a couple of hours. We had a cup of coffee, and he went on his way." Quinn's words were flippant, but her eyes had hardened at the reminder of Scully. Stepping forward, Quinn gave Angie a hug. "We should get going."

Before Angie could protest further, Quinn released her and hurried across the sand. "Have fun!" Angie called after them.

Quinn didn't look back when she waved at her. "I'll drive," Julian offered when they got to the Jeep.

"Nope," Quinn replied.

Chris shot him a look; he made an odd gesturing motion with his hand as his eyes pleaded with Julian to try again. Julian smiled at him before sliding into the passenger seat. Melissa and Chris both hesitated before reluctantly climbing into the backseat again.

CHAPTER 12

Quinn pulled up in front of the large house at the far edge of town, pulled the emergency break, and turned the Jeep off. Dim light shone from around the navy curtains covering the windows on the lower floor of the building. The front stucco façade was a deep orange in color and reflected the moon shining upon it.

Chris leaned forward in his seat and propped his elbow on the shoulder of her seat. "Nice place."

"It was a movie theatre at one time, but it's been remodeled since then," she told him.

"Must be pretty interesting inside."

"I imagine so." Quinn could hear country music playing inside as she studied the building. It was a welcoming, mellow beat after the pulse of the strip club and the competing melodies at the bonfire. "I barely know the couple who owns this place. They come into Clint's once in a while. They're about ten years older than me, and I'm not sure how they're going to feel about me walking in there," she told them.

"They'll get over it," Julian said and slid out of the seat.

Quinn didn't know how to respond to him, but then again, she never knew how to respond to half of what came out of his mouth. She watched him as he walked in front of the Jeep and stopped to study the large building.

Her attention was drawn to the shadows next to the building as she spotted people moving amongst them. The couple was mostly hidden behind a large cactus. When she heard the sound of giggling and then a slurping kiss, she hastily looked away. She'd had enough of naked bodies and people groping each other for one night.

Grabbing the keys from the ignition, she jumped out of the Jeep. "Are we going to have to couple up in order to gain entry?" Julian asked her and looked pointedly at the keys in her hand.

The teasing glint in his eyes caused a strange flutter in the area of her deadened heart; she forced herself to scowl at him. "If you put your arm around me, I'll break it."

He leaned so close to her that she realized the white band encircling his pupils actually had inflections of pale turquoise within them. She tried not to lose herself to his striking eyes, the smile curving his luscious mouth, or the intoxicating pull of his power.

"One of these days Quinn, you're going to admit you like me."

Her lips compressed into a flat line. She gave him a disapproving look, but she couldn't deny the excitement sliding over her at having him standing so close. He rose back to his full height and turned toward the house. Chris and Melissa's eyebrows were in their hairline when he stepped away from her.

She looked quickly away from the pointed glances Chris and Melissa swapped with one another. They may not be saying anything, but plenty of silent conversation was being exchanged between them.

Moving past them, she followed Julian to the front door. He knocked on the door and stepped back when the sound of feet approaching from the other side could be heard. Quinn didn't recognize the woman who opened the door, but it didn't matter as the woman's eyes found Julian and stayed there.

The three of them could have been wearing ninja costumes and waving katanas around, the woman still wouldn't have spared them a glance. She tossed back her bleached blond hair and stuck a hip out in a seductive gesture. If she pushed her lips out any further, she would be giving Daffy Duck a run for his money, Quinn decided. The woman lifted a hand, wrapped it around the doorframe, and thrust out her ample breasts.

"Hello there," she purred. Quinn tried to remain impassive, but she felt her eyes narrow upon the woman. Images of knocking those lips back into place and stopping the fluttering of those lashes filled her mind. She didn't know how the woman opened her eyes with all the goop she'd coated onto those lashes. "Have you come to join the party?"

"We have." Julian waved at the three of them when he spoke, but the woman's eyes still didn't flicker in their direction. The sexy smile, and subtle lean in toward the woman that Julian gave her, caused her not to hesitate before stepping aside. She waved her hand in a welcoming gesture, it still wasn't enough to grant them entrance. "Are you sure we're welcome?" Julian prodded.

Smooth as grease, she thought. She couldn't help but admire his suave manipulation of the woman though.

Yep, she wouldn't mind plucking every one of those lashes from the duck mouthed woman across from them as she leaned close enough to Julian to press her obviously fake boobs against his arm. "You're welcome anywhere I am," she purred and Quinn couldn't stop the disgusted sound that escaped her as the woman stepped aside. "Come in."

Julian slid gracefully past her, but Quinn's movements were more measured. She stared at the woman who gave her as much attention as she would a speck of dust. Melissa and Chris followed her into the dimly lit, massive foyer of the home.

Quinn could just barely make out the bones of what remained of the movie theatre in the two massive doorways across from them. She could picture holding her popcorn and drink as she made her way into one of those doorways to see the show. One of the doors had thick red drapes blocking it; the other had black drapes pulled back to allow people entrance.

On her right was a kitchen so large she felt the urge to cook for the first time in six years. Stainless steel appliances sparkled in the dim glow coming from the recessed lights. Shiny copper pots hung from a rack over the island in the center of the room. Nothing remained of it, but she assumed the kitchen had once been the concession area.

To her left was a dining room with a table large enough to seat twelve people around it. The china cabinet behind it had at least a year's worth of her pay tucked behind its glass doors. Maybe it had once been the ticket and entrance area of the theatre, or perhaps it had been some backroom for employees only, either way it was magnificent now.

"This way." Duck lips wrapped her hands around Julian's bicep and began to walk with him toward the room with the open drapes.

Quinn tried to focus on her surroundings, but she felt herself glaring daggers into the two backs in front of her. She really hoped this would be their last stop of the night so she could go home and bash the crap out of her punching bag. The idea of pretending the bag was Julian made her almost giddy with anticipation.

She tried not to think about what the feelings rolling around inside her might mean. She didn't want him in her life and she wasn't going to *let* him any further into it. However, she still wouldn't mind kicking old Ducky in the ass.

Shock rippled through her when they stepped into the room. Across the way, the stage that had once held the movie screen had been turned into a dance space with wood floors. The bar behind the dance floor easily rivaled the size of the one at Clint's. All of the movie seats had been ripped out and replaced with red couches and black chairs that were set up so they faced each other. The people lounging within those seats could talk to each other without having to raise their voices to be heard over the music.

The idea had never once crossed her mind before, but looking around she realized it was pretty freaking awesome to live in an old movie theatre! She found it difficult to keep her mouth closed as she tilted her head back to look into the space above her. Numerous speakers were set within the rafters; the music drifting from them wasn't overwhelming or too loud. There were various movie posters hanging from the ceiling that had all been stitched out of cloth. They depicted classic movies with the newest one being Anthony Perkins', *Psycho*.

"Impressive," Chris murmured from beside her.

"Yeah," she said and finally tore her attention away from the rafters. "I guess I should see if those men are here."

Chris nodded and she stepped away from him. She refused to look at Julian and that woman again as she began to mingle with the crowd. The few people she knew greeted her, but most of the people within the room weren't the type to spend much time at Clint's. She searched for someone she recognized from the fight, and finally spotted one of the men standing at the bar.

With ease, she weaved her way through the crowd toward the stage. The sound of the music was louder up here but still not overwhelming. She climbed the two steps and walked across the stage toward the stranger. Stepping beside him, she rested her hands on the bar and leaned forward to study the bottles lined up before the glass. The assortment of liquor lining the shelves would have made Clint jealous.

"Would you like me to make you something?" the man beside her offered.

"I'm having a tough time deciding," she replied with a smile as she tried to recall his name.

He grinned at her. "I'll make you something special." He made his way around the bar and began to study the bottles on the shelves. "You work at Clint's."

"I do," she answered though it hadn't been a question.

"I was part of that fight last night."

"Oh really?" she feigned. "It was all so crazy; I didn't know what was going on." Ugh, she kind of disliked *herself* right now. Weak, confused female wasn't a role she played well. She hoped he'd been preoccupied enough he hadn't seen her break the other guy's nose.

He lifted his head to meet her gaze and smiled as he placed a bottle of rum on the bar. He may like fragile women, but at least he knew how to pick a drink. "It was a little hectic. You should have stayed out of it, but I'm glad you weren't hurt."

Her teeth clamped together; she forced a smile. "Me too."

She leaned closer to him while he dropped some ice in the glass. *What am I doing?* She wondered. This wasn't her; she wasn't a flirt. She sure as hell didn't pretend to be demure and weak, especially not around someone who could possibly be the next Jeffrey Dahmer.

Then she heard the cackling laughter of Ducky and she knew immediately what she was doing. She was staying away from that shit show. If she was honest, she might admit she could be trying to make Julian jealous, but she found she much preferred to lie to herself right now.

The ice clinked against the side of the glass when he slid her drink toward her. "Thank you." Her voice had stopped being flirty and airy though.

She'd been many things over the years, but one thing she'd always prided herself on was being independent. She couldn't deny that Julian affected her; she wouldn't change herself for him though. Julian would be able to find out if this man was a killer just by touching him. Her leading him on would get them nowhere and only make her feel worse about herself.

She grabbed hold of the glass and swallowed the contents. The man's eyes lit up as he took her glass to refill it. This was the most she'd ever drank. Thankfully, her digestive system processed alcohol far faster as a vampire than it had when she'd been alive. She didn't even have a buzz after all of the alcohol she'd consumed tonight. Which was a good thing because Clint would kick her ass if she crashed his Jeep, his baby.

He refilled her drink and pushed it toward her. Propping his elbows on the bar, he leaned toward her. "So," he said, and before she knew what he intended, he ran his finger down the scar on her chin. "How did you get this?"

Quinn recoiled from him; memories flooded her mind. For one horrible minute, she was trapped in a place she'd spent the past six years trying to avoid. Closing her eyes did nothing to block out the blood splattering the room. It did nothing to shut out the image of the only woman who'd ever been a mother to her falling before her. The screams of the dying echoing in her ears drowned out the music filling the room.

A shudder ran through her. She forced herself to open her eyes and shake off the memories of the past as she strained to concentrate on the present. He'd thrown her off when he'd asked the question. Most people pretended not to see her scars, others stared openly at them, but in the six years since her face had been sliced open, no one had ever outright asked her about them. She didn't know if she hated him for asking, or if she had a grudging admiration for having the balls to ask when no one else ever had.

She forced herself to shrug. "Accident."

It had been far from an accident but she wasn't about to tell him that. Her hand was steady when she picked up her drink. Instead of drinking it, she placed it back on the bar.

"Car?" he asked.

"No," she replied abruptly. "Thanks for the drink."

He seized hold of her wrist when she went to turn away. Her first instinct was to zap his hand away from her, but she managed to suppress it. With the mood she was in, she might just cause him to fall into the bottles lining the glass shelves and attract far more attention to them than she was looking for right now.

"What's the rush, honey?" he inquired.

"I'm not bear food, my name is Quinn. I have to get back to my friends." She tugged on her wrist but he didn't release it. Her teeth ground together. The cells in her body began to slide toward his; she could feel the crackling energy within them as they sought out his skin. "Let me go."

The flood of her energy pooled against the palm of his hand. It would be so easy to pull the life force from him, to feed on it and absorb it. She was a vampire in every sense of the word, a drainer of life in every possible way, and the idea of taking it was so very enticing.

No matter how tempted she was to give him a jolt he would never forget, it wasn't enough of a reason to flirt with the lure of darkness that came with her ability. There would be so much pleasure if she ever gave in and allowed herself to wield her ability freely, but she could never let herself become one of the monsters she'd always despised. She would walk into the sunlight first.

His lips skimmed back to reveal his teeth in a strange smile that looked more like a grimace. "What's going on?" She'd been so focused on the man she hadn't felt the pulse of power that signaled Julian's arrival.

Quinn gave up on pulling her wrist free as she turned to face Julian. She disliked Cowboy holding her wrist, but she didn't need someone to rescue her. Not when she could blast Cowboy's grip off of her or rip out his throat.

"Just getting a drink," she replied. Julian's gaze slid from her to the man and back again. The man released her. Instead of pulling her arm away, she left it resting on the bar and smiled up at Julian. "Where's your friend?"

Julian's eyes twinkled; he put his elbow on the bar and leaned against it. Cowboy glanced between them before leveling a resentful look on Julian. "She's around," Julian replied carelessly.

"I'm sure she is," Quinn said and lifted her drink.

"We were talking here," Cowboy protested. He definitely had a set of balls, she decided as Julian had a good two inches and thirty pounds on him.

Julian gave him the amused look most people gave to a toddler talking into their toy phone. Quinn bit on her inner cheek to keep herself from laughing. "And?" Julian drawled.

Cowboy made a huffing noise. Deciding Julian wasn't worth fighting with, he turned his attention back to Quinn. "Would you like to dance?" he asked her.

Not at all, she thought, but she pondered the proposition while she stared at Julian. The smile slid from his face; his eyes burned into hers as he waited for her answer. Quinn lifted her drink and finished it off. She pushed the glass away from her. The guy went to grab for it at the same time Julian did. Their fingers bumped against each other before Julian pulled his hand away.

She gave him a questioning look; he shook his head no. Quinn's shoulders sagged, all the energy drained from her. Before she'd been looking forward to pummeling her punching bag, now all she wanted was to go home, crawl into bed and sleep until she had to go to work tomorrow night. That wasn't going to be an option, but at least she didn't have to deal with Cowboy anymore.

Ignoring the drink Cowboy placed before her, she turned away and hurried down the steps to the main room. Her gaze ran over the few dozen people gathered within. Chris and Melissa were talking with another one of the men from last night, but she didn't see the other two. The crackle of energy against her spine alerted her to Julian's presence behind her.

"Where are the other two men?" she inquired.

"In the room next door would be my guess," he answered.

She weaved her way through the crowd and back out to the main entryway. Her eyes traveled to the red velvet draped over the other massive doorway. "Are we allowed in there?" she whispered.

"Dewdrop we're allowed to go wherever we want, once we're invited in of course," he added with a wink.

"People have a right to their privacy."

"Not tonight." Before she could stop him, he pulled back the curtain and stepped inside. Quinn hesitated outside, unwilling to intrude upon someone's space. He turned back to her, his eyebrow arched as he studied her. "Scared?"

"Are you going to double dog dare me next?" she scoffed.

"Triple dog dare."

"For someone who was alive when Columbus set sail, you have the maturity level of a teenager," she retorted.

Damn she hated that smile, or not so much the smile, but the strange flips and flutters it caused to erupt in her belly. "I'm young at heart. Let's go you cranky old fart."

Her nostrils flared as she glared at him, but she still followed him into the dimly lit hallway beyond the drapes. This area of the movie theatre was far different than the remodeled one they'd just left. She felt a little claustrophobic, as the black walls were only inches away from her arms.

"I think we just stepped into the nineteen seventies," she muttered.

"I really hope there are no black lights somewhere. Even *I* didn't enjoy that little trend. With as pale as vampires are, we all looked like freaks under those things."

"I'm more afraid of the key party you mentioned before."

"I don't think it's that either," he muttered as he surveyed the hall.

Quinn didn't like the constricted hallway, but she sensed no impending danger from the shadows surrounding them. They passed by a few doors that were open to reveal the rooms beyond. A library, stuffed full of books and two comfy looking sofas almost made her stop to go snoop. The other two rooms had small beds tucked within the orderly spaces. No pictures, perfume, jewelry, or other personal items marked the rooms. Looking in at them, she assumed they were guest rooms.

At the end of the hall was a closed door of another room she thought might be the master bedroom; she certainly wouldn't want people looking in on her sleeping space. Beside the closed door was a set of stairs leading up. The scent of cigarettes and cigars drifted down to her, along with the aroma of stale booze and beer.

Craning her head, she stared up the stairs but could only make out a faint light above as the stairs curved out of view. It didn't smell like anyone was having sex up there, but she really didn't want to take the chance that they might be.

Unfortunately, Julian didn't have any of the same reservations she did; he immediately started up the stairs. If the scents changed to something more intimate by the time they arrived at the top, she planned to turn and bolt back down the stairs. She'd leave him behind if he decided to join the party.

She planned to live years, and experience many things, none of them involved discovering her neighbors involved in an orgy. She fought the urge to cover her eyes when Julian made it to the top and stepped out of view.

A clinking noise came from above; she could also make out a distinct rattling sound. She couldn't quite place what was creating the noises as she stepped off the stairs behind him and into a large room. The smoky haze filling the air caused her eyes to water; she rapidly blinked away the tears. Her forehead furrowed as she stared around the room. It took a minute for her to process that she hadn't walked into some sort of bad porno movie.

Poker chips clinked together as the people sitting around one of the poker tables tossed them onto the pile in the middle. Two other card tables were set up in what had been the old projection room. There was also a roulette and craps table in the room. All of the card tables were filled with people, and there were more people standing behind them waiting to take a seat.

"Not what I was expecting," she murmured.

"Get your head out of the gutter, Dewdrop," Julian replied.

She shot him a look, but he was too busy watching the room to notice her. A few heads looked up when they entered, but for the most part no one paid them any attention and remained raptly focused on their games. She spotted the other two men from Clint's last night at the roulette table. They had beers in their hands as they watched the ball spinning around the wheel.

A lanky brunette approached them in a dress Quinn would have considered more of a nighty. Apparently it was perfectly acceptable public wear for this woman as no one else gave her a second glance. The woman raked Quinn with a scathing gaze from head to toe; it seemed she found Quinn's outfit as inappropriate as Quinn found hers.

"It's a hundred dollar entry fee," the brunette said, her attention solely focused on Julian.

Julian pulled his wallet out of his pocket. He searched through the wad of cash as he spoke, "It's just me playing, but I'd like to keep my lucky charm here with me."

Quinn groaned inwardly as the trashy brunette looked her up and down again before glancing at the stairs behind her. It was obvious she didn't think he could possibly be calling *her* his lucky charm. Quinn didn't know what possessed her, she stepped closer to Julian and wrapped her arm through his. She smiled sweetly at the woman as Julian lifted his head to stare at her in disbelief.

"Call me lucky," she said through her teeth.

The woman gave her a disdainful look, but she took the hundred Julian handed out to her and slid it into her ample cleavage. "You can call on me for anything you need," she said to Julian before turning on her heel and walking regally through the crowd.

Quinn glared at the woman's back, a back she could clearly see through the mesh of her dress. "Careful, people might think you like me."

"Hardly," she snorted. "I just don't like snot bag, stuck up women."

He looked down at where her arm was linked through his before his eyes came back to hers. She tried to deny it felt good to feel his flesh against hers. Even at its slightly cooler temperature, it heated her in a way she'd never experienced before. His eyes dilated, his fingers sliding over her skin caused shivers of pleasure to dance across her flesh. If she still breathed, she would be breathless, if she still had a heartbeat it would be racing. She felt trapped within his gaze, unable to move as his fingers continued to brush sensually over her flesh.

Her ability coursed to where their arms connected. To her surprise, it wasn't seeking out his life force but looking to connect with him in some way. The rush of power she felt when she linked with him caused her to remember why she'd been trying to avoid touching him to begin with. Terror pooled through her, she jerked her arm away as if he'd burned her and took a hasty step away.

Fighting to regain her composure, she ran her hands nervously over her arms. How much had he seen of her? *What* had he seen? The spinning of her mind caused the world to blur a little.

Inwardly, she kicked herself in the ass; her temper had gotten the best of her. However, she had to admit she'd been craving to touch him again ever since that first time. In the heat of the moment, she'd completely forgotten the riskiest thing she could do was let her guard down around this man and allow herself to touch him.

The longing look on his face unsettled her even more. He stretched a hand toward her, but dropped it back down when she took another step away from him. "Dewdrop…"

"We should get this over with. Sunrise is only a couple hours away."

Before she could hear what he had to say, or what he'd learned of her, she made a bee-line for the roulette table. She had no idea how the game was played. Julian handed out more cash in exchange for chips.

"Have a lucky number?" he asked her.

"Thirteen."

"Good thing I'm not superstitious." He smiled at her, but she was still so rattled she couldn't come up with a snappy retort. He placed a number of chips on the black number thirteen. Quinn remained immobile as she watched the ball bouncing around the spinning wheel before it finally landed on the number thirteen. "You really are my good luck charm," he said with a grin as the chips were pushed toward him. "Pick another number."

Her fingers trembled as she shook her head. She didn't care about picking another number, all she cared about was getting out of there. Before she could turn away, he grabbed hold of the hand she'd rested on the table.

A zing of pleasure ran through her; she tried to tug her hand away from his unyielding grasp. Power grew in her fingertips, her skin crackled with the life force she could feel swirling between them. She didn't want to harm him, but he refused to release her.

"Pick a number, Quinn." His gaze was as unrelenting as his hold on her. She had to be hurting him; he showed no sign of it as his face remained blank. The full force of her power didn't flow into him but it was enough to inflict pain. Like the rolling tide, she pulled his energy from him and shoved it back into him in equal measure. He kept his hand wrapped around hers when he placed them both on the table.

"Twenty-three." Her gaze remained riveted upon his as he held her stare. "Please, let me go."

He released her hand instantly, turned away from her and placed the chips onto the number twenty-three. He didn't look at her as the little ball began to bounce around the wheel again. She was still staring at him when the number two was called. All the chips were claimed by a little man with a cigar hanging out of his mouth sitting opposite them at the table.

What had he seen of her?

Her stomach churned with apprehension as she pondered this question. But even more than her anxiety over what she might have revealed to him, the loss of contact with him left her feeling hollow. She dropped her hands down before her and rubbed at the back of the hand he'd been holding. Julian moved around her to stand next to the men who had been a part of the fight last night.

A waiter arrived to take their drink orders. Julian waved him away, and as much as she would like to chug down a bottle of rum right now, she also shook her head no. She remained rigid beside Julian as she fought to keep herself from bolting out of the room, and this place.

The wheel on the table began to spin again. She paid no attention to the bouncing ball; she felt as if she were looking through a fog as she watched Julian maneuver through the men. His arm brushed subtly against the arm of one of the guy's.

She didn't know exactly when he came into contact with the other man, but after a few more minutes he bent low to whisper near her ear, "It's not them. We can go."

Quinn forced herself to nod. She followed him mutely to the stairs and watched his back as he descended. The muscles beneath his form-fitting shirt rippled with every step he took. She opened her mouth multiple times to speak with him; every time she clamped her lips shut again.

They were halfway down the shadowed hall when the question she'd been fighting against asking, finally tumbled from her lips, "What did you see when you touched me?"

He spun toward her so rapidly that even with her vampire vision she barely saw him move before he had her pinned against the wall. He rested his hands on either side of her head and bent lower to look her in the eyes. She shrank away from him; doing everything she could not to touch him.

A muscle twitched in his cheek, his eyes were as cold as the ice their color mirrored. "I can turn it off you know."

"Turn what off?" she managed to croak out because it certainly wasn't *her*.

"My ability. I can turn it off."

She swallowed as she searched his eyes. "Julian…"

"I didn't see anything when we touched because I wasn't trying to. Whatever your secrets are Quinn, they're yours to keep." Relief swelled through her; she had only a second to relax before his finger slid over her cheek. She tensed at the hungry gleam that lit his eyes when his finger dipped toward her lip. "For now, but I think you'll tell them to me one day. So you can stop going out of your way not to touch me."

His arrogance caused her temper to rise, but the feel of his finger against her skin turned her insides to goo. "I don't have any secrets," she managed to force out. "And I have not been going out of my way to avoid your touch."

"Don't lie Dewdrop, it's unbecoming." She fought the urge to drive her knee into his groin. He must have sensed this as his mouth curved into a smile and his finger stilled on her lip. "Easy tiger."

The hair on her arms stood up, her skin became electrified when he leaned closer to her. How could she long to punch him in the face so badly and yet find herself so irresistibly drawn to him? Stepping away from him would be the best thing for her to do, but right now she found herself aching to know what those lips would feel like pressed against hers. She wanted the answer to that question more than she wanted to make him scream like a girl.

The smile slid from his face, his eyes searched hers for a minute before he slowly bent his head. She'd contemplated what it would be like to kiss him, had been denying the truth she'd been yearning to do this since she'd first seen him. But no matter what she'd expected it would be like, nothing came close to the reality of it as his mouth took firm possession of hers.

Heat sizzled over her body at the same time goose bumps broke out on her flesh. His hand encircled her neck; he pulled her closer to him as he deepened the kiss. Unable to stop herself, Quinn wrapped her hands around his powerful forearms and clung to him. His sinewy muscles flexed beneath her grasp, his tongue slid over her lips in a sensuous motion that made her head spin. She relented to the gentle pressure of his tongue and opened her mouth to him.

A low groan escaped him; he tipped her head back further and tasted her in deep, thrusting pulls. His kiss was a drug that ensnared her as his tongue pushed her to heights of ecstasy she'd never dreamed she could attain. His body covered hers, his thigh slid between her legs as he pushed her into the wall. What his tongue did to her was nothing compared to what the feel of his firm body pressed flush against hers did. Every part of her begged for more of him, to feel bare flesh against bare flesh...

Of its own volition, her power surged toward him. She could feel it connecting with him, drawing the essence of him forward and into her in a dance that caused her excitement to increase. Unlike the other times when she drained the life from someone, now she took and gave to him in equal measure. She tried to shut her ability down, but it had spiraled beyond her control, so had the reaction of her body. Releasing him, she slid her arms around his neck and pulled him closer.

Constraint became a thing of the past; the press of his fangs against her lips caused a moan to escape her. Another low rumble emanated from him when her tongue brushed over those fangs. He nipped at her lower lip, not hard enough to draw blood, but enough to make her almost scream with desire. She impatiently tugged at his hair, pulling him closer but unable to get close enough.

She struggled to regain control of herself when he broke off the kiss. Cloudy with passion, his eyes had deepened to the blue of the Mediterranean Sea as they held hers. He was the most magnificent man she'd ever seen, and if he said one conceited, asshole comment right now, she would blast him so violently she'd shoot him straight through the wall across the hall.

He didn't say anything stupid though. Instead, his finger brushed over her lower lip again before he took a small step away. Her hands twitched to grab him and pull him back against her, but his next words stopped her, "The sun will be up soon."

CHAPTER 13

Jerked from sleep, Julian blinked against the sparse illumination filtering through the heavy drapes. Frowning, he tried to figure out what had woken him when he heard a low moan from Quinn's bedroom. He swung his feet to the floor and rose swiftly. He moved so fast across the small space it felt as if he were flying over the floor. Grabbing hold of the knob, he thrust it open before he could stop to think about what he was doing.

Quinn lay in the middle of the bed, her pale skin vibrant against the midnight blue sheets and her chocolate colored hair. Sweat beaded over her forehead and across her upper lip; her hair stuck to her cheeks and forehead. The faded red t-shirt she wore had bunched up around her stomach to reveal her cotton shorts. His eyes narrowed on another red, puckered scar just beneath her sternum.

Another scar? What had happened to this girl?

His mind spun through the possibilities, his blood boiled at the torment she'd experienced in her short lifetime. If anyone could relate to cruelty, he could. He'd bestowed enough of it upon this world and he'd also experienced more than his fair share. The Commission had been the worst of it, but he'd been beaten and brutalized by older vamps before he'd been old enough to defend himself against them.

When she revealed her secrets to him, he'd gladly tear the head off of whoever had done this to her. Until then, he'd have to bide his time and hopefully earn her trust enough to get her to open up to him.

He stood in the doorway, uncertain what to do as she thrashed to the side and released another low moan. She was having a nightmare but wasn't in any real jeopardy; he knew she wouldn't want him here. When tears began to streak down her face, he found himself unable to resist her.

She moaned again and thrashed to the side. The sheets tangled around her legs and fell across the floor. Reaching out, he placed his hand on her shoulder to wake her. He'd braced himself and shut his ability down before touching her, a barrage of images still slipped through to flood his mind. The images of her nightmare were too much to keep out; they were too vibrant and real for her.

Screams resonated in his head; blood splattered around the room much like paint being thrown onto a canvas. A man fell to the ground, followed by a teen-aged girl with hair as dark as Quinn's, and brown eyes. Life still glimmered in the man's eyes, but the teen girl stared sightlessly at the ceiling over her head. He remembered the man and girl from the family picture he'd seen the first time he'd touched Quinn.

The pull she had over him wasn't broken until she bolted awake; her golden eyes were dazed as they rolled toward him. She stared at him unseeingly before reality crashed over her. She didn't bolt up in the bed or grab at the covers. She simply stared at him with tears sliding down her face.

"You were having a nightmare."

Her gaze slid away from him; she focused on the small TV on her bureau. "No more zombie movies for me before bed," she murmured.

He didn't question her on the lie; she'd only be angry with him for seeing things he knew she preferred to keep to herself. He'd never intended to tell her he could shut his ability off, but he'd grown so tired and frustrated with her going out of her way to avoid him that he'd caved on his decision. Now that he'd touched her and tasted her though, he wanted even more of her, or at the very least he wanted to curl up beside her, draw her into his arms and chase her nightmares away. It killed him not to be able to hold her, to console her and kiss the tears from her silken skin.

"Quinn…"

"I'm fine," she whispered. "I'm sorry I woke you."

"Don't be sorry." Unable to stop himself, he bent and placed a kiss to her forehead. "I'm here if you need me."

The wounded look in her eyes when they met his made his heart ache. He'd never felt this urge to protect someone so fiercely before, not even with Cassie. But then, Cassie had never been his to take care of, and Quinn was staring at him with eyes that shimmered with moisture.

"I'm fine," she whispered again. "You can go back to sleep."

He brushed the hair back from her face before stepping away from her. It took everything he had to keep walking, but he knew when he wasn't welcome somewhere.

"Julian." He turned back in the doorway to look at her. Her hair tumbled around her shoulders as she sat up on the bed. "Thank you."

"Anything for you, Dewdrop," he told her with a smile and left the room.

Walking back to the couch, he knew there would be no more sleep for him tonight. Not now that he realized those last four words had been the truest four words of his life.

***

Julian kept his arm draped over his eyes as he listened to the sounds of Quinn moving about her room. He gritted his teeth together and launched up from the couch when the shower turned on. Prowling the living room, he felt like a caged lion as he paced from the doorway to the window and back again. His skin felt too small for him. All he wanted was to go into the bedroom, pull her into his arms and crush her against him. He could lose himself in her again like he had for those few minutes in the movie theatre gaming house.

He never should have kissed her; he never should have gone into her room last night, but there was something so damn irresistible about the stubborn woman. He was supposed to be trying to keep her safe, not molesting her in the hallway of someone else's house. He wasn't supposed to be entering her room when she was vulnerable and trapped within the memories haunting her, but it was impossible for him to fight the pull of her.

But he should be fighting against her in every way in order to ensure she was never hurt again. All he'd ever done in his life was bring misery to others. And death, he'd brought a lot of death into other's lives. From what he'd seen she'd had far too much of that already in her life.

He'd never hated his ability before; there had always been things he'd never wanted to see from a person, but he'd always been able to use that to his advantage. Tormenting people and vampires with his knowledge of their pasts and loved ones was something he'd thrilled in. He'd wielded his ability with more lethal intent than he'd wielded his fangs over the years.

Now, he cursed it. Now he found himself wanting to comfort someone rather than use his knowledge to crush her with it; something he most likely would have done just two years ago. Quinn was everything he would have despised then. Good, loving, caring, and able to keep her murderous impulses under control when he'd never bothered to even try.

Frustration built within him. He had this knowledge, and there was nothing he could do with it. Not until she opened up to him, but she was willful and hiding behind her trauma.

And he might be the worst possible man for her to open up to. He wasn't right for her, he'd never been right for anyone. There was too much in his past. He'd spent these past two years trying to be different, but there were things he'd done in his lifetime no one should know or be exposed to.

She was a vampire, but she was also an innocent, something he never had been, not even when he'd been human. He'd only bring her more hurt, something he refused to do. She was just so tempting with her full mouth, haunted eyes, and that defiant thrust of her pointed, scarred chin.

The vibration of his phone drew his attention to where he'd plugged it in by the rickety TV stand. If he didn't think she'd kick him in his nuts and stake him in his sleep, he'd replace all of her shitty furniture, but going against her wishes would only push her further away and that was the last thing he wanted. Grabbing the phone, a smile curved his mouth when he saw Cassie's name on the screen.

"Hello Buttercup," he greeted. "How are things in the tundra?"

Her cheerful chuckle caused him to smile more. He may not be in love with her anymore, he'd managed to move on from that over the last two years, but he still loved her dearly and she would always be one of the most important vampires in his life. He'd discovered he was capable of becoming a better man because of her; he owed her his life and so much more.

"It's not that bad up here, if you came back to visit more often you would know that," she chided.

"We'll be back soon. I'd prefer to wait till spring but I'm sure we'll be back before then. How are things?"

He could feel her sober up across the airwaves, feel the smile leave her face and her laughter fade away. "Everyone is doing well; Barnacle misses you." Barnacle was one of the children they'd taken under their protection a couple of years ago. They'd found him, and other orphaned children under the control of The Commission. It was also where they'd first encountered and befriended Lou. "Devon does too. He's a little outnumbered by women up here right now."

"Better him than me," he replied with a laugh. "Now, what's wrong?"

"How can you always tell?"

"It's in your voice; what's wrong?"

"I had a vision."

He turned away from the closed door of Quinn's room and paced toward the kitchen. "What did you see?"

Silence drifted across the airwaves. He could hear her moving about; picture her walking out of one room and into another. "A desert, a woman with brown hair and golden eyes." Julian stopped pacing; he turned in the doorway to look back and make sure her door was still closed.

"What about her?"

"She's in danger. I didn't see what is after her but I got this…" she broke off as she searched for words. "This *impression* of danger. She must be kept safe. I don't know why, I only know we have to protect her. I don't know how you're going to find her…"

"I think I already have," he said quietly. "Scars on her face?"

"Yes."

His hand tightened around his phone as the water of the shower turned off. "We've found her. Her name is Quinn."

"You have to get her somewhere safe."

"That's a problem seeing as she won't leave. She kind of reminds me of someone else in that way."

Cassie chuckled. "I have no idea who you're talking about."

"I'm sure you don't. We've already encountered a group of vampires after her. One of them informed us that a vampire also had a vision about her. The vamps are hunting for her, but they don't know where she is or what she looks like. There's another evil in this town too." He quickly explained what had happened in the bar the other night and the hunt he'd been on ever since.

"You'll find them." He could hear her fingers tapping against a countertop. "Why are they hunting her?"

"She's powerful, *extremely* powerful, and I think they're trying to become the new Elders. Or trying to regain a threshold of their former power in the world by forming an alliance."

She made a hissing sound. "Julian…"

"It's not going to happen, Cass," he assured her. "I won't allow it. Besides, just because some of them may be amongst the oldest still in existence that doesn't make them an Elder. None of them will be able to make it through me."

"Maybe we should come down there."

"No."

"But what if something happens?" she asked worriedly.

"We'll be fine," he assured her.

"We can help keep her safe."

"And you could end up becoming a target for them. She is extremely gifted and stronger than she should be, but they'd completely bypass her if they believed they had a chance of getting their hands on *you*. No matter how powerful she is, you're stronger, Solar."

He could practically hear her teeth grinding over the airwaves. "I hate it when you call me that."

"I know."

The sound of her laughter helped to ease some of the tension. "You'll let me know if you need our help."

"I will."

It was a lie, what he'd said before had been the truth. He didn't think many vampires knew what Cassie was capable of, but if they ever figured it out she would become their biggest target. They'd either try to take her out or try to find a way to bend her to their will.

At heart, she was one of the purest souls he'd ever met, but she'd do anything for her loved ones, especially Devon. He would never take the chance of putting the most powerful vampire in the world into the hands of vampires who would destroy her. He'd have to call Devon later and make sure he knew Cassie wasn't to come anywhere near Arizona, or Quinn, until everything was sorted out.

"Liar," she muttered.

"You know me so well."

Seconds stretched by before she spoke again. "You take care of yourself and the others, Julian."

"Of course."

"You're still so annoyingly stubborn."

He laughed as he turned away from the bedroom again. "So are you, but if you come down here I'll kick your ass and so will Devon. Think of Barnacle and stay safe, for once."

"Yeah, yeah, yeah... I'm going to be calling and pestering you all, and I'll be on the first night flight out if it becomes necessary."

"I wouldn't expect anything else."

"Stay safe."

"I will," he promised.

"I love you."

"Love you too."

He hung up the phone and turned to find Quinn standing in the doorway of her bedroom. Her hair hung in wet tendrils around her face. The look in her eyes was one he'd never seen before. For the first time since he'd met her, she appeared almost vulnerable as she stared at him.

The scar on her chin, and across her eyebrow, stood out more sharply against her paler than normal skin. He suspected the one cutting across her temple was also more noticeable, but her hair covered it. Even in her simple black pants and shirt she wore for work, she was incredibly alluring. The shirt hid most of her curves but the pants hugged her muscled thighs and calves.

"Did you get any more sleep?" His voice came out gruffer than he'd intended, but seeing her brought his lust racing back to the forefront. He ground his teeth against the urge to take her into the bedroom and spend the rest of the night barricaded in there with her.

"No."

Her gaze slid to his phone; she didn't ask who he'd been talking to as she moved away from her bedroom and toward the kitchen. He stepped out of the way when she turned sideways to walk past him. The fresh scent of her cucumber shampoo filled his nostrils; he resisted the urge to grab her and pull her into his arms.

"That was my friend, Cassie." She didn't look at him as she opened the fridge and pulled out a can of Mountain Dew. There was a subtle stiffening in her shoulders though. "She had a vision that you're in danger."

"She has Melissa's ability?"

"She has many abilities." She finally shot him a questioning look over her shoulder. "She's a rarity."

"I see," she murmured as she opened the can.

"Like you."

Below her left eye, a muscle began to twitch in her cheek. Her scar stood out starkly against her skin when she clamped her lips together. "So I remind you of her?"

He sensed he'd somehow entered shaky ground. "No, you don't."

Her stony expression didn't ease as she placed her soda on the counter. "I have to feed."

"Let me shower and I'll go with you."

"I'd prefer to be alone."

"That was hardly an option before Cassie had her vision; it's even less of one now."

He could almost see the smoke coming out of her ears as her hand clenched around her can. "I never asked you to become a part of my life."

"Maybe not, but you're stuck with me until you're not at risk anymore."

Dropping the can into the sink, she turned away and folded her arms over her chest. She focused on the back wall. "Hurry up."

"If you leave this apartment, I'll…"

"You'll what?" she demanded.

"I'll tie you to the radiator for the rest of the week and spoon feed you blood."

A new muscle began to twitch on the other side of her face. "And I'll suck the life from you until you're nothing more than a husk if you try."

A startled sound escaped her when he flew across the room and slammed his hands onto the countertop on both sides of her waist. "Do you honestly think you can?" he grated through his teeth.

"You don't know what I'm capable of!" she shot back. "You have no idea the extent of what I can do."

He grabbed one of her hands and pressed it against his chest. "Then do it."

"Stop it!" she shouted and tugged at her hand. He refused to relinquish it.

"Come on, Quinn, *do* it."

A sneer curved her upper lip; she tugged more forcefully at her hand. She struggled to keep her ability suppressed. However, he could feel the growing tidal wave rising between them. He'd realized when they'd kissed last night that she didn't always have control over her ability, but it wasn't always painful, not when she was giving and taking in equal measure.

Last night, it had been a pleasant sensation one that had slid beneath his skin and escalated his desire for her. What he felt swirling up between them now wouldn't be pleasant and more like what he'd experienced with her that first night. He would withstand it if it helped to get his point across. She may not like it, but she was stuck with him. He only wished she didn't hate the idea as much as she did.

"Let. Go. Of. Me!"

The words were spat succinctly at him. However, they weren't what caused his mouth to drop and his defense against her to slip enough that his whole body jerked from the zap he received from her. That zap was nothing compared to the astonishment rolling through him right now. He'd assumed that after nearly six hundred years on this earth nothing would dumbfound him anymore. Especially not after what he'd gone through with Cassie and the others, but he'd been completely wrong.

The air between them began to crackle; it felt as if little snaps of electricity rapidly fired into his skin. He could actually see little bursts of golden sparks building between them. She blasted him with enough force to knock her hand away from his chest and finally free herself of his grasp.

Her chin lifted defiantly; her eyes had a wary air about them as they held his. He'd never seen eyes like that before, he'd believed Cassie's eyes were the strangest things he'd ever encountered, but Quinn's were something entirely different. They were spectacular and eerie; they caused a chill to run over his skin as they also drew him forward with their enchanting beauty.

They hadn't turned entirely red; instead, the honeyed hue of her eyes had deepened to a molten gold color. Red danced around the outer rim of her pupils, like flames they actually seemed to be leaping and burning as she glared at him. The odd thing was that like Cassie's eyes, the whites of hers had also become completely red.

What is she? He wondered as he tried to assimilate what he was seeing with everything he knew about vampires.

He rested his hand upon her arm again; she went to throw it off, but he kept hold of it as he blocked the rush of images trying to fill his mind from the contact. "What are you?"

"I'm a vampire."

"No, you are much more than vampire, Quinn. Your eyes." She flinched and dropped her head down. He took hold of her chin and nudged it up, so she had to look at him again. The color of her eyes hadn't changed at all, her posture had eased a little though. "Were you a Hunter before you were changed?"

Just because Cassie's eyes had become entirely red after she was changed didn't mean it would be the same for every Hunter turned vampire. Cassie had always been an anomaly amongst the Hunter species.

"Quinn, if I'm going to keep you safe, you have *got* to tell me what is going on. What I'm dealing with, what we could be up against, and how many others know you're different?"

"No one knows," she murmured. She tried to drop her head down, but he kept his finger under her chin.

Flames leapt higher in her eyes; she didn't jolt him again, something he was thankful for.

"What were you before you became a vampire?" he demanded.

"What makes you think I was anything other than human?"

She may be the most stubborn, infuriating woman he'd ever come across, but if the look she gave him was any indication, she felt exactly the same way about him. "I've seen what a Hunter's eyes look like after they become a vampire. Your eyes aren't exactly the same, but there are similarities. You knew Hunter's heal faster, you know more about Hunters and Guardians than any vampire your age should. And your power is *far* stronger than it should be at your age. Talk to me."

Her eyes shot around the room, he couldn't tell if she was looking for an escape or contemplating punching him in the face. "I'm going to keep you safe, Quinn. Please, talk to me."

Her eyes were filled with resignation when they finally came back to his. "The only people who ever knew about me are all dead."

"It takes a lot to get rid of me, many have tried, all have failed."

"I don't blame them." He couldn't help but smile at her, his thumb traced over the scar running down her chin. "Don't. They're hideous." She tried to push his hand away; he kept hold of her.

"No they're not," he assured her. "You're still beautiful…"

"I don't care what they make me *look* like. I'm glad people can see them." She seized hold of his hand and tried to pull it away again as desperation filled her. "You don't understand what they mean! Don't touch them, I can't… Just *don't.*"

The fire in her eyes blazed higher, the air between them crackled. She was keeping herself restrained but only barely. Her obvious desperation bothered him more than any of her anger, resentment, and fight ever had. He removed his hand from her chin and dropped it back to the counter beside her in an attempt to help ease her somewhat.

Her shoulders slumped, the sizzle in the air lessened. He contemplated pulling her into his arms and hugging her instead of continuing to push her to finally get the answers he wanted from her. He knew if he backed off now though, he would lose the weakening he felt in her defenses.

"Quinn…"

"You've barged into my life and turned it upside down. This is my life! They are *my* scars!"

The hitch in her voice broke him, before he could think he reached out and pulled her against his chest. She remained rigid against him, her arms hung limply at her sides. His lips dropped down to her ear, her damp hair tickled his nose as he buried his face against her neck and inhaled her enticing scent.

He didn't know what he'd been looking for when he'd grabbed her, but when her body finally eased against his and her arms slid around his waist, he knew he'd found it.

CHAPTER 14

Quinn cursed herself as she remained unyielding against him. The one thing she'd been taught all of her life was to keep control and never slip up. It was impossible to hide what she was when she was overemotional. There had been no way to pass as a human in the beginning of her life, and then no way to pass as a vampire after her life had ended.

She'd slipped up in front of him, something she hadn't allowed to happen in years. Control and restraint, they were the cornerstones of her life. He'd knocked her off all of her foundations with his sarcastic words, tender kisses, constant meddling into her life, overwhelming presence, and his *I love you* to another woman.

Those words had been her complete undoing, a wound that cut deeper than any scar on her ever could have. Chris and Melissa had told her about Cassie and the way Julian felt about her, but there had been no way to prepare herself to hear him say those words to her. Then, he'd never even given her a chance to try and recover. Instead he'd continued to come at her, and torn at scabs that would never heal.

Now he was holding her within his solid embrace. The heat of his mouth warmed her and caused her skin to tingle as his lips pressed against her neck. Everything in her screamed to give him a zap he would never forget. The power swirled up within her like an avalanche, determined to take out everything in its path. She'd been ready to strike out against him; she found herself easing into his embrace instead. Her arms wrapped around his waist; her cheek pressed against his chest.

This was not supposed to happen, but as the realization blazed across her mind, she found herself melting further into the formidable man holding her. His hand slid into her hair, he cradled the back of her head as he held her closer. "I only mean to keep you safe; you have to help me do that."

"You're asking me to reveal things only dead people knew and to revisit things I've spent the past six years trying not to recall."

His lips brushed over her face before he pressed his cheek against hers. "We've all done things we'd prefer not to recall. I was a monster, a vicious brutal murderer who took a lot of pleasure in destroying lives and inflicting misery upon others. No matter how different I am now, that monster is still there, just beneath the surface. I may not give into my more savage urges anymore, but I *will* do whatever is necessary to keep anyone I care about safe." She closed her eyes as she absorbed those words. "You're not a monster, Quinn."

A shudder ran through her; her hands clenched involuntary upon the thick muscle of his back. "You don't know what I've done."

"There's nothing you could have done that would be any worse than anything I've done in my extended life." He nudged her chin up with his thumb and held her so she had to look at him. "There's nothing you can tell me about your past that will make me turn against you."

She so desperately wanted to believe him. No one had ever known what she'd done; she'd never planned to tell anyone about it. It was her dirty secret, her shame to live with; her nightmare to face whether asleep or awake. What would it be like to tell someone and not have them stare at her in revulsion? What if she *did* tell him and he stared at her as if she were lower than vomit running through sewage?

"When I was a mere three hundred years old, I helped to slaughter over thirty people on a whim with the woman I was involved with." Her eyes widened at his words. "She had a bigger sadistic streak than I did and attacked the handful of children also present. I may have been a monster at the time, but even I had my limits. When it was over, I destroyed that woman even though she fancied herself in love with me. I'm the last man who should ever condemn another, but she enjoyed killing those children, and I decided to be her judge and executioner. I didn't have many standards back then, I was surprised to discover killing children was one of the two things I found beneath me. I've slaughtered thousands of other humans and vampires. *Thousands.* And it's not something I'm proud of."

She remained unmoving as she tried to process his revelation. He'd taken so many lives... But who was she to judge anyone? She'd taken lives too, most in self-defense, but one of those lives had been worth more to her than a hundred others.

"What is the second thing you find beneath you?" she inquired.

"I've never raped anyone, *ever*." That was a relief to know. "Are you repulsed by me now?"

The desperate look in his eyes pulled at her heart as his gaze searched hers. He'd opened himself up, and now he felt exposed as he waited for her answer. Her heart melted; she'd never expected to see such vulnerability coming from him. Her fingers slid over his back as she sought to comfort him in some way.

"No." The word had popped out, but now that she'd said it, she realized she meant it completely. "I would never condone it, and if it was something you still did, I wouldn't feel the same way, but…"

"We all make mistakes," he finished for her when she stopped speaking.

"Yes," she whispered.

"Would you like to hear more of the things I've done? I can keep going all night with the countless torments I've inflicted upon others."

She shook her head. "If you want to tell me about it, I'll listen. You don't have to tell me anything you don't want to though."

His forehead furrowed; the line between his brows deepened. He bent and pressed his lips against her forehead. "Maybe one day," he murmured. "But first we have to talk about you."

Her shoulders slumped; she bowed her head. "Ok."

Taking hold of her hand, he led her over to the table and pulled out a chair for her. Quinn sat awkwardly in the chair and clasped her hands on the table. He rested his hands on top of hers, but she couldn't stop her foot from tapping. Her gaze slid past his to the clock on the wall behind him.

"I have to get to work soon," she told him.

"There's plenty of time still."

She couldn't put it off forever; she knew she couldn't, but she didn't know how to start. He remained mute, his gaze unwavering as he waited for her to speak. "I guess there's no better place to start than the beginning."

A smile curved the corner of his upper lip. "So I've been told."

Quinn found she couldn't do this while sitting. Rising to her feet, she paced over to the fridge and pulled out another can of soda. Popping the top, she took a swallow before walking over to her window. She stared out at the red, pink, and orange spreading across the darkening sky as the sun had already slipped beyond the horizon.

"My mother and father were Hunters." She didn't turn to look at him when she spoke. She thought if she looked at him she would never continue. "My father was killed by vampires when my mother was four months pregnant with me. During the attack my mother was also killed and turned."

Wood creaked behind her; he shifted in the chair, but showed no other reaction. "The vampires who turned my mother took her back to where they were holed up. I don't know what their intentions were for her; I doubt she ever knew what their plan was either. Maybe they meant to see what would become of her, or maybe they knew she was pregnant with me and wanted to see what *I* would become. Thankfully, whatever they had planned was ruined when a couple of Hunters found the vampire's nest and destroyed them."

Quinn turned away from the window and paced over to the kitchen sink. "My mother's sister and her husband were the Hunters who found and rescued her. They took my mother back with them and kept her hidden, my aunt told me she was never the same though. She never attacked them, but she'd been broken by the change and never recovered from losing my father. When I was born only two months later, perfectly healthy and normal weight, she handed me over to her sister and walked out into the sun.

"My aunt and uncle raised me. Even before my strange birth, they'd decided to tell their Guardian and The Commission we'd all perished in the attack. After my birth, they put two vampire bodies into their house, lit it on fire, and fled to Alaska with me. They had no reason not to trust their Guardian, but they knew my existence would either be completely unwelcome, or it would create more questions and a possible case study of me. They knew how Hunters were created, and they didn't want anyone experimenting on me."

"Wise choice," he murmured. "Did anyone ever search for them?"

"They were declared dead in the fire so there was no reason for anyone to."

"Besides your early, and healthy birth, did you exhibit other nonhuman signs?"

She fiddled with the tab on her can as she spoke. "I always needed blood. Nowhere near as much as a normal vampire, but I required a few drops of blood with my formula. As I got older raw meat was the way I got it. I had a heartbeat until I changed; I never had fangs, but when I got mad my eyes would start to change color."

"Like they did earlier?"

"Sort of. Only my irises changed color before, and they looked exactly like what you just saw without the whites of my eyes turning red. I was also stronger than a normal Hunter, I grew faster, and my ability was more lethal. The sun affected me too. It hurt my eyes, and only a half an hour under its rays would burn my skin. My cousin Betsy was born six months after me, the differences between us were impossible to ignore. My other cousin, Barry, was two years younger than me. They both went to school; I was kept home."

Her hand went to the heart locket as her thoughts turned to Betsy. For years her cousin had been her best friend, her confidante. They'd spent many nights talking until almost daybreak about dreams and boys. She'd lived vicariously through Betsy; listening to her stories about school and a world she didn't think she'd ever get to be a part of.

"When The Slaughter occurred, we were still in Alaska, and my family fled once again. They'd been listed as dead, but they weren't willing to take any chances with our safety. They settled in a town a couple of hours from here in California. I wasn't able to go out as much after the move, but we blended in with the people and assumed an entirely human lifestyle. Even with all of my abnormalities and the knowledge of what I was, my aunt and uncle treated me like their own child, and they loved me.

"When I was thirteen, I'd gained control of my ability and my strength, but I was still too afraid of losing my temper to be around other people so I remained hidden away. I didn't think I'd ever go out in the world. By the time I was sixteen, I felt confident enough of my restraint to risk going to high school. I knew I was different but my family loved me, and they encouraged me to try and live as normal of a life as I could. My happiness was the only thing they wanted for me."

"I've never heard of a vampire being born before," he murmured.

She popped the tab off her soda and dropped the can in the sink. Leaning against the counter, she turned to face him again. "Apparently I'm a rarity." A stab of sorrow slid through her as she remembered he'd already called her that, had already compared her to Cassie.

His gaze slid over her from head to toe and back again. "You most certainly are. So they raised you as a Hunter?"

"For the most part. I was always aware of my real heritage. They never could have kept it hidden from me, and it would have been irresponsible to try. I learned the lore of the Hunters and Guardians and was taught to fight vampires, something I do well." She wasn't bragging it was a simple fact. "I was determined to one day take revenge on the species who had killed my parents and slaughtered countless others, but I also enjoyed my role in the human world. When I turned eighteen, I started to prepare for high school graduation, and talk of college was eagerly discussed at the dinner table. Betsy and I were going to be roommates. Two days after graduation it all came crumbling down."

She wrapped her hand around the locket and clasped it in her grasp as memories flooded her. It had been six years, yet the screams still echoed in her head as vividly as they had that night. The nightmares still came to her at least a few times a month.

"I'm still not sure how the vampires got in the house. One minute Barry was opening the front door, and the next thing I knew they were on us. In our *home*." She lifted her head to look at him. "We'd mistakenly assumed we were safe there."

"One of them probably had the ability of mind control. It takes age to be able to use it with a lot of force, but I've encountered at least a dozen mind controllers over the years. The most powerful one I know is Devon. His ability can be chilling, and he can do some impressive and lethal things with it, but at seven hundred and fifty-four years old, he's the oldest one of us now."

"Do you think he could have been the one who did it?" she hissed.

Julian snorted and shook his head. "No, Devon most definitely was not involved in the murder of your family."

"How can you be so certain?"

"Because until Cassie walked into his life, Devon hadn't killed anyone or drank human blood for almost a hundred and fifty years. Cassie's blood was the first he'd had in all those years. The only reason he would kill another is to keep those he cares for safe."

Quinn tilted her head. "Why did he give up human blood?"

Julian folded his arms over his chest and leaned back in his chair. "Devon fancied himself in love."

"With Cassie?"

"Oh no, this was before Cassie. A pretty girl named Annabelle he became fascinated with. She was sweet and innocent and Devon was determined to destroy that in her."

Quinn's stomach turned. "He sounds like a monster."

"He was, but so was I back then." The relentless hold of his stare made her realize he was gauging her reaction. She didn't know what he expected to see from her, but she couldn't fail him. "We were both monsters." The underlying current in his flippant tone made her realize this was far more important to him than he was letting on. "And we both enjoyed it."

"I've seen what vampires are capable of."

Julian sat up in the chair, folded his hands before him and rested his elbows on his knees. "You've only seen the tip of the iceberg, Dewdrop; I can assure you of that much. What Devon and I did all those years, together, are things you probably can't even imagine. Then one day Devon came across Annabelle. The only problem was Annabelle loved a human, Liam. Determined to destroy their love, Devon turned her into a vampire, and everything blew up in his face."

Despite the lethal light in his eyes, she found herself drawn into his story. "What happened?"

"Annabelle turned out to be Devon's downfall, or at least that's what I considered her at the time. The night Annabelle turned, instead of becoming a mindless killing machine who turned on Liam like Devon had hoped, she slaughtered a field of cows. Devon found her there. He realized that instead of destroying her, she'd retained the characteristics that had made her good as a human. She made him realize *he* could be better. He stopped killing and stopped drinking human blood. After a couple of years Annabelle went to Liam, told him everything, and changed him when he agreed to it."

"What became of them?" she asked.

"Annabelle and Liam have been mated ever since he turned. Devon remained a boring do-gooder. I hated him for it."

"Why?"

"Why would I like him? He'd been my best friend; he'd helped to mold me into the monster I'd become, and then he walked away from it all because of a *girl*. I became determined to break him as punishment. I bided my time and I waited; Devon may have been good, but he was still stronger than me. Then he met Cassie, and I saw my opportunity to take him down by taking *her* down."

The challenge in his gaze only intensified. "I see," she murmured.

He rose to his feet and walked with the lethal grace of a puma across the room. Quinn remained frozen as he stopped before her and rested his hands on the counter beside her again. The tantalizing scent of him engulfed her; she became mesmerized by the eyes burning into hers. "Do you really see, Quinn? Do you really understand what I was? I tried numerous times to kill Cassie, in order to destroy him. I missed my friend, but even more I wanted to destroy the good in them and the love between them, because I'd been engulfed in the evil, death and blood for centuries."

"What happened?" The bare whisper of her question probably wouldn't have been heard by a human.

"That's a horror story for another time."

She grabbed hold of his arm when he went to turn away. The powerful muscles of his forearm rippled beneath her hands, the warmth of his flesh sent little tingles into the palm of her hand. She ignored the attraction blazing to life between them.

I will not look at his lips, she chanted in her head.

"If you want to know about me then you'll tell me what happened," she said.

He glanced pointedly at her hand. "I could already know about you."

It was a tactic meant to unnerve her, and it did, but she refused to release his arm. It was also a challenge. He was trying to see if he could drive her away; she wasn't going to let him. "But you don't."

His eyes were callous as he stared at her. "Not yet."

"Maybe not ever."

He leaned closer to her, the mantra in her head kicked up as his mouth hovered only inches away from hers. "Dewdrop, you're a mystery I'm going to solve no matter what it takes."

Were there bones still left in her legs? She didn't think so as his words caused his lips to brush over hers before he stepped back.

"The Commission was determined to try and create new Hunters." He walked away from her as he spoke and over to the table. He didn't return to his seat but rested his fingertips on the table and turned to face her. "They felt the best way to do this was to use a current Hunter and an Elder, if they could get their hands on one. Cassie had no abilities when she was a Hunter, a perilous rarity amongst your kind. They were determined to capture her if they could, but they knew it would be difficult, if not impossible, to take her *and* Devon."

"So they went after you?"

"They took me. I never saw those bastards coming." The flash of red in his eyes revealed more about his fury than the growl he emitted. "A Hunter with telekinesis and some members of The Commission teamed up to take me down. They drugged me with something strong enough to knock out ten elephants and took me to a hidden laboratory under a school in upstate New York. There they locked me up and they waited."

"Waited for what?"

"For Cassie. For their fun to begin. And then they unleashed every torture they could think of upon us. They were trying to get Cassie to turn into a monster, and I was their vampire pincushion. The only one we had to talk to was each other; we helped to keep each other sane while we were in there."

"And you fell in love with her?"

His head tilted to the side, his hair fell across his forehead. "I did," he confirmed.

"Did she fall in love with you?"

"No. She loves me, she always will, but she never could have fallen in love with me. After being in there with her though, I finally understood why Devon had walked away from what he'd been, and allowed Anna-belle to go to Liam. I understood everything about him. Including the realization I would let Cassie go."

"Why?"

"Because she was never mine to have. She's Dev-on's mate."

Quinn's gaze slid to her window. "I'm sorry." She didn't know what else to say. He'd been through hell and back; he'd been locked away like an animal, tor-tured, and he loved a woman who didn't love him.

"Don't be, I'm not. Being in there was awful, but if it hadn't happened I may have killed her or died myself. Instead, I got my best friend back; I got more friends and a family out of it. I also realized that blood and death doesn't have to be my life. Loving her gave me a whole new life, a better one, and I wouldn't change anything that happened in order to bring me to this point."

She still felt as if she should comfort him in some way, but he didn't look upset. He was an ancient man who was extremely aware of who and what he was. A man who was perfectly accepting of the twists and turns his life had taken.

"What is this mate thing you keep talking about?" she inquired.

"It's an intense bond between vampires. They're soul mates and can't be separated from each other once the bond is completed through the exchange of blood and sex. If one mate dies, so does the other."

Quinn's hands wrapped around the edge of the countertop. "I see."

"And I came to see Cassie was the same thing to me as Annabelle was to Devon. She showed me how to love again."

"And maybe one day you will find your mate."

A snort escaped him; a smile curved his luscious mouth. "Doubtful, but I'm quite content with living the single life. I may not be a killer anymore, but I'm certainly not a saint."

"That's for sure," she muttered.

He released a small laugh before dropping into the chair again. "Now Quinn, I've told you my secrets, it's time to hear the rest of yours. How did you become a vampire?"

"I'm sure you have plenty more secrets."

"You've only asked for some of them, and I've already told you that if you would like to know every horrid, juicy detail of my life I will happily reveal all to you one day, but not today. Quit stalling and tell me, or I will take the answers from you." His eyes burned as he leaned toward her. "I am not playing a game; I won't allow my friend's lives to be placed in jeopardy. I gave and now so shall you, one way or another."

Quinn bristled over his highhanded attitude, but he was right. She'd asked for him to reveal his secrets, and he'd done so. For her to not return the favor was wrong but she'd been determined to never go down this road again.

"I don't like threats," she told him.

"I don't like to give them, but I know you understand."

"I do," she said.

"Now, I'm guessing the vampire with mind control got to your cousin before they arrived at your door that night."

"You think they knew we were Hunters." She'd always suspected that, but it was the first time she'd said it aloud.

"They knew what you were," Julian confirmed. "Or at least what your family was. I highly doubt they knew what *you* were. You wouldn't be standing here if they did."

She shuddered at the idea. "How would they know what we were?"

"The vampire with mind control was older; he'd have to be to accomplish what he did, but he somehow figured out you were Hunters. For years, many vamps didn't look for Hunters and Guardians because The Elders had told them they were all wiped out during The Slaughter. With the death of The Elders, most now know it wasn't true. How many of vampires came into your house?"

Her gaze went beyond him, but she didn't see the wall there, she saw an entirely different scene. "Six."

"What happened once they were inside the house?"

She closed her eyes and shuddered. Her hand instinctively went to the scar at her temple, her fingers traced over the puckered flesh. "They killed Barry first, and then they came for us. My power wasn't as strong then, but I managed to give one a good enough zap that I sent him through the wall. The next one came at me with a bowie knife over a foot long. He sliced me across my temple first and slammed the handle of the knife into my skull. I was still trying to get my bearings from the blow, and I'm pretty sure a fractured skull, when he cut me from my lip to under my chin."

Her fingers slid over the faded scar there. "I don't remember falling, but the next thing I remember is him leaning over me and that knife plunging into my flesh, pinning me to the ground." Her hand fell upon the scar beneath her sternum; she rested her palm there as the agony of the moment slid back over her. "Then, he took my hands and pinned each one of them to the ground with nearly identical knives, like I was nothing more than a bug. I will never forget his face, those eyes, or one single detail about him. I *will* find him one day, when I'm stronger, and I will make him pay for what he did to my family. I *will* destroy him.

"I laid there and listened to the slurping sounds of him *feeding* on me. The screams of my loved ones filled my ears, but there was nothing I could do as my blood seeped out of me and the world faded away," she said. "And then I don't remember anything else until I woke again. Dead."

CHAPTER 15

She stared at him but he knew she didn't see him; he was certain the only things she could see right now were the memories of that night. Memories he'd glimpsed when he'd first touched her. The color had faded from her already pale skin; her eyes were shadowed. Crimson color had bled into the whites of her eyes again and the gold of them had red flames flickering around the edges once more.

"The vampire who attacked you gave you his blood," he prodded when she remained mute.

Quinn shook her head; her hand fell away from her stomach. "No. Apparently being born a vampire and a Hunter was enough for me to transform without having an influx of vampire blood. It wasn't an easy one."

"None of them are," he murmured. "But I imagine without that influx it must have been brutal."

Going on his own experience with how excruciating the transformation was, and the strained look on her face, he imagined it had been far worse for her. Julian rubbed at his forehead as he tried to process what she'd just revealed. Six hundred years and he'd never heard of anything like this; six hundred years and he was still able to be surprised. It would have been amusing; however, this situation was anything but.

"Do you have any other abilities, besides being able to master souls?"

"No, it's the only thing I can do."

"What happened when you woke?" he inquired.

Her forehead furrowed, the red of her eyes deepened further as her fingers rubbed at the scars on her palms. "It was still night when I woke again. I was still pinned to the floor. I remember everything being strangely quiet and loud all at once. I'd died listening to the screams and I woke to the booming tick of a clock on the second floor of the house. My head throbbed; my skin felt as if someone had peeled a layer of it off. I could feel my blood congealing at my back but more than that I could smell the blood of everyone else…"

"And you were hungry."

A muscle twitched in her cheek, tears pooled in her eyes before she blinked them away. "I was hungry," she said in an ashamed whisper. "I felt like I was being consumed by flames, as if the hunger was eating me alive from the inside out, and there was nothing I could do to sate it. My fangs dug into my lips and tore at my mouth. A part of me knew what I'd become, all I cared about was stopping the incessant burn though. After what seemed like hours, but was probably only minutes, I succeeded in ripping my right hand over top of the blade still embedded in the floor. It tore my hand open further, but I didn't care. I was mindless, crazed.

"I pulled the other knife from my left hand, and then the one from my stomach. Before I knew what I was doing, I crawled over to Betsy, and I began to feed. I took what little was left in all of their bodies before turning to what was still drinkable on the floor. I was like a wild creature, a *monster*."

"You were a newly turned vampire who already had a thirst for blood before you were turned. There was nothing you could have done to stop what happened, Quinn. Stop blaming yourself for it."

Her strangely colored eyes were pitiless as they met his. "My uncle raised me like one of his own; he loved me like a daughter. He protected me more than either of his children. It wasn't a clock I heard upon waking but the faintest beat of his heart. A beat I stopped when I sank my fangs into his neck."

This wasn't shocking to him. He'd seen many a new vampire awaken and go on a rampage. The only two he knew who hadn't gone straight for human throats were Annabelle and Cassie. If there had been puddles of human blood and bodies lying around them, it may have been a completely different story, at least for Annabelle. Cassie only had one mission upon waking and that was getting to Devon.

"Was your uncle going to survive his injuries?" Julian inquired.

"What does that matter?"

"It matters because it means you didn't kill him. Maybe he was still alive when you got to him, but you are *not* the reason he's dead now. I know you don't want to hear this; I know you'll continue to blame yourself, but just keep reminding yourself that you didn't kill him. Maybe one day it will sink into that thick skull of yours. If those vampires had never walked into your house you would still be human, well mostly, and your family would still be alive. You're not to blame here, *they* are."

Her face remained impassive; he knew it would take more than his words to get through years of her self-inflicted shame, but he would do everything he could to help her stop blaming herself for things far beyond her control.

"Was he going to live?"

"No."

Her response was stony; a muscle twitched in her cheek when he rose to his feet and deliberately advanced on her. She was exposed right now in a way she never had been before; he was afraid she would bolt if he approached her too quickly. Thankfully, she remained where she was and didn't pull away from him when he took hold of her hands and held them out before her.

His thumbs traced over the two-inch long scars marring her flesh. The scars ran across the centers of her palms; they had faded enough that they weren't raised up anymore. He turned her hands over and saw the same faded lines on the other side.

The pain and helplessness she must have experienced caused anger to swell within his chest. He would gladly help her find the vampire who had done this to her. What he would do to that vamp would make what was done to her look like a day at the carnival in comparison. He'd make the man watch as he leisurely carved him into pieces; make him see parts of himself no one was ever supposed to see, and no man ever wanted removed.

"Why didn't the scars heal during your transformation?" he inquired.

Her hands twitched in his, but she didn't try to jerk them away. "They started to."

He studied her as he waited for her to explain, but realization dawned on him. "You didn't allow your flesh to heal."

"I gathered the bodies of my loved ones, and took them to a nearby lake to bury them by the shore." Her voice was flat when she said this, but a single tear slid down her cheek. "I returned to the house to gather what I would need, but the sun came up before I could go. Trapped there with the realization of what I'd done, I put the knives back into my palms and stomach as I waited."

"Why?"

The haunted look in her eyes pulled at his heart when she met his gaze. "Because I deserved it."

Julian's hands clenched around hers. He didn't argue with her though, she wasn't ready to believe she hadn't deserved it. "Did the police come?"

"No one came, not for me."

He would have come for her, but he kept the thought to himself. He didn't even know where it had come from. "When did you leave?"

"At nightfall, and I never looked back."

His fingers traced over her hands again. "How long did you keep these wounds open?"

"I reopened them every day for a month."

"Quinn…" he breathed.

"They are my reminder of what I must do, the mission I have, what I have lost, and the atrocity of the acts I committed."

"They're your punishment."

"Yes."

"Do you still reopen them?" he demanded. She shook her head but wouldn't look at him. "When was the last time you reopened them?"

"Six months ago."

She'd spent five and a half years reopening her wounds; years atoning for sins she never should have been made to pay for. "I'm sorry for what happened to you," he told her honestly.

"Don't," she whispered. Her lower lip trembled but she stalwartly held back her tears as she shook her head.

He clasped hold of her face with his hands and leaned forward to kiss her forehead, her nose, her cheeks, before finally pressing a chaste kiss upon her lips. "I can't take it away from you but I will make sure it never happens again."

A single tear slid down her cheek. "You can't promise that."

"Yes. I can."

The fire slid away from her eyes as her gaze searched his. "No one else can ever know what I did."

"I have to tell Luther and the others what you are. They need a better understanding of your ability, and what we may be up against if someone else were to realize what you are. *No* one else will ever know about the events that transpired after your transformation."

She closed her eyes and nodded. Lifting her face, he kissed her tenderly on the lips again before pulling her into his arms. He held her against his chest as she buried her face in his neck and leaned into him. She didn't let another tear fall free, but he could feel her sadness in the limpness of her body and the fingers digging into his back as she cuddled closer.

"Do you mind if I tell Luther your last name? He won't let anyone know you're alive. It's definitely better your family line remains dead to any other Hunters or Guardians."

"You don't trust them?"

"I don't trust many people, but I *do* trust Luther and the others with my life. I know they will keep you safe, and I think it would be good if Luther knew as much as he can about you."

She bit on her lower lip when she looked up at him. "It's Martin." He smiled as she gave another sign of trust in him. "And yours?"

"Aasen."

Her eyebrows rose. "Unusual."

"It's Swedish." He tugged at his hair. "I told you this was all natural."

Her chuckle caused pleasure to spread through him as she rested her head on his chest again.

***

"She's a what?" Chris slumped onto the bed in Luther's hotel room. "Is that even possible?"

"Apparently it is because she exists," Julian replied. He stepped out of the room and glanced down the street toward the increasingly packed parking lot of Clint's bar. He hated the idea of leaving her there unprotected, but he had to speak with the others about what he'd learned tonight. She would be fine on her own, but he still much preferred to have her in sight.

"Now I don't feel like as much of a freak," Zach said.

"She's not a freak," Julian snarled. "And if you ever call her that I'll tear your tongue out through your throat."

Zach's eyes widened, he took an abrupt step back. "Julian behave," Melissa admonished. "He's only kidding, Zach."

"No. I'm not. And if you think I am then just try me."

An awkward silence descended over the room. He could hear the increased heartbeats of those surrounding him. Maybe his reaction had been a little too volatile, but he continued to stare at Zach.

Luther covered his mouth and gave a little cough before stepping forward. "It's fascinating indeed, but we've dealt with a Hunter turned vampire before. This isn't so different. I've never heard of a vampire being *born* before though."

"No one has," Julian said. "It's never happened before, at least not to my knowledge."

"Did you ask Devon about it?"

"I spoke with him earlier. He has no knowledge of it ever happening either."

"How is it possible that she survived? Wouldn't her mother's heart have stopped beating when she was turned?" Chris asked. "Wouldn't Quinn have died too?"

They all looked to Luther. His mouth pursed as he tapped his foot on the ground. "As a Soul Master she may have been able to pull on the life force of her mother, which could also explain her rapid growth in the womb."

"She could have done *that*, as a fetus?" Melissa asked in disbelief.

"It's possible, and most likely what she did, since she was born with a heartbeat."

"Wow, just wow," Chris breathed. "It explains why you felt so much more power coming from her. Is her Soul Master ability the only one she has, or is she able to do other things, like Cassie?"

"It's the only thing she can do," Julian confirmed.

"Good," Chris said. "I've known Cassie my whole life; the things she can do still unnerve me a little."

Cassie's ability had unsettled him in the beginning too, it still did. No one should have that much power, but if anyone could handle it, it was Cassie. "If the vampires learn about Quinn, they'll come after her with everything they have. If they also learn what Cassie is capable of, they'll see her as a way to counteract Cassie," he told them.

"Wait you don't think Quinn would be able to kill Cassie, do you?" Melissa demanded.

Julian shook his head. "No, I don't. She doesn't have that much power, but that won't matter to them. They'll see her as a Hunter turned vampire who they might be able to get their hands on. One that they might be able to twist to their way, and a Soul Master is a powerful asset to begin with. You've seen what she can do. Imagine if that power was warped and fueled by death and blood. Quinn is good at heart, but we all know how brutal a vampire can be, how they can twist and manipulate things. And if they're unable to bend her to their will, they'll kill her."

Chris shuddered at his words, Julian's hands fisted, but he managed to keep his temper over such a notion covered up. Or he believed he did but when he turned his head, he found Melissa watching him with assessing eyes.

Luther lifted his glasses to rub at the bridge of his nose as he spoke, "With her knowledge of the Hunter line and her strength, she'll be a double threat if the vampires get their hands on her."

"It doesn't change anything," Chris said. "We already knew she had to be protected."

"True. A born vampire," Luther said. "Amazing. How was she changed into a full vampire? Who changed her?"

"The vampire blood already in her from being born, and from her Hunter heritage were enough to bring her back when she died," Julian answered.

"How did she die?" Chris asked.

"Vampire attack."

"Awful." Melissa gave a sad shake of her head. Aside from him, everyone in this room had lost at least one of their parents to vampires. Most of them had lost both. "What of the family who raised her?"

"They were killed in the same attack," he answered.

"The Hunters have never had an easy life, or a lengthy one for that matter. Hers was made doubly difficult because of the circumstances of her birth," Luther said. "We cannot allow them to get their hands on her, Julian."

"I'll kill anyone who tries," he vowed. "Her last name is Martin. I don't know if that will help you in any way."

"I remember seeing a Martin line in one of the journals. I'll look into them. Her aunt and uncle were assumed to have died in a fire?"

"Yes. I can find out their names if it will help."

"No, her last name is enough info to be able to locate them." Luther walked over to join him in the doorway. "I need a shower, and I'll take a look through the books. I don't think info on her family will help in this situation, but it can't hurt. I'll join you at the bar shortly."

Julian watched the smaller man walk away from the door. "I have to get some clothes."

He didn't bother to look back at the others as he walked out of the room and down the row of rooms to the one he'd yet to sleep in. He watched the people gathered outside the door of the bar, smoking. Quinn briefly materialized by one of the windows, she delivered a round of drinks and turned away swiftly. He couldn't help but smile as he watched the sway of her hips.

Slipping into his room, he tossed a few articles of clothing into a duffel bag. He didn't acknowledge Chris or Melissa when they appeared in his doorway. Turning away from them, he walked into the bathroom to gather his toiletries. Chris was leaning in the doorway when he reemerged from the bathroom.

"You like her," Melissa stated as Julian tossed his deodorant into the bag.

"Who?" he asked.

"Quinn," Chris replied. "You like her."

He zipped up the bag. "I like many things, Christopher."

"I've touched a nerve." Julian glared at him; Chris only smiled more. "You only ever call me by my full name when I aggravate you."

"I must call you by it all the time then."

"Shockingly, no. You like her."

Julian lifted the bag and tossed it over his shoulder. "She's a nice girl."

"She is." Chris folded his arms over his chest. "And you think you don't deserve her."

"Don't try to read me."

"I couldn't if I tried; you're too old for that. I'm not a moron though. You like her, and it scares you."

"Nothing scares me."

"She does."

"Christopher..."

"You're worried you'll lose her or hurt her in some way," Melissa interjected. "You've never felt like this about anyone before."

"First off, you're both really starting to grate on my nerves," he growled. "Second of all, are you forgetting I loved Cassie?"

"No," Chris said. "Come on, admit it, you let yourself love Cassie because a part of you always knew she could never be yours. It was easy to let yourself love someone when you already knew the outcome. But Quinn, she's a mystery to you. She's not a monster, and she's not unattainable."

"You're pretty bored lately aren't you?" Julian asked.

"You can pretend to deny it all you want, but we know the truth and so do you," Melissa said.

Julian refused to think about their words. "Whatever helps you sleep at night," he told them as he strode across the room. They both stepped out of his way. "I'm going to drop this off at Quinn's place, and then I'm going to try and hunt down whoever is killing in this town. Go to the bar and keep an eye on her."

Julian would have much preferred to be the one watching over her, but after their words he needed some time to himself. "We will," Chris said.

"Make sure she stays safe." He hadn't intended them to, but the words came out a snarl.

"Of course," Chris replied.

Julian turned away from them and strode rapidly down the wooden walkway running along the front of the motel. "Julian." He turned to look back at them. Melissa stepped forward as she continued to speak. "Just so you know we said you liked her; *you're* the one who brought love into this."

Julian's upper lip curled into a sneer. Chris's laughter trailed behind him as he hopped off of the walkway. Melissa waved at him before turning and following Chris. They both whistled innocently as they strolled toward the bar.

CHAPTER 16

Over the next week, Julian spent every night trying to find the person who had touched him the night of the fight, but the more he looked the more frustrated he became by it. Or perhaps it was his purposeful separation from Quinn frustrating him. The others watched over her at night, and he still slept on her couch during the day, but there had been little interaction between the two of them.

He'd purposely put a wall between them, the last thing he wanted was to make things more complicated than they already were, but he wasn't the only one with a wall. She barely made eye contact with him and seemed as determined to stay away from him as he was from her.

The few conversations they had were clipped and usually in the presence of the others. Ever since she'd revealed her history to him, he didn't know how to act around her. She walked around with this hard outer shell protecting her, but inside she was damaged and he was frightened he would somehow make it worse.

He wasn't a good man, and she deserved some-thing wonderful and some*one* good in her life. She deserved better than him.

So he threw himself into finding the monster hunt-ing the innocent people in this town.

That there were no bodies only made things hard-er. It was difficult to track a killer when he didn't know where to start. No one had been reported missing, and the person doing the killing was smart enough to hide the mess they were creating.

In the brief flash of images he'd seen, the women and children all had darker skin with black hair and deep brown eyes. Their faces had been round, with broad cheekbones. The lack of missing people reports, the lingering images of those innocent faces, and the fact they were only a half an hour from the Mexican border had led them all to the conclusion this killer hunted illegal immigrants crossing over. The killer may be a brutal monster, but they weren't stupid.

By the third day of the search, Quinn insisted they'd run across everyone who had been involved in the fight, but there *had* to be someone they were missing. His ability had never been wrong before; he knew what he'd experienced from whoever it was he'd touched.

The lack of progress was making him testier with every night that passed. Trying to keep Quinn safe should be his main concern, and he wanted this checked off of his list of things to be taken care of, or taken out was more like it. He didn't understand how he couldn't find the man or where they were hiding from him, but the longer the killer eluded him, the more determined he became.

He placed his beer on a table and shifted his pool stick into his other hand. He'd been avoiding the bar until closing time, but with the dead ends he'd been hitting in his search, he'd decided it was time to go back to the beginning. The clinking of balls sounded in his ears as his gaze drifted to Quinn. She smiled as she placed some drinks onto a table surrounded by a group of young men.

One of them said something and went to slap her on the ass. Julian's jaw clenched; he placed his pool stick against the wall and stepped toward them. He'd break their hand before he ever let them disrespect her.

Before he could intervene, Quinn's hand shot out and caught hold of the guy's hand in the air. The smile was still on her face, but even he would have been put off by the chill in her eyes. The guy was an ass, but the human wasn't a fool, he dropped his hands back into his lap like a good schoolboy.

Julian couldn't help but smile while he watched her walk away. He found Chris grinning at him when he turned from the scene. "You're so lucky Cassie made me promise not to kill you," he muttered.

"I didn't say a word," Chris replied innocently.

Julian was really beginning to rethink his promise to Cassie. He didn't have to kill Chris; he could always just make it so he couldn't speak again. But he'd probably miss talking to Chris, seventy-five percent of the time at least.

Unwilling to deal with him right now, Julian turned away and watched as Quinn returned to the bar. Hawtie, having resurfaced in Clint's four days ago, was sitting at the end of it. Quinn rested her elbows on the bar and leaned forward to talk with her. He couldn't hear what they were saying, but the smile on Quinn's face was genuine now.

"Julian…"

"I'm not going to discuss this. This is the one thing that is off limits, Chris."

The hand Chris had wrapped around his pool stick turned white as he bit back his words, finally he gave a brief bow of his head. Julian took a step away from him and moved into the main barroom. There wasn't anyone in here tonight, he hadn't seen over the week. There might still be a chance he could find some people he didn't know if he returned to Hawtie's, the bonfire, or the Mitchum's, but he couldn't bring himself to look again tonight. Tonight he wanted to be close to *her*.

A human murderer in this town was nothing compared to the vampires he feared might be closing in on her. He'd been hiding from her this past week, he wasn't so oblivious he couldn't admit that to himself, but he couldn't do it forever. They were going to have to stay close to one another if he was going to keep her alive. The vampire community had taken a huge hit when the Elders were killed, and their main source of leadership had been disrupted.

He and Devon may not have fallen into line with The Elders when they'd been alive, and preferred to be on their own, but many had looked to The Elders for guidance and protection. Without The Elders, the vampires had been lost and scattered these past two years. The hopeful promise of her might be enough for them *all* to regroup, something that would be treacherous for them all.

Apprehension twisted in his gut, the urge to get closer to her drove him as he swept across the barroom. Few people paid him any attention, but more than a couple instinctively leaned away from him. Quinn's eyes widened when she saw him approaching;

she paused in the act of placing some glasses into the dishwasher.

Hawtie's eyes lit up when she spotted him; her gaze slid pointedly toward Quinn and a smile curved her mouth. He grinned back at Hawtie as he stepped beside her.

"You may be twenty years too young for me, but I still wouldn't mind teaching you a thing or two," Hawtie teased.

Quinn snorted before returning to stacking dishes in the washer. Julian couldn't help but chuckle over Hawtie's statement either. If she knew the truth about his age, she'd fall off her barstool. "I'm a lot older than I look."

Hawtie laughed and flirtatiously hit his arm. "Still too young for me."

"I ain't afraid to shoot you, Eminem," Clint grumbled as he walked behind the bar.

A burst of laughter escaped Quinn; her eyes twinkled when she glanced up at him from under her sweeping lashes. Julian stared at the old man as Clint eyed him up and down and rested his hand on the revolver holstered at his waist. There was a time he would have leaned over and snapped the old man's neck before ordering his next drink, now he found himself oddly amused by him.

"Point taken," Julian assured him.

Clint grunted in response; he glanced at Quinn before giving Julian another glaring look. "Clint behave, and leave the children alone," Hawtie admonished and rested her hand on Clint's arm. The old man relaxed visibly beneath her touch.

Quinn finished loading the dishwasher and dried her hands on a towel. "What can I get for you?" she asked him.

He shook his head as he simply drank in the sight of her. She wasn't beautiful in the classic sense, but she was pretty, and he believed she might be the most intriguing woman he'd ever seen. Her features were striking, the air of pride surrounding her almost irresistible.

"Nothing," he told her.

"Nothing? You came over here like you were on a mission."

His only mission had been to get closer to her, but he couldn't say that to her, not after their estranged week of who can avoid whom most. He should walk out of this bar and go back on the hunt, but now that she was looking at him again, he found it impossible to do.

"I'll take a Bud, on tap."

Quinn dropped the towel and walked down to the taps. "If you're going to keep staring at her like that, you should at least buy her dinner," Clint griped.

Julian frowned at the man. He found him amusing for the most part, but there was a fine line between amusing and starting to piss him off. "You know why you're finding him so annoying right now?" Julian had been so focused on Clint, he hadn't realized Chris had come to stand beside him.

"Please enlighten me, Yoda," Julian retorted.

"Oh I will young Skywalker. He annoys you because he's so much like you. Just ask Zachariah."

Julian glowered at him before turning away, but as his eyes landed upon Clint's, he realized Chris was right. "Crap," he muttered.

Chris laughed harder and slapped him on the back. "I really like that old guy."

Quinn gave them both a questioning look as she handed Julian his beer. "What's so funny?" she asked Chris.

"Your boss," Chris replied.

Her mouth quirked in a smile; she glanced at the man who had moved further down the bar to talk with some of his other patrons. "He's one in a million."

"Miss!" Julian's attention was drawn to the group sitting at the table and waving to get Quinn's attention.

"If you'd like, I'll teach them some manners," he told her. "And I'll make sure their hands never travel to places they shouldn't again."

"Believe me their hands won't be traveling anywhere anytime soon," she retorted.

"They could still use some manners."

"So could you."

He lifted an eyebrow at her as he leaned against the bar. "Come now, Dewdrop, you have to admit you enjoy my more *uncivilized* manner."

She scowled at him, but he caught the hint of a smile tugging at her lips when she turned away from him. Julian drank down his beer and turned to Chris. "Are you following me now?"

"No, I actually came to tell you Melissa had a premonition."

"About what?" Julian demanded.

"She told me to grab you before she said anything."

Julian nodded and followed Chris to the poolroom. He spotted Melissa and Zach sitting at a table in the corner. Melissa's shoulders were hunched up, her head bowed as she stared at her folded hands on the table. When she lifted her troubled eyes to his, he knew whatever she'd seen had been bad.

Melissa's premonitions ranged from the mundane to the life changing. She could brush off the smaller ones and continue on as if nothing had happened. The bigger ones left her looking older and wiser than her tender years. They drained her, and they were more noticeable to anyone around her as they took hold of her and held her immobile until they revealed every detail to her.

He glanced around the room, but the dozen or so people playing pool and shooting darts hadn't noticed anything different. Julian turned toward Angie as she walked by. "Can you get us a water?" he inquired.

"You got it," Angie replied and hurried away.

Julian grabbed hold of a chair and pulled it up to the table. "What did you see?"

"I saw whoever it is you're looking for." Her voice sounded as if she'd swallowed a handful of sand. "Or not what they look like, but what they're going to do. I haven't caught any hint of their presence until this vision, but I was there." She leaned closer to them. "I was in their head. I saw it from *their* point of view."

Zach rested his hands on her back and began to rub it when she shuddered and closed her eyes. Melissa's shoulders relaxed as she leaned into his touch. He still didn't like the guy, but he had to admit it was good to see Melissa unwind a little.

Quinn's presence in the room caused warmth to spread through him before she stepped beside him. His left elbow, the one she stood closest to, tingled. He almost took hold of her hand, but restrained himself at the last second.

"Whoever is doing this is going to kill again, soon," Melissa whispered. "A little girl."

"Was there anyone with the little girl?" Julian inquired, his voice edgier than normal.

Melissa shook her head and swallowed heavily. She lifted her head to look at him. "I didn't see anyone else. I don't know what that means; I don't know if there is someone else in the background or if it was only the little girl. I do know we still have a chance to save this child."

"Shit," Julian hissed from between his teeth. He ran a hand through his hair, tugging at the ends of it as his mind spun. His gaze drifted to Quinn.

"You have to go," she urged. "There's no one here you haven't seen before. If there's a chance you can save the child, you *have* to go."

It was the right thing to do, but up until two years ago right and wrong had mattered to him about as much as dirt. Looking at Quinn, he realized right and wrong were on the backburner. He didn't want the child to die, but her safety mattered more to him. He'd left her to the protection of the others this past week, but he couldn't shake the feeling their time was running out. That vampires were closing in on them even now.

"I can take care of myself," she murmured. The feeling of being torn in two filled him. If he went she could be put at risk, if he stayed she may end up hating him. "If you don't go, I will. I'll tell Clint I'm sick or something, and I'll walk out of this bar. I'm safer here, in public, than out of it."

Her eyes were determined as they held his, her jaw jutted out defiantly. He rested his palms flat on the table and rose to stand beside her. "You're not to leave this building until I get back." The muscle in her cheek began to jump. "The others will stay here with you."

"You need someone to go with you," she protested.

"No, I don't."

She stepped closer to him and cast her voice low. "I can drain the life from someone, I'm stronger than most, and I don't need a babysitter."

He rested his hands on her shoulders. "You have to be kept safe. That *is* my number one concern. If the vampires were to capture you…" He broke off as he bit back the words, *I don't know what I would do.* Instead, he continued with, "It could spell doom for all of us."

The hopeful shimmer in her eyes faded away by the time he finished speaking. Confusion swirled through him as he sensed her disappointment and hurt. He had no idea what to make of anything happening between them. What did she want from him? Or better yet, what did he want from her? The frightening answer to that question hovered at the edges of his mind, but he refused to acknowledge it.

Where he'd just been unwilling to leave her, he now found himself eager to escape the suddenly cramped bar.

She gave a brisk nod and moved away from his hands. "I have to get back to work."

In his mind he made a move to stop her, but his hands remained by his sides. The others all stared at him with expressions that made him think he might have somehow sprouted a third eye in his forehead. "She doesn't go to the bathroom by herself," he commanded gruffly.

Spinning on his heel, he stormed out of the bar before he could stop to contemplate everything that had just transpired and the tumultuous feelings rolling through him.

CHAPTER 17

Quinn put her hands in Chris's back and pushed him toward the door. "But we're supposed to stay with you," he protested.

"Not after closing," she told him.

"Julian's going to kick my ass."

"And Clint will fire me if he finds out I let anyone stay in here after closing. Stand outside; I'll be out in half an hour."

Melissa and the others were already gathered in the parking lot when they arrived at the door. "But…"

"Don't forget there's a backdoor," she said and closed the door in his face.

"Talk about some barflies," Angie said and shook her head. "I didn't think they were ever going to leave."

"Me either." Quinn gathered the last of the glasses from the tables and placed them on her tray. She dropped them off at the bar for Angie to put in the washer.

"Where did Julian go?" Angie asked.

"He had some things to take care of," she replied evasively.

Angie's eyes were probing when she met Quinn's gaze. "I think he likes you."

Quinn shrugged and began to wipe off the tables. She had no response for her or any idea of what she and Julian were to each other. It was all such a confusing mess, one she would have preferred not to have in her life, yet she also didn't want him *out* of her life. She didn't have a choice on that matter though, not as long as he believed she could possibly become a menace to them if she was caught.

She'd opened up more to him than anyone else in her life, and then she'd shut him back out again. It had been difficult to do, but necessary. Tonight the reasons why had slapped her over the head again.

Sometimes she thought he might care for her, and then he reminded her the only reason he was still here was to make sure she couldn't be used as a weapon if she fell into the wrong hands. Of course that was his number one concern, his heart belongs to another, she reminded herself for the thousandth time.

It felt like a weight had been tied around her heart, but she couldn't shake the heaviness dragging her down since he'd left. She hated that she'd come to care for him and opened herself up to him in such a way. It made her vulnerable, made her feel exposed and like a fool for thinking he could feel anything more than pity for her.

But his kisses…

She could vividly recall every one of his sizzling kisses, but he hadn't kissed her since she'd told him about the horrific events of her transformation. Nothing pissed her off more than being pitied, and that's exactly what she felt she was now. As she scrubbed one of the pub tables she debated giving him a good ass kicking so he would stop thinking of her as fragile.

"You're taking the paint off it," Angie said with a laugh.

Quinn stepped back as she realized she had indeed scrubbed off a layer of varnish. "Just distracted," she muttered.

"I bet I know by what or should I say, *who*," Angie teased.

Quinn smiled at her, however she felt anything but cheery as she moved onto the next table. Angie sprayed down the bar; she was beginning to wipe it off when a loud bang on the roof froze them both.

"What was that?" Angie asked breathlessly. Everything within her went completely still as she strained to hear another sound. It remained completely silent, unnaturally so. "Quinn?"

Quinn lifted her finger to her lips in a shushing gesture. She studied the roof over their heads. There were no trees in the area, nothing could have fallen onto the roof, but a vampire wouldn't have been so loud and obvious. Not unless they were trying to create a distraction. Quinn dropped the rag onto the table and took a step away.

Her eyes searched the inside of the bar, but whatever was happening outside hadn't made its way inside, yet. "Stay there," she commanded Angie.

"Quinn," she whispered with a trembling lower lip.

Reaching the front of the bar, she slid to the side of the large, plate glass window. She stared outside, passed the cursive Clint's emblazoned on the glass. Melissa, Zach and Lou stood across the street. Melissa shifted back and forth and cupped her hands to blow on them. None of them showed any sign of having heard the noise.

Her head tipped back to stare at the roof. The other buildings were close enough someone could jump from one rooftop to another; kids had done it in the past during the daytime. If it was only teens out on the town, looking to have some fun up there, why would they be loud on the initial landing, but not make a sound afterward? She cast a glance at Angie, she was as pale as the rag in her hand.

"I'll be right back," Quinn told her. "Keep watch up here."

Angie watched her walk around the bar and toward the back; she didn't move a muscle. Quinn stepped into the hall leading to the kitchen doors. Before she approached the doors, she bent down to pull one of the stakes from her boot and a knife from the holster strapped to her side.

She stopped outside of the swinging doors to the kitchen and placed her foot against one of them. Carefully, she pushed it open and craned her neck to look inside the small room. The stainless steel counters of the island in the middle of the room shone in the light. She pushed the door open further to reveal the shining silver stove and fridge before she stepped into the room. The harsh scent of the stringent cleaning chemicals made her nose wrinkle.

Only twenty feet across the room was the back-door. She could see the deadbolt still in the locked position and the window in the door remained unbroken. Her gaze ran over the small room as she cautiously advanced on the door.

She walked past the pizza oven and the fry station, before stepping around the island. Her eyes constantly flitted around as she waited for something to jump out at her. If she'd still had breath, she would have stopped breathing, as it was her body vibrated with the adrenaline pulsating through her tensed muscles. She kept her hands up by her head, ready to drive her weapons into anything that came at her.

She didn't dare bend down to search under the island, it would leave her too exposed if she did, but she was gripped with the certainty a hand was going to shoot out and seize hold of her ankle. It would be the last time that hand gripped anything, she'd make sure of it.

She'd assumed making it to the backdoor would ease some of her tension; she'd been wrong. Pulling aside the curtain, she peered out at the night. Shadows from the streetlights lining the road danced and played across the sand and the roadway behind the building.

She spotted Luther at the back of the building, staring at the roof, but she didn't see Chris with him. Placing the knife handle between her teeth, she swiftly turned the deadbolt and pulled the door open. She took the knife out of her mouth and braced herself as she nudged the door the rest of the way open with her foot.

Luther turned toward her and shook his head no in response to her questioning look. She craned her head and looked up and down for Chris; she didn't see him near the garage or anywhere out in the sandy desert behind the bar. A chilly wind blew the hair back from her face, the hair on her neck stood on end as she felt eyes watching her.

She was about to step forward when something dropped down from the roof in front of her. At first she was so surprised she took a startled step back. Then, as she stared at what she barely processed was a face before her, she realized its sudden entrance was nothing compared to its grisly appearance.

What the hell is that? Her mind screamed at her, but the more she tried to assimilate what it could possibly be, the less she knew about it.

It hung upside down, its feet gripping the edge of the roof so it could dangle into the doorway like a wacked out bat. A hiss escaped it, cracked and bloody lips skimmed back to reveal fangs far too long to fit into its mouth. A full thirty seconds went by before she realized the black cloud hanging into the middle of the door was hair. The unsightly hair would have been amusing in any other circumstances, now it only added to the unrecognizability of this creature.

Red eyes gleamed at her, blood ran from its mouth, up its cheek, around its right eye and dripped onto the floor. *Vampire.* And yet, somehow, that made no sense either. The features were strangely distorted, and not because it was acting like Batman, but because they were scrunched together in a way she'd never seen before.

With a croaking yelp that reminded her of a stepped on bullfrog, the thing flipped from the roof and landed in the doorway. A sinking sensation crashed through her body. She'd been expecting some kind of cracked out elf, not that elves existed to her knowledge, or some other strange ass creature she'd never heard of. She had *not* been expecting what stared back at her.

The hair was going the right way now, but it was still a tangled puff around the distorted features. Blood trickled down its chin; the single drop falling on the floor was as loud as a gunshot in her ears. She realized now why the features were so distorted as she stared at the small four-foot frame across from her.

A child's face wasn't designed to contain the fangs or the fiery eyes blazing like a demon's at her. A *girl*, she realized though it was only a guess and mostly because of the long hair. That strange, squashed bullfrog sound escaped it again before it charged.

Quinn had been so thrown off by the realization there was a vampire child standing across from her that she hadn't been fully prepared for its attack. Lunging to the side, she rolled across the steel island in the center of the kitchen and landed on the other side. She spun, her knife and stake at the ready, but she had no idea what she was going to do with either of them as the child turned toward her. The idea of plunging either weapon into the child made her stomach burn with acid.

Not since The Exorcist had she seen a child as frightening as the one on the other side of the kitchen. If this thing started spitting pea soup at her, she wouldn't be the least bit amazed, and it would have made more sense to her right now.

The child came back at her again screaming as rage made its tiny features even more indiscernible. At least she assumed it was screaming; the hideous croaking noise was all that came out, but its mouth was open and its hands waved through the air as if it were trying to frighten away a bear.

Quinn leapt onto the two steel carts used to move dishes around and went to leap off again. The child charged straight into the carts, roughly shoving them backwards. Quinn's arms spun, she leapt off of the back cart and landed on the first like some kind of demented surfer.

Her clumsy leap brought her right in front of the girl. She couldn't kill a child, but as spittle flew from its mouth and its teeth clacked from the snapping of its jaws, she realized she might not have a choice in the matter.

"What is that?"

She didn't turn at the sound of Chris's gasp; instead, she danced away from the grotesque fangs in the child's small face. The fangs sliced into the bottom of the young girl's chin, causing more blood to flow forth. She now understood the trail of blood trickling down the child's face when it had been hanging upside down.

Needing to put some distance between them, Quinn did a backflip off the cart and landed soundlessly on solid ground. Better than a torpedo honing in on its target, the child's eyes followed her. When the young girl charged at her this time, she was more prepared for it.

With a graceful dart to the side, she left Chris in the girl's direct line of attack. His mouth dropped; he braced his legs apart in preparation for the attack. Before the child could reach him, Quinn launched forward and brought it down. The spitting noises escaping it caused her skin to crawl, the child flailed wildly at the ground, but she refused to let go.

Quinn dodged the tiny fingers trying to tear the flesh from her face as she pressed the child more firmly into the floor. Those awful sounds wouldn't stop. Unexpected tears burned in her eyes; she'd once been in a position similar to this, once been helpless and unable to escape. She fought the tears back as she succeeded in pinning the child's arms to the floor. Her head bowed, she took a minute to steady herself before looking at Chris.

Chris no longer stood in the door; instead, Julian loomed within the frame. His broad shoulders encompassed the doorway; his ruby colored eyes met hers over the thrashing head of the child.

"Are you ok?" he demanded.

"Yes."

His eyes held hers for a minute before sliding to the child. "I'll take her."

For once, she was more than willing to hand over control of something to him. She slid away from the child's back when he knelt to take hold of her. Luther shoved past Chris and moved closer to the child, his face was stony as he stared at the girl. The sound of her name coming from the other room caused Quinn to shoot to her feet.

"Who is that?" Julian asked.

"Angie," she whispered. "I'll be back."

She hastily returned her weapons to their hiding places and smoothed back her hair as she fled the kitchen. Angie was coming around the corner when she emerged from the kitchen. "Is everything ok?"

"Fine," Quinn replied smoothly. "Just a raccoon."

"Mighty big raccoon."

"Yeah," Quinn muttered.

"I thought I heard some banging in the kitchen, did it get inside?"

"I got it back out," Quinn assured her.

"I should have helped you."

"That's ok. We had to make sure someone didn't try to break in the front."

"Yeah, I guess," Angie murmured.

"I probably should have left the raccoon for Clint tomorrow."

Angie released a short burst of laughter as she shook her head. "We'd both be out of a job then."

"Yeah," Quinn agreed, but her eyes slid back to the closed kitchen doors and the horror that lay beyond.

CHAPTER 18

Quinn stepped out the front door with Angie then locked it behind them. She slid the keys into her pocket and climbed down the steps with far more calm than she felt. Her body was twitchy with the urge to double around to the back, see what was going on, and help the others.

"I'll see you tomorrow!" Angie called and branched off to the left, toward her apartment.

Quinn watched until she was out of sight before turning to go behind the restaurant. She didn't make it all the way through her turn before she smacked up against a solid chest. Startled, she took an abrupt step back and shook her head. He moved as noiselessly as a wraith if he'd managed to sneak up on her, either that or she was way off her game.

Despite the fact she was annoyed with herself, she couldn't help but admire the way the moonlight lit his white blond hair and shimmered across eyes made even more arctic by the hostile air surrounding him. His gaze went to where Angie had disappeared before settling on her. With a sharp jerk of his head, he indicated the small alley between Clint's and the bank next door.

"How is the girl?" Quinn asked anxiously. "Is there something we can do to help her?"

"No." His blunt tone caused her to stumble over her feet a little.

"What do you mean *no*?" she demanded. "There has to be something we can do."

"She's dead."

Quinn's mouth dropped, for the first time in her life, she believed she might throw up. "What?"

Julian turned toward her. "There was nothing we could do for her, Quinn," he said quietly. "The few children who survive the change are crazed monsters, but she didn't survive it."

"I saw her," she whispered. "She was alive."

"She wasn't done with the change. She was too small. Her body couldn't handle the influx of vampire blood, her system shut down. It was for the best; she would have been irrational and we would have had to put her down anyway. Children can't handle the thirst; they can't control themselves. There's a reason why vampires can't procreate."

Her gaze drifted back toward the bar; she couldn't shake the sickness in her stomach. "She was so helpless, so broken."

He wrapped his hand around the back of her head and pulled her against his chest. She pressed her hands against the unyielding flesh of his ridged abdomen. To curl up in his arms and lose herself was an enticing prospect, but it wasn't a possibility. Not today, not ever. She didn't respond to his hold on her, but he kept his hand around her head. He bent and placed a kiss against her cheek.

"We have to get back in there."

She nodded at his words and reluctantly stepped away from him. His eyes were still frigid when they came back to hers, but his face had softened a little. She walked with him to the kitchen door and braced herself before stepping inside.

Melissa was kneeling by the child; tearstains streaked her face, but she'd stopped crying. Chris stood on the other side of the island, his hands rested on the steel. He glanced up at Julian, but his attention quickly returned to his hands. Lou and Luther knelt on the other side of the child; Zach had retreated to stand by the stove.

"It's the same girl," Melissa whispered. "She looked far different, but this was the same little girl in my vision."

Images flipped rapidly through Quinn's mind, screams echoed in her head as she stared at the body. The past surged up around her, it tried to pull her into its murky depths and bury her beneath an avalanche of fear and misery.

"How is that possible?" Quinn managed to get out. "I thought we were looking for a human. There were no vampires, other than the two of us, in the bar the night of the fight."

Luther leaned back and rested his arm over his bent knees. "I have no idea."

Despite herself, she felt her eyes flicker to Julian. He'd been the one saying the killer was a human. Melissa hadn't seen who the killer was in her vision, and he'd been away while the girl had been changed. No matter how much she tried to push it away, she couldn't stop the suspicion growing within her.

She hated it; she didn't want to be skeptical of him. She'd trusted him with things she'd never trusted anyone with, but she couldn't shake her growing uncertainty. His gaze slid to hers, and though she wanted to look away, she forced herself to meet it head on. She would know if he had done this, she would know if he was a killer, wouldn't she?

His gaze burned into hers, she knew he wasn't a mind reader, but she became certain he knew exactly what she was thinking. Hurt flickered through his eyes before he turned away from her. Standing there, she felt more exposed now than she had when she'd revealed her hideous secret to him. She had every right to doubt him; he hadn't been here when this girl had been changed, and he *had* been a killer.

Then why do I feel so awful about it? She wondered as he turned his back on her.

"Whoever is doing this is playing with us," Julian said. "They sent this child here to prove that to us."

"Why would they do that?" Melissa asked.

"Because they're letting us know they're here, and they're coming for us."

Quinn couldn't tear her gaze away from his back. Who would be coming for them, vampires she wasn't even sure existed, or *him?*

***

Julian's mind spun as he stared at the ceiling and tried to sift through everything that had happened tonight. The killer was a vampire, but he *knew* there had only been two vampires in the bar the night of the fight. He also knew he wasn't the vampire who had caused the events of last night to unfold and neither was Quinn.

The only problem was Quinn didn't know both of those truths. He'd seen the look in her eyes last night, the uncertainty, and the *doubt*. She was looking at him with far more doubts about his innocence than he was at her.

He'd been a heartless, murdering bastard once. He'd told her as much; he couldn't blame her for doubting him now.

So then why did it make him feel like a razor was repeatedly slicing at his deadened heart? He'd loved two women in his life. One had created a monster when she'd turned him, and the other had helped him to become a man again. And now there was Quinn, a woman who affected him in ways that neither Victoria, his creator, nor Cassie, his savior, ever had.

She frustrated him and made him feel protective but even more, he realized Chris and Melissa had been right. He'd always known Victoria had never truly cared for him, and that Cassie's heart could never be his. When Quinn looked at him, she didn't see him as a toy she could play with and turn into a monster like Victoria had. She didn't look at him like a friend and battle partner like Cassie did.

No, when Quinn looked at him she simply saw a man. When she'd kissed him, she'd done so with enthusiasm and an openness he'd never experienced before, or at least she had before the events of tonight had placed misgivings into her head.

Unlike Victoria, she had a soul to care for him with. Unlike Cassie, she had a heart that didn't already belong to someone else. This wasn't love between them, but damn if she hadn't wormed her way into his heart with her unshakeable pride and determination, yet there was a vulnerability within her that touched a piece of his soul. He would do anything he could to keep her safe.

Rolling off the couch, he climbed to his feet and stretched his cramped muscles. This couch was far more pleasant than the other one, but a bed would be better. Preferably, the one in the room next door, but he had a saint's chance in Hell of getting in there after last night.

Walking over to the blinds, he pulled them up and stepped away from the fading rays of the sun spilling inside. Slowly, as the sun dipped lower toward the horizon, he moved his body in front of the window.

It felt as if sand from the ocean stuck to his skin and rubbed over his flesh when the sunlight spilled over his bare chest. The sensation was like multiple needles firing into his skin, his flesh prickled, but he could tolerate it. Warmth slid over his skin, his head tipped back as he savored in the heat encompassing his body.

He became so lost to the sensation, he didn't realize Quinn had emerged from her room until he heard her startled gasp. He lowered his head and turned it toward her. Her hand covered her mouth; her golden eyes were wide as she stared at him.

He should probably move away from the window, but his gaze remained riveted upon her slender frame. The oversized t-shirt she wore hung down to her knees and slipped off of one of her creamy shoulders. Her chocolate hair fell around her face and shoulders in tumbled disarray.

She was striking without meaning to be, enticing without even trying. His hands fisted at his sides; he fought the urge to go to her. She distrusted him, he reminded himself, and maybe she had a reason to, but it still cut him.

"How?" she whispered.

He stepped away from the sun's rays. His skin had turned redder but the burn would fade soon. "Lots of time spent gradually exposing myself to it."

She approached him and stopped at the edge of the sun's rays. The yearning on her face pulled at his heart. As she stretched her fingers into the rays, smoke began to curl from her reddened flesh. With a hiss, she jerked her hand back and twisted the blistered skin over before her. Her eyes were questioning when they came back to his.

"It's taken me two years and I'm still not able to stand it for very long, or directly," he explained.

She continued to stare at her red, swollen hand, but the blisters had already healed. "How did you know you could do this?"

Julian dropped the blind back into place. He walked away from the window and around the couch to grab a t-shirt from the bag on the floor. He pulled the shirt over his head and pushed the hair back from his face before turning to face her. "One of The Elders was able to do it, and Devon can also withstand it."

"Devon is Cassie's husband?"

"I guess you could call him that."

"It doesn't bother him that you're in love with his wife?"

All of his amusement vanished as he turned to face her. A muscle in his cheek began to jump as his teeth clenched. "Cassie means a lot to me, she always will, but I'm not in love with her. Not anymore."

"You're not?"

He believed he detected a hint of hope in her voice but he couldn't be sure if it was actually there or if he just really wanted it to be.

"No, I'm not." Her eyes flickered, but her face remained impassive. "I always knew there was never

215

going to be a chance for us, but the past is the past, if we become bogged down in the things we did or who we were, we'd never be able to move on and actually live again."

"It sounds rather sad," she murmured.

"I suppose you could look at it that way. If it wasn't for her though, I wouldn't be here, I would still be a vicious killer." Her gaze flickered away at his words, her fingers played with the edges of her t-shirt. "You think I still might be."

"I don't know what to think." Her eyes came back to his. He had to give her credit for not trying to deny it. "I don't have your ability to see into people and know things. The killer is a vampire, yet we were the only vampires in Clint's the night of the fight."

"You have instincts Quinn, what are they telling you?"

"That I should run as far from you as possible."

Her blunt answer caused his eyebrow to rise. "Why?"

"Deep down I don't believe you're a killer, anymore, but you were once and you scare the crap out me."

"I'm not frightening."

"You're terrifying. The way you make me feel, the things I've told you. You barged into my life, you tore it apart, and I don't know what to think or do anymore."

He'd been steadily approaching her while she spoke. She went to step away from him, but he clasped hold of her wrist. "Do you really find me terrifying?" he inquired as he tugged her up against his chest.

Her eyes were the color of gold as she tilted her head back, her lips parted. His fingers entwined with hers; he pulled her arm gently up and behind her back.

Excitement pulsed through his body; he took a step back, pressing her against the wall.

"Julian." The husky whisper of the word only electrified his skin further.

He rested his hand beside her head and bent to look into her eyes. He could feel the pulse of her power, the flow of it reminded him of the waves washing in and out on the shoreline.

"Am I really that frightening, Quinn?"

"Yes," she whispered.

He smiled at her. "If it makes you feel any better, I find you more than a little scary too." Her eyes searched his face, his hand tightened on the fingers he held behind her back. "I'm not a killer, not anymore. Not of innocents anyway. You have to believe me."

Until he said the words, he hadn't realized how badly he'd needed to hear her say she believed him, that she had faith in him. He needed it more than he'd ever needed anything before in his life.

Her eyes remained locked on his, the ebb and flow of her power notched up a level as she gave and took from him in equal measure. He could feel his own ability trying to break free, trying to search her mind in order to see what she felt for him, but he wouldn't invade her in such a way.

"I believe you." He continued to stare at her as he tried to process what she'd said. "I do."

He wrapped his other arm around her waist and releasing the hand behind her back, he lifted her off the ground. A startled sound escaped her seconds before he claimed her mouth with his. Her lips parted to allow his tongue to sweep into her mouth, the minty taste of her toothpaste greeted him.

A growl escaped him, his hand slid over the delicate contour of her cheek before sliding through her thick, silken hair. He'd kissed more women than he could count over the years, but she was the first one who made him feel as if he were drowning in the waves of pleasure she aroused in him.

Turning her around, he took four steps before placing her down on the couch and following her onto it. Pushing her back onto the plump cushions, he leveled his body over top of hers. Her hands pushed the back of his shirt up, his skin bunched beneath the fingers skimming across his flesh. He couldn't get enough of tasting her, as his hands slid up her silken thighs to the bottom of her baggy t-shirt.

The almost cinnamon scent of her blood was an alluring temptation that only excited him further. The silky feel of her creamy skin ensnared him; pushing her shirt further up, he flattened his hand against her stomach as he tried to steady himself. He'd never be satisfied until he possessed her in every way, but he wanted to savor her and take his time.

The prick of her fangs against his bottom lip rattled his resolve to go slow and nearly sent him over the edge. His hand slid further up to brush over her ribcage. She jerked beneath him; her hands dug into the flesh of his back as he ran his hands over her skin. Unable to control them, his own fangs lengthened in eager response.

He nipped at her bottom lip before drawing it into his mouth and lightly licking over the area he'd just offended. Drawing on his firm restraint, he fought against biting down on her full bottom lip and bringing forth the blood he so desperately craved.

The deep, probing thrusts of his tongue sweeping into her mouth caused her to tremble. A small moan escaped her; she arched up beneath him, her hips thrusting against his. Hunger for her body and her blood surged as insistently in him as lava from an erupting volcano.

He'd been walking a fine line with her, trying to keep his distance, his control. He felt that line fraying as the blood in her veins called to him. With a more forceful growl, he withdrew his hand from her shirt to clasp her face in between his palms.

"Julian!" His name was a pant that drove him further beyond the thin layer of control he was barely holding onto.

Her head fell back as his mouth slid away from hers. He kissed her cheek before taking her ear into his mouth and sucking on it tenderly. Her hands slid up his back, leaving a trail of fire over him.

The heat of her skin burned into his as he pressed his lips against her neck and the vein running just beneath the surface. His lips skimmed back, he raked his fangs over her tender flesh but didn't pierce it. Her blood was there, begging to be tasted. All he had to do was bite down.

Her body stilled beneath his, her warm mouth turned into his neck, and her lips rested against him. The pull of her blood was so potent it caused saliva to rush into his mouth, but he remained still against her. This was different than any of the other times he'd exchanged blood with a vampire. He cared for her, but this line wasn't one he was ready to cross. It would leave him vulnerable in a way he hadn't been since he'd been imprisoned and tortured in that hellhole with Cassie.

Pulling his mouth away was one of the most difficult things he'd ever done, but he pressed a kiss against her skin and did so. His disappointment vanished as he dropped his hands down again to skim over her body. He wouldn't taste her now, but he had his control back and he planned to take his time and enjoy her like he'd originally intended.

His palm flattened against her thigh as he pulled back to look into her smoky honey eyes. His finger traced over the scar on her chin, her penance, her punishment for a mistake she'd had no control over. He touched the scar running across her temple before bending to press a kiss to the one on her chin.

"Julian, no…"

"Shh," he whispered as he kissed the one on her temple next. She remained rigid against him, unable to relax as he gently touched the heartrending reminders of her past. "You don't deserve them."

Bending his head to hers again, he was about to reclaim her mouth when a knock sounded on the door. A low grumble of displeasure rumbled through his chest. Judging by the scents in the air, Chris and Melissa stood on the other side of the door.

His upper lip skimmed back, the words, *go away*, lodged in his throat, but no matter how badly he wanted to continue this, there were more important things they had to deal with.

His fingers slid through her silken hair as he turned back to her. Her enticing lips were swollen from his kisses, but the smokiness had faded from her eyes. She'd briefly let her walls slip; he could see them going back up now.

"Don't shut me out," he told her as he ran his finger over her bottom lip.

"I'm not."

He tilted his head to study her. "Dewdrop, I can almost see the fortress growing behind your eyes. Don't shut me out."

"You won't let me."

He laughed as he bent to press a kiss against her lips again. "No, I won't."

He kissed the tip of her nose before reluctantly pulling away from her and rising to his feet. Holding his hand out to her, he helped her to stand. She hastily fixed her t-shirt and pushed back her hair.

"I have to take a shower," she mumbled.

The idea of her in the shower caused his blood to flash boil with lust. He briefly contemplated kicking Melissa and Chris out of here, but he didn't think the action would be well received by anyone. Forcing himself to release her arm, he took a step away from her. She gave him one last look before hurrying away.

Keeping his face impassive, he walked to the door and pulled it open to let them in. "Everything ok?" Chris asked.

"Fine," Julian assured him as he closed the door behind them.

"Took you a while to answer the door."

"Some of us like to sleep."

"Uh huh," Chris said, his gaze went pointedly toward Quinn's closed door.

Julian abruptly stepped in front of him to block his view of her door. Melissa smirked at him and plopped onto the couch. Chris whistled maddeningly as he walked over to join his friend.

"Cassie's still itching to come down here," Melissa said.

"I've talked to Devon, he knows to keep her away," Julian replied.

Chris laughed. "Let's see how good that works out for him."

"I definitely don't envy him."

"So, any theories on how a vampire is the one committing these murders without any of us knowing a vampire was in our presence the night of the fight?" Melissa asked.

"Not one," he admitted and dropped onto the couch beside Chris. "Maybe it's some kind of cloaking ability we've never encountered before."

"Fantastic," Chris mumbled.

Julian agreed as he propped his feet on the milk crate and rubbed tiredly at the bridge of his nose. Whatever was going on, he had a feeling he wasn't going to like the answer.

CHAPTER 19

Quinn stepped away from the coyote she'd caught and fed from. It glanced over its shoulder at her before vanishing behind one of the numerous outcroppings of rock rising up from the desert. The cool air slid over her skin, causing goose bumps to break out on her arms. She tilted her head back to take in the moon hanging just above the horizon and the thousands of stars glowing from the midnight tapestry above her.

She hadn't been born in the desert, but it had become her home over the years. With her inability to deal with the sun, she'd often considered going somewhere safer for her, but she felt at home here amongst the shifting red and orange sand though. Felt at home amongst the numerous wildlife, large and squat prickly cactuses and the wildness of the terrain around her.

Maybe staying here was another way to punish herself by having to be locked away for large portions of the day. Or perhaps it was the barrenness of the desert, the loneliness of the rolling dunes and cactuses dotting the landscape that called to her.

It didn't matter what it was, all that mattered was she'd somehow always felt safe hidden away here. Until now. Now a monster had invaded her home and was killing innocent women and children. And not just killing them, it was turning them into monstrosities, and she had no idea who it was or how to stop them from doing what they were doing.

She wiped away the blood on her mouth with the back of her hand. Her gaze involuntarily drifted over her shoulder as Julian released the coyote he'd been feeding from. The moonlight spilled over his chiseled features and lit his hair with its silvery radiance. The memory of what had transpired between them earlier flooded her mind; her lips tingled as she recalled the heat of his mouth burning against hers.

She'd been kissed before; felt up and nearly had sex with a boy she'd dated for two months during her senior year of high school. If her family hadn't been murdered, she probably would have stayed with that boy, at least through the summer and maybe even her first semester of college.

After the murders, she'd locked herself away from people until she was certain she could be trusted around them. When she'd reemerged she'd been guarded, caged, unwilling to care for anyone again. She was a monster, she'd killed her uncle, she'd consumed the blood of her loved ones; she deserved more than the scars marring her face and body. At least the scars showed the outside world a small piece of the hideousness within her.

She'd made friends in this town, but she'd always known those friendships were tenuous at best. One day she would have to leave here, and people died far too easily.

This man had managed to break past the walls she'd so carefully constructed around herself over the years, and she didn't know how to handle it. He wasn't in love with Cassie, or so he said, but what was it he wanted from *her*? And why did he have to keep tearing at her walls, keep coming at her until she had nothing left to defend herself with?

His gaze mirrored the Arctic Ocean when it slid to her. It was a chilling color but warmth still spread throughout her as she held his unwavering eyes. A smile curled his mouth as he rose with the flowing grace of a river rippling over rocks.

She could watch the mesmerizing way he moved every day, but then she realized she was getting way ahead of herself. There was no way of knowing how long he would be in her life.

Still, she couldn't deny that seeing him standing in front of the window, his arms open to the warmth of the sun, had been one of the most magnificent things she'd ever witnessed. He'd been so achingly beautiful that it had tugged at her heart in ways she'd never experienced before.

She glanced away from him and back toward the shifting sand of the desert as the wind rippled over the dunes. The fresh influx of coyote blood had helped to ease her hunger, but it did nothing to dampen the desire he'd managed to create within her.

She brushed back the hair from her face and wiped the sand from the knees of her pants as she tried to gather her scattered thoughts and emotions. What was she going to do about him? She didn't think she'd ever figure out the answer, but when his hand wrapped around her elbow she wasn't entirely sure she wanted to know it.

He walked with her toward the back of Clint's bar. If they started to run they could cover the three miles to the bar in less than two minutes; she found she far preferred walking with him. She stayed close to his side, welcoming the heat of his body. Just touching him warmed her from the tips of her toes to her hair.

"Are you going to search for whoever is doing this again tonight?" she asked.

"I don't know," he answered. His thumb stroked over her arm as they walked, sending a firestorm of yearning through her body. "I don't like the idea of leaving you."

"I can take care of myself."

His head tilted as he studied her with an amused twinkle in his eyes. "I know you can, but you also don't want to come up against a child again."

"No, I don't," she admitted. "But if it's going to die…"

"Not all of them die from the change, but all of them have to be put down." Quinn shuddered at his words. "I don't think there will be any more children coming for us though."

She swallowed before turning to look at him. "Why not?"

"Whoever is doing this made their point. They think they're smarter; they're playing with us, and they're going to pay for that."

The cold didn't cause her to shiver this time; the merciless flash in his eyes did as they met hers again. His kisses could melt her like a flame melted chocolate, but there was only so much warmth in him.

"How are we going to find them?" she inquired.

He pondered her question before shaking his head. "I'll find a way. They may have some kind of cloaking ability that makes them appear human. They can't cloak their memories from me though. And I think they want to be found; they mistakenly believe they're stronger than me, but they don't know who they're messing with."

His voice was a lethal rumble. She knew, without a doubt, if he discovered the vampire who had turned the girl, there would be little left of them. It was the matter of finding the vamp before they could kill any more children.

***

Quinn dropped the tray onto the bar and pulled her apron off. A hot bath sounded like a little bit of heaven right now. She'd forgotten the extremely popular, local band, *Kerosene* was playing tonight.

Not only did her feet throb and her head ache, but she'd been groped more times than a tour guide in a dark haunted house. At least a dozen men had walked out of here tonight having received a good zap; she'd smacked more than her fair share of hands, and one of them wouldn't be having sex again for a good week.

She had bills to pay, but there was only so much she would tolerate. If she was too tired by the time she got home to take a bath, she was at the very least going to scrub herself down.

Chris, Melissa, and the others were still in the pool-room, talking with the members of the band as they packed up their equipment. They were all that remained in the bar, and she couldn't wait for them to head home.

Angie glanced up at her from behind the bar, her eyes were bloodshot and her hair straggled around her pretty face. Quinn was about to ask her how she'd faired through the night when the door opened. Her hand instinctively went to the stake strapped at her side; it fell away when Julian stepped inside.

He met her questioning gaze and gave a barely discernible shake of his head no. Quinn's shoulders slumped, she plopped onto the bar stool and dropped her chin into her hands. It was more than the crowd that had worn her down, but also the ever-present worry some Chucky-like child would barge in here to try and kill them. She didn't think she could take that horror again.

Her skin prickled from the aura of power he emitted seconds before Julian's hands came down on her shoulders and he began to massage them. Quinn relaxed into his touch, her body swayed instinctively closer to his. Angie's mouth parted, her eyes shot back and forth between them.

"Long night?" The low rumble of his voice caused her body to tingle all over.

"It was a ball buster," Angie replied. She dropped her rag on the bar and leaned across it toward them. "Good tips though."

"Yeah," Quinn murmured but she didn't care about anything else as his hands continued to knead her flesh. He could work miracles with those hands, something she knew well from earlier. Right now, he made her feel cared for in a way she hadn't felt in the past six years.

Her eyes closed, her back pressed against his chest. His hands slid from her shoulders down her arms, the warmth of his lips pressed against her ear as he spoke. "If you like, when we get back to your place, I can get some lotion and give you a proper massage."

Her eyes flew open; her mouth went dry as she met the wicked twinkle in his eyes. She'd thought he was teasing, but meeting his gaze now, she knew he'd been dead serious. She didn't know how to respond.

"If you're ready for me?" he murmured.

That was the question, was she ready for him? She definitely felt more for him than anyone else she'd ever encountered, but was she ready to give herself over to him so completely? Her heart had been destroyed once already; she'd spent many years keeping it safely tucked away, but this man insisted upon wiggling his way into it.

"We haven't even been on a date yet," she managed to choke out. It wasn't the best way to deflect his question, but it was the best she could come up with right now.

His gaze searched hers; his smile was endearing as he leaned forward and pressed a kiss against her forehead. "We'll just have to remedy that now won't we, Dewdrop?"

The vulnerability in his eyes pulled at her but the idea of having her heart shattered again caused a lump to form in her throat. He was putting himself out there right now, and she couldn't think of one word to say in response.

Thankfully, she was saved from having to answer by the band trudging into the main bar area. "Quinn, Angie," the lead singer said with a tip of his cowboy hat. "I'm sure we'll be seeing you ladies soon."

"Have a goodnight, Raylan," Angie said and Quinn gave a brief wave of her fingers.

"You guys should be getting out too," Quinn said to Julian. "While we lock up."

She reluctantly moved away from the fingers making her muscles quiver and rose to her feet. Angie walked around the bar and began to gather empty glasses from the tables as Chris, Melissa, Luther, Lou, and Zach emerged from the poolroom. Melissa and Zach had their heads bent close together; they were both laughing as they walked.

Luther had told her earlier he'd looked up her family and confirmed they'd been listed as dead years before their actual deaths. Her birth had never been recorded, her existence never known about. These were things she'd already been told, but it was still a relief to know that no one had ever known about her, until now. Luther hadn't discovered anything else of importance in his search through her family's history.

"I'll be right outside," Julian told her.

"I wouldn't expect anything less." Placing her hands in his back, she nudged him toward the door.

"Oh wait!" Melissa cried and spun back toward the poolroom.

Lou, thrown off by her abrupt change in direction took an awkward step to the side. His foot became entangled in the bottom of one of the tables. It skittered to the side when he fell heavily against it. Angie let out a startled yelp and lunged forward as a glass slid over the wooden surface toward the floor. Julian's hand shot out; he snagged hold of the glass before it could crash to the floor and create a much bigger mess.

Angie gawked at the hand that had moved with the speed of lightning. "Ah, thank you," Angie stammered, her fingers brushed over his when she took the glass from him. Quinn started to turn away when Julian stiffened perceptively, his nostrils flared and his hand shot out to wrap around Angie's wrist. "Hey!" Angie cried out. Julian kept hold of her wrist, his eyes burned into Angie's as he searched her face. "Let go of me!"

He released her so abruptly that Angie took a stumbling step back. Grabbing hold of her wrist, she held it against her chest as she rubbed at it. Julian continued to loom over her, his jaw locked as he stared at her relentlessly.

"Asshole," Angie muttered before hurrying past Quinn and toward the bathroom.

Quinn rounded on him when the bathroom door closed. "You hurt her!" she accused. Julian's eyes remained focused on the bathroom. "Julian…"

"It's her."

"What?" Quinn demanded and even the others looked at him as if he'd just said the sun had fallen from the sky.

"She's not a vampire but she *is* who the memories came from."

"Impossible," Quinn said flatly. "Angie's a good person, she'd never harm anyone."

The muscles in his arms stood out as his hands clenched and unclenched. She was half-afraid he was going to launch himself across the bar, break down the door to the bathroom and rip Angie out of there. He remained where he stood, a muscle jumping in his cheek as his teeth grated together.

His head turned toward her. Quinn's eyes widened when she came face to face with the barely leashed savagery running below his surface. He'd told her he was lethal and not to be messed with. Looking at him now, she fully realized how brutal he could be.

"She's a good person, Julian," she insisted again.

"Maybe she is, but you're not going to be alone with her in here again."

"Angie would never hurt me and she's *human*."

"She is," he confirmed. "But she's mixed up in this somehow, and there's a vampire involved. I will *not* take the chance of you getting injured."

"Julian…"

He was on her so fast she never saw him move. His arms wrapped around her waist; he jerked her up against him and spun his back toward the window. Less than a blink later the large front window shattered inward with a resounding crash that echoed through the bar.

A startled cry escaped her; flying shards of glass sprayed the air around them. It had to have sliced into his back, but he showed no sign of injury as he dragged her to the ground and plastered his body over the top of hers. Glass fell to the ground in a tinkling wave; loud bangs resonated throughout the building. Confusion swirled through her; it took her a few more seconds to realize it was bullets rattling through the building and shattering the bottles and glass mirror behind the bar.

Julian's hand wrapped around her head, his weight pressed her more firmly into the floor. Across the way she saw Melissa, Chris, and Zach with their backs against the wall. Lou and Luther were lying on the floor with their hands over their heads as more bullets smashed into the walls and shattered bottles. Bits of wood exploded around the room and fell to the ground around them.

"Julian we have to help them!" she cried. The bullets wouldn't kill the two of them, they'd sting worse than a Box jellyfish, but they'd survive. The humans wouldn't.

"They'll be fine. Stay where you are," he growled in her ear.

He wrapped his arms more protectively around her face as a jagged piece of wood sliced across her cheek, spilling blood. The sound that issued from him when he spotted her blood brought to mind a wolf defending its mate.

His cheek pressed against hers as more bullets crashed throughout the building. The smell of gunpowder and chipped wood filled the air; she flinched away from more splinters of wood shooting around the room.

The blessed hush that descended upon the bar seemed almost too good to be true. Terrified to draw more fire on the bar, she didn't move. Her gaze drifted back to the humans still huddled in their defensive postures. They all remained unmoving, waiting to see if more bullets would come flying into the building as the seconds stretched into a minute.

She was still trying to get her bearings when Julian launched himself off of her. Quinn flipped herself over in time to see him leap out the missing front window in one easy bound.

"Julian!" His name tore from her throat, leaving it raw and brutalized.

Adrenaline pulsed through her; she shoved herself to her feet and bolted across the floor. She leapt out the window behind him, landed easily in the parking lot and dashed into the road. She spotted Julian's rapidly fading figure already halfway down the road. Putting her head down, her arms pumped as her legs eagerly ate up the ground in between them. She would never be able to catch up to him, but she had to keep him in view or else she could lose him completely.

The world raced by her in a blur of speed she'd never achieved before. The driving urge to get to him gave her a powerful strength she'd never felt before. She didn't know how far or where they were running to, location didn't matter right now. All that mattered was staying on his trail.

Rounding a corner, she saw Julian zipping in between two buildings. Following behind, she had to turn sideways in order to squeeze in between the two houses. Forced to slow down her rush, she attuned her senses to her surroundings as she searched for any hint of menace up ahead.

She didn't hear, see, or smell anything out of the ordinary, but she knew they might be running into a trap. The wood of the one house nearly pressed against her nose, the scent of the old, rotting wood of the abandoned home filled her nose.

Pausing halfway down the narrow alley, she pulled her stake from its holder at her waist before continuing. At the end of the alley, she stuck her head out cautiously. Julian stood around the corner, pressed against the wall. He glanced back at her and made a staying gesture with his hand. She saw nothing abnormal behind the two homes. Her head tipped back, the rooftops above her appeared to be clear.

Julian's eyes were upon her when she looked at him again. 'Stay,' he mouthed.

Like hell, she thought as he slipped further into the shadows.

She glanced around again before stepping out from between the two buildings and following him down another alley running behind the double line of homes. The sagging and dilapidated houses had been beyond their prime twenty years ago, now they looked like a good wind would blow them over.

She was half-afraid some of them might fall down upon them if they hit the structures the wrong way. If she was right about where their run had taken them to in the desert, these homes had all been abandoned years ago when the bridge in this town had washed out during a flashflood. The economy had quickly followed the collapse of the bridge and the people had left the town behind.

The rotting houses faded away to be replaced with the crumbling buildings and store fronts that had once made up the center of the deserted town. Being stuck in this maze of dilapidated buildings, and unable to see more than ten feet in front or behind her, was a disconcerting sensation she didn't like. Nor did she like that she kept losing Julian in the maze.

If something happened to him...

She refused to let herself think about the possibility. *Nothing* would happen to him if she had anything to say about it.

Turning the corner, she nearly ran into his back. He'd stopped in the middle of the alley and turned to face her. "I told you to stay," he whispered.

"And?"

Tension radiated through his vibrating muscles; he gave her one of those smiles she'd hated so much in the beginning. Even now, she scowled back at him, but she couldn't deny the smile put her a little more at ease. It bolstered her to know he was still so cocky while standing in the middle of a ghost town, hunting vampires. It sounded insane in her head and yet so entirely right for her life.

He gave a brisk jerk of his head and pointed upward. Before she could figure out his intent, he braced one foot against the back of one building and the other foot against the back of another. Like some kind of humanoid monkey, he began to climb rapidly up between the structures. Quinn stifled a groan; she put her stake back in its holster and braced her feet and hands against the buildings too.

She'd never done anything like this before. As she moved rapidly up the three feet of space dividing the structures, she felt like Spider-Man and had to admit it made her feel a little badass.

Reaching the top, Julian leaned back over to look down at her. He took hold of her hand and pulled her onto the roof of the building. Quinn warily eyed the sagging roof that bowed and dipped toward the middle. The last thing she needed was to fall through the thing, with her luck she'd be staked upon landing. Julian started across the roof toward the front of the building.

Her gaze fell on the tears and blood crisscrossing the back of his shirt from the glass and wood that had sliced across his flesh during the attack on the bar. There may even be a bullet embedded in his flesh, but the wounds were already beginning to heal, his skin had knitted itself back together. Even still, she couldn't help but wince at the reminder of the damage he'd sustained while protecting her. Her heart ached for him, she longed to reach out and soothe him in some way, but there was no time for that now.

Quinn followed behind him; they stayed toward the more stable looking edge of the roof. Julian knelt against the two-foot high wall running around the entire roof. She knelt beside him and rested her shoulder against the wall. He placed his hands onto the wall and rose to peer over the side before ducking back again.

He pulled his phone out and began to type something into it. "What are you doing?" she whispered.

"Letting the others know where we are and turning on the tracking app on my phone."

"You have a tracking app?"

He slid his phone into his pocket. "We all do. With what we do, we tend to get separated far more often than we'd like."

"Oh." She didn't know what else to say to that.

He leaned closer to her. "I don't suppose telling you to stay here would do me any good, would it?"

"None at all."

"That's what I thought. When we get in there you have to be prepared for at least one of them to be able to control minds."

Her hand flew to her mouth as realization dawned. Sickness churned within her stomach, anger rose up in her. "Angie," she whispered.

"Yes."

Her nostrils flared as another notion hit her. "My family."

Julian rested his fingers against her cheek and shook his head. "No. This one is newer than the one who killed your family."

"How do you know that?"

"Because Angie's memories weren't solidified, there are holes in them. She doesn't recall what she's witnessed, but I was able to see it the first time I touched her. I made the wrong and stupid assumption the killer was a human male and not a human with tampered memories. The vampire who murdered your family was smart, he had a lot more power if he got to your cousin and recognized what you all were. He was far older than these vamps. We'll find the one who killed your family, but he's not in there."

Uncertainty swirled through her; she so badly wanted one of the bastards inside to be the one she'd been preparing to run across for the past six years. But even if he wasn't in there, these monsters deserved to die for what they'd done to Angie. He clasped hold of her cheeks, leaned forward and kissed her.

"Stay calm and stay near me," he whispered against her lips.

He sat back to study her; she nodded her agreement. She had no idea what he'd intended when he'd climbed onto this roof. She didn't get a chance to ask as he rose to his feet, climbed onto the wall, and then stepped off of it.

Quinn shot up like a firecracker. The sight of him standing only a foot beneath the wall and grinning up at her doused her panic. "Ass!" she hissed.

"Shh," he said and put his finger against his lips.

He was lucky she had to be quiet; otherwise, she might have staked him herself. Instead, she swung her leg over the wall and suppressed a gasp when he grabbed hold of her waist and lifted her effortlessly into the air.

Goosebumps broke out on her flesh when he slid her back down the broad expanse of his chest. Wrapping his arm around her waist, he kept her pinned against his body on the set of fire stairs running down the front of the three-story building.

"Don't move."

She thought he might actually be enjoying this, and she couldn't deny the thrill of pleasure the feel of him gave her, but she kept her senses focused on the world around them as they remained immobile on the stairs. She tried not to think about how old these stairs were and when the last time they'd been maintained was. If the stairs gave out beneath them there would be no keeping their presence here a secret. Every vampire in a hundred yard radius would know where they were. And they would come for them.

The breeze tickled her hair and chilled her skin. She didn't move so much as an eyelash as she strained to hear. She thought she caught the sound of voices and tuned out the lonely howl of the wind over the sand. Yes, there were definitely voices.

She couldn't make out what was being said or how many there were, but they were coming from inside the building. Grunting and the hollow thump of fists hitting flesh followed the voices. She frowned at the noises, unable to understand why they were fighting amongst each other.

She turned her head and rested her mouth against his ear. "How many?"

"Seven, maybe eight," he whispered. "You really should stay here."

She shook her head. "You're not going in there alone."

"You're to stay near me, Dewdrop," he told her again.

He released her and slid around to stand in front of her. She followed noiselessly behind as they crept down the dilapidated stairs. With every step they took, she was certain the stairs were going to collapse beneath them. Miraculously, the stairs held firm until they arrived at a second floor window.

CHAPTER 20

Julian kept hold of the remaining pieces of glass as he knocked them out of the already broken window. He dropped the glass silently onto the floor inside the building before noiselessly slipping inside. He had no idea where the vampire who had shot up the bar had gone. He could have continued to follow him, but his attention had been drawn to this building by the overwhelming stench of decay, and the presence of even more vampires.

He'd find the one who had fled the bar eventually, he would definitely pay for what he'd done tonight, but he couldn't ignore the nest of vampires here. A nest he was certain the vampire he'd been chasing belonged to, but he'd purposely gone in a different direction. The vampire hadn't realized Julian wouldn't be so easily lost or led off the real trail.

Turning back, he took hold of Quinn's hand and helped her inside. He didn't like the idea of her in here with him, would have preferred to keep her far away from this, but that would have been impossible. It was better to have her with him while entering the building then to have her sneak in later.

She bent over and pulled two stakes from her boots. She handed one out to him, but he waved it away. 'Keep it,' he mouthed to her.

She shook her head and shoved it into his hand. Before he could protest further she tugged a knife free of a holster on her waist. He'd known she was armed at all times, but he hadn't realized she was a walking death trap as she shoved the knife into his hand and pulled another one free.

Her eyes were the color of amber when they met his again; they brought to mind a hawk's eyes when it honed in on its prey. He hesitated, his gaze slid back to the window as he briefly contemplated dragging her back outside and far away from this place.

The vampires in this place may not be old, but they were still volatile and lethal, especially to her. She jerked her head forward and jutted her chin out. She would never agree to leave here without a fight. Julian turned away from her and focused on the cavernous room they'd entered.

The expansive space took up the entire second floor of the building. Heavy cobwebs hung from the rafters above their heads, their feet left prints in the thick dust as they crossed the floor with care. At least half a dozen five-foot tall mannequins of torsos were shoved into the shadowed corners of the room. Some had sheets draped over top of them, but the sheets had fallen off of others and were a dusty heap pooled upon the ground.

He didn't pay any attention to the floor squeaking beneath him. The rats he heard in the walls and scurrying through the shadows were more than enough to cover a noisy floorboard or two. At the end of the room was a single wooden board running from the wall to the set of stairs winding down to the first floor. Light flooded up from below, it bounced off of the dark ceiling beams and illuminated the first five feet of the loft area they stood in.

Voices reverberated through the room. A low moan sounded; he could hear the solid thwack of a boot connecting with someone's ribs. Something cracked, a squeal sounded from below and then the hollow thuds stopped. Small mewls and whimpers continued, but the beating had ceased, for now.

"What is his problem? Why did he flip out like that?" a voice demanded from below.

"I don't know," someone else answered.

Bending down, Julian crept forward the last few feet, and held his arm back to keep Quinn at a safe distance away. He peered over the edge of the loft at the eight men gathered below. One of the men was curled up in the fetal position on the floor. The pitiful noises were coming from him as he kept one hand clasped against his caved in cheekbone, and the other against his concave chest.

"Kill me," the pitiful, bloodied and broken vampire moaned. "Please, just kill me."

"Shut up," one of the others said and spat at the writhing man.

Julian's lip curled in revulsion as his gaze drifted away from the pathetic excuse of a vampire lying on the floor. Before he'd looked over, he'd already known what to expect as the stench of rotting flesh and coppery blood filled his nostrils. The spectacle of the piled bodies below was enough to make even *his* stomach turn.

He rested his hand against the railing and wrapped his other hand around Quinn's arm in order to hold her back. It would be impossible to keep this from her, but he'd like to be able to do so for a little bit longer.

There were at least a couple dozen bodies of women and children lying in a heap near the back of the building. These vampires were the worst form of life. They killed innocents, and slept and lived with the remains of their food. Animals had more care for their environment and conditions than this.

He was going to enjoy killing these bastards.

Bloodlust built within him, excitement pulsed through his body; his fangs tingled as his body swelled with power. Quinn's hand wrapped around his bicep drawing his attention back to her. She crept closer to him and rested her hand on his cheek.

She affected him in some strange ways, but he wasn't prepared for the sense of calm that slid through his body at her touch. He placed his hand over top of hers and turned his lips into her palm. She tried to take a step closer to the edge; he kept her back and shook his head no.

'Not yet,' he mouthed against her palm.

Her eyes flickered toward the lower room, but she didn't try to fight him on it. From below the sounds of more blows falling upon the flesh and bone of someone drifted up to them. He leaned over to see three of them beating the one on the floor again. With the way they were going, they were going to kill him before Julian had to worry that he and Quinn were outnumbered four to one.

Julian pulled Quinn back when the front door opened and moonlight briefly spilled inside the building. Thick leather boots resounded on the wooden floor as the vampire he'd been chasing strolled inside with a cocky grin on his face. His long brown hair stood up in spikes on top of his head. Julian's fingers flexed on his free hand, as he imagined driving his fist into the smirk on this guy's face.

"Where have you been?" one of the others inquired.

"I decided to pay our friends a little visit," the shooter replied.

A man who had been hanging back, watching the others beat on the broken vampire on the floor, held up his hand to halt the others. They reluctantly stepped away from the now unmoving form curled into a ball.

"What?" the man who had halted them barked.

The shooter shrugged and ran his hand through his hair. "It will make them think twice about snooping around again."

"Are you out of your mind?" The man strode across the open floor toward the shooter. The shooter's eyes darted nervously toward the others, but they all stayed where they were. Julian focused on the one approaching the shooter; the one he assumed was their leader. "Who gave you permission to do that?"

The shooter took another step back. "We can't continue to hide from them, I thought…"

"No one said you could think!" The bellowed words reverberated through the rafters of the building and shook the walls. "You just poked at a nest of rattlers."

"They're only two vampires," the shooter stammered as he began to back peddle faster.

"I told you last night, after you sent the child, to leave them alone! I won't tell you again!"

The crunching sound of a punch hitting shooter's cheekbone echoed through the building. He felt the small flinch that ran through Quinn's body. She was tough, she'd been through a lot, but she didn't have this level of viciousness and cruelty within her. He pulled her closer against his side in the hopes his touch would be able to pacify her as much as hers did him.

The piercing snap of a bone cracking was followed by a squeal that reminded him of a frightened pig. The shooter hit the floor with a loud thump. His going down didn't stop the other vampire from continuing to pummel him.

He knew he could take them out, but he worried about Quinn. She would never agree to stay up here and out of danger. The others would be arriving soon, he could always wait for them but he'd never been one to wait, or require help. He'd also never had anything worth waiting around for. He squeezed Quinn's hand reassuringly again.

The shooter lay unmoving upon the ground; blood seeped out around him and covered the one who had been beating upon him, but Julian knew he wasn't dead. Kneeling down, the one who had been beating on the shooter removed a knife from the holster at his side. Julian pulled Quinn further back; he shot her a silencing look when she started to protest. She didn't need to see the man having his head methodically sawed off.

When he finished separating the head from the body, the vampire Julian assumed was the leader of the group holstered his knife, rose to his feet and kicked the head carelessly aside. It rolled across the floor before knocking up against the wall. "We're going to have to go and finish what this moron started."

"But you said we should stay away from them, Drew," one of the others protested.

"That was before this *idiot*," he punctuated the word with a severe kick to, "idiot's," headless body on the ground. "Went and declared war on a vampire that's easily a hundred years older than us."

Julian scoffed at their deadly wrong assumption that he was only a hundred years older than they were. They had absolutely no idea what they were dealing with, which only led to his growing belief that the oldest amongst them was at most a hundred.

The Elders had needed to be destroyed, but jack-asses like these guys were the bad side of having the hierarchy of vampires removed. Even if The Elders had mostly faded away into oblivion after The Slaughter, the knowledge of their existence had been enough to keep vampires like these assholes from stepping out of line.

They'd spent the past two years concentrating on trying to gather the straggling remainders of the Hunter and Guardian lines together, but he realized now they'd made a big mistake by ignoring the vampires still out there.

They'd given little consideration to the younger and therefore less of a hazard, vampires. Vampires like these were a big menace to society and their way of life, if they believed it was remotely ok to start shooting up human establishments and attacking other vampires in public.

"Let's go," Drew commanded.

Those words made his decision for him, he couldn't allow them to leave this building.

Turning toward Quinn, he tugged her up against him so he could whisper in her ear. "I'm going down there. Wait here until I tell you differently." He could see the argument building in her eyes as they shimmered with defiance. "The two of us in here, without them knowing is our biggest element of surprise right now. If we don't go down there together, they might assume I left you behind when I chased our attacker. Just wait."

Her eyes narrowed on him, he had no doubt she wouldn't wait for long; he could only hope he'd be able to take out a couple of them before she followed. He wrapped his hand around the rail and gave it a forceful tug. Dust fell down from it, but it held up beneath his jerk. Switching both of his weapons into his left hand, he seized the board with his right and climbed onto it. He remained crouched on it for a second before launching himself over top of the stairs and out over the first floor.

Air rushed up around him, it whipped his hair back from his face and beat at his clothes as he fell from the sky. He didn't make a sound as he landed in the center of the building with his knees bent to absorb the impact. His left hand rested on the floor, the knife and stake pressed firmly into his palm as he met the startled eyes of the men surrounding him.

He remained crouched as he stared at the men. Three of them glanced wildly toward the front door. "I'll rip your head off before you make it ten steps," Julian promised them.

"Hey now," Drew's tone of voice made Julian's fingers curl into the wooden floor as his upper lip curved into a sneer. "We're all the same kind here; we're all friends."

"You may be vampires, but you're not my kind, and we are *not* friends."

They exchanged uneasy looks, but none of them made a move. His gaze flickered over all of them as he waited for the telltale niggle at the base of his skull that would alert him to who he was searching for.

And then he felt it, the distinct sensation of something trying to wiggle its way into his mind like a worm slithering into the earth. His nostrils flared, his head turned to take in the one he sought. His eyes settled on the disheveled man across from him. He looked no older than twenty, his collarbones stuck out from his torn shirt and there was enough dirt on his face to give Pig-Pen a run for his money.

The boy's eyes were focused on Julian, the niggling at the back of his skull intensified. Julian held his gaze as he broke into a slow smile and gave the kid a wink. The boy did a double take, his forehead creased in confusion before he took a step back. With a burst of speed, Julian sped toward him, grabbed him by the neck and drove him into the floor. A startled cry escaped the boy; his fingers tore at Julian's hand.

"Don't poke at those whose minds are far older than yours," Julian snarled before driving the stake into the boy's chest.

The boy convulsed beneath him; his fingers clawed at the stake before he went limp. Julian jerked it free and spun to face the other six as they started toward him. Though he hadn't given the signal, Quinn leapt onto the railing of the loft and swung out to grab hold of a beam over her head. He'd been hoping to take more down before she decided to disobey him, but his biggest concern of taking out the one with mind control had at least been accomplished.

Quinn swung across to another beam while the others charged at him. Julian braced himself for their rush as she began to fall from the sky. The impact of her weight falling onto one of the vampire's backs knocked him down; his face pressed into the ground as she raised her stake above her head and drove it through his back. Two of the others split off to go at her while the other three continued to hone in on him.

Unwilling to lose sight of her, Julian stepped to the side. The men circled with him, but the other ones continued their rush at Quinn. The knife she whipped through the air buried itself to the hilt in the throat of one of the men running toward her. Blood burst from his neck; his hands scrabbled at the knife as he fell away from her.

Quinn spun to the side and swung her arm out as the other vampire tried to attack her. She drove the stake in her hand deeply into his chest and ducked the arm swinging toward her that would have knocked her over. Placing her foot against his hip, she pulled her stake free as she shoved the man remorselessly away from her.

One of the men who had been stalking him spun toward her. Julian leapt forward, and seizing hold of his head, jerked it harshly to the side. The breaking bone resonated through the building. Julian didn't stop until he'd wrenched the head completely around and tore it from the man's body. Dropping the head on the ground, he took out his knife and whipped it at another vampire rushing at Quinn. The knife plunging into the man's back did nothing to stop his momentum toward her.

The vamp's hands wrapped around her upper arms, but even as they did, her hands encircled his forearms. The man's mouth dropped; he jerked as he tried to break free of her grasp, but she continued to cling to him. Before his eyes, the man began to wrinkle like a prune left out in the sun. Quinn shuddered; she didn't let go of him as she absorbed more of his life force.

Drew and his cohorts' mouths dropped. Before they could spin to get away, Julian grabbed the one who still had the knife in his throat by his shirt and jerked him backward. He thrust his fist into the vampire's chest, breaking through flesh and bone to wrap his hand around the non-beating heart within.

He met the startled eyes of the vampire across from him before he wrenched vehemently backward, taking the heart with him. Dropping it to the ground, he crushed the heart beneath his foot and spun toward Drew.

The man Quinn had been holding fell in a heap upon the ground. Quinn gasped; her hand flew to her mouth as another shudder ran through her. Distracted by the life force racing through her, she didn't have enough time to get out of the way as Drew dove at her. His arms wrapped around her waist, a startled cry escaped her when they crashed to the floor and bounced across its hard surface.

Panic tore through him as he raced across the floor toward them. Drew didn't appear to be at all thrown off by what she'd done to his friend as he scrambled to get a firm purchase of her.

Recovering from the influx of life she'd sucked from the other vampire, Quinn released a rapid fire of blows into Drew's face. His nose and cheek caved from the force of her fists, but it didn't knock him free.

Grabbing hold of her hair, he lifted her head up and smashed it into the floor. A bellow of fury tore from Julian when the scent of Quinn's blood permeated the air. Her fingers tore chunks of skin away from Drew's face as he lifted her head and bashed it into the floor again. A cry escaped her; she briefly lost her purchase on his face. It was all Drew needed to strike at her.

Red suffused Julian's vision when Drew's teeth sank into her neck, and a scream of agony erupted from her. Her hands flattened against Drew's chest; Drew's body began to twitch and shake. There wasn't enough power left in her to kill Drew, or knock him free though. Drew's throat worked as he eagerly swallowed her blood.

It felt like an eternity had passed since her fight with Drew started, but it was only seconds before Julian snatched hold of his neck and jerked him backward. With a mighty heave, he flipped Drew over his shoulder and sent him flying across the room.

He crashed into the back wall with enough force to shake the building. Dust and debris rained down from the rotting and sagging ceiling, the decaying building gave a low groan but held firm. Drew slid down the wall to land on his head. Julian's muscles rippled as his lips skimmed back to reveal his fangs.

Quinn scrambled to her feet behind him. Her skin was whiter than normal, but she was steady on her feet. "Are you ok?" he demanded.

"Yes." She wiped the blood away from the already healing tears in her neck.

Julian stalked forward as Drew started to get his bearings. Before he could get back to his feet, Julian flew at him, lifted him up and slammed him into the wall again. His lips twisted into a leering grin, his hand traced over Drew's chest and stopped over his heart. Drew squirmed within his grasp; his feet kicked against the wall.

"I am far more than a hundred years older than you," Julian murmured as he began to push his hand leisurely into Drew's chest. Drew's mouth dropped, strangled sounds escaped him as his ribcage began to cave in. His hands tore and beat at Julian's arm, but he barely felt any of it. "That was your first mistake. Your second mistake was touching her." Drew's cries became more fervent, his legs kicked rapidly against the wall as

Julian mercilessly inched his hand forward at an excruciatingly slow pace. "Your *biggest* mistake was harming her."

Drew's ribs gave way completely, leaving the tender flesh of his heart exposed. Julian smiled grimly at him; his hand encircled Drew's heart and he gave a gentle tug. There was no color left in Drew's face; his mouth opened and closed as rapidly as a baby bird's looking for food.

Julian leaned closer to him and gave another subtle tug on the heart; coldness engulfed his body as he continued to toy with Drew. This was the part of himself he'd been trying to keep under control for the past two years. This awful, merciless piece of himself that relished in the thrill of death and missed the torment he'd once gleefully handed out.

There was no burying it again now. Now it had been set free to do as it pleased. He relished in the freedom that came with finally allowing this sinister piece of himself to rule again. Drew's eyes rolled back in his head as Julian crushed his heart within his chest and tore it free. It hadn't taken anywhere near as much time as he would have liked it to, but he wasn't going to expose Quinn to anymore brutality than necessary. He callously dropped the heart on the floor and stared down at it.

Bracing himself for what he'd see from her; he turned guardedly toward her. He didn't think he could stand it if she looked at him with disgust or fear. Lifting his head, he met her gaze. He'd expected to see revulsion in her eyes, but it wasn't reflected there.

Instead, he saw an understanding and acceptance of what he was, what he could do. His skin felt alive, the thirst for more blood and death pulsed through him in waves he was certain were going to bury him. She hadn't turned against him now, but if he returned to the vampire he'd been, she would. She was too good for that, too good for *him*.

Even still, all he craved was to touch her right now. He didn't understand how he knew it, but she could calm him. She could ease this swamping feeling of barely controlled destruction pulsating through him.

He took a step toward her, but the low moan of the last beaten vampire on the floor drew his attention. Julian's bloodlust notched up again. There was one more to be destroyed before he could go to her. The beaten vampire released a hysterical laugh as he stared at Quinn.

"What's so funny?" Julian snarled.

He rapidly strode forward and stopped in front of the man on the ground. The man didn't notice him as his eyes remained on Quinn. Julian knelt down and grabbed hold of the man's chin, jerking it toward him. "*What* is so funny?"

The man still wouldn't look at him. "Vampires have been looking all over for her... and I didn't realize... it was Quinn," he got out in between hitching bouts of laughter broken up by wracking waves of coughing. The blood pooling in the man's mouth from his internal injuries sprayed outward and dribbled down his chin.

Julian turned toward Quinn; she looked as confused as he felt. Moving closer, she studied the filthy, bruised and swollen face of the man lying on the ground. Then, her forehead cleared and her mouth dropped.

"Seanix?" she gasped.

"I'm a little different now," the man giggled.

"What happened to you?"

"I think that's fairly obvious," he said with another manic laugh. "The same as you."

"When? How?"

"A couple of years ago. I was on a truck run in Alabama when I got jumped by a group of guys. I woke up later as this *thing*."

Quinn's hand pressed against her mouth as she gazed at the man in sorrow. "I'm sorry," she whispered.

Chuckles rolled through Seanix, he wiped at his mouth but only succeeded in smearing blood from one side of his face to the other. His eyes flashed from red to brown and back again as tears began to roll down his cheeks. Julian almost thrust the disturbed man away from him, but he found even he couldn't be so cruel to the pathetic vamp.

"I don't think Seanix made it through the transition with his mind still completely intact." Julian had already known Chris, Melissa, Zach, Lou and Luther had arrived before Chris had spoken.

He didn't turn to look at them when he replied, "It happens sometimes, the trauma of it can destroy an already fragile mind."

Seanix began to laugh louder, his arms wrapped around his belly as his laughter shook his slender frame and more blood sprayed from his mouth. Julian released his shirt and moved away in order to avoid the spray.

"I'd thought we'd missed all the fun," Melissa said dryly as she stepped over a body. "But apparently this guy is a barrel of laughs."

"Yeah." Julian ran his fingers through his hair as he studied the man before him. It felt cruel to kill someone who so obviously wasn't all there, but Seanix couldn't be allowed to live either, not in this condition.

"If I'd known it was Quinn they were looking for I would have told them. They would have let me have Angie if I had!" Seanix burst out through his fits of laughter and sobbing.

Any sympathy Julian felt for the man vanished. His hand shot out and wrapped around his throat as he shoved him into the ground. "What do you mean by that?" he snarled.

His anger didn't break through to Seanix as he continued to chuckle like a clown high on pot. "They wouldn't let me have Angie, wouldn't let me turn her, wouldn't let me near her. They told me lookie but no touchie. They said I was too young, they said I had to earn her, but they would bring her here, tease me with her, and let me know what I could have if I brought them people and helped them to find *the* vampire. The one of the prophecy. They wouldn't let me touch Angie; they'd sit her there, just beyond my grasp, and then they would take her away again. Then, when they realized you were in town." His eyes fell on Julian. "They said I couldn't see her anymore. As awful as it was to have her here, it was far worse not to be able to see her."

"Oh, Seanix," Quinn breathed as she stepped forward and knelt at his side.

Julian went to grab her hand, afraid to let her anywhere near this man after what he'd just said, but she shot him a look and shook her head. Julian's upper lip curled into a sneer; he kept his eyes focused on the man, ready to tear off his head if he so much as twitched in her direction. Ignoring the blood, Quinn rested her hand comfortingly on his cheek.

"I wouldn't have wanted them to hurt you Quinn, but I missed her *so* much." His laughter had completely vanished, now only sobs shook his slender frame. "I would have given anything to be able to touch her one more time. I loved her with everything I am."

"Shh, I know," Quinn said soothingly. "She loves you very much too. She's missed you terribly over the years."

"She would have stopped loving me if she ever remembered what they made her witness here. I would have done anything to get her away from them, even…"

"Turn me over if you'd known," Quinn finished when he closed his eyes and curled into a tighter ball.

"Yes," he moaned.

"Who is looking for me?"

"All of them are. All of the vampires believe you're the key to taking their power back. They won't stop. They will find you. No matter where you go, they won't stop until they find you."

A shiver of dread swept down Julian's spine, he pressed closer to Quinn as his gaze shot over the building. Scully's group and this group of vampires vanishing from this area wasn't going to help keep her hidden, but then vampires were never known to stay in one area for long. Settling somewhere for too much time was a good way to get discovered and killed. If either group had been in contact with other vampires, outside of their tight nest, it was more than likely that neither group would be giving a daily update of their locations.

It would be best if he could talk her into leaving, but he doubted she would relent and he didn't know where he would take her. Canada was out, as long as someone hunted her, he couldn't take her there and risk putting the young Hunters and Guardians in jeopardy.

"Do they think I'm in this area of the country?" Quinn asked nervously.

"As far as I know they're not sure where you are, exactly." Quinn's shoulders slumped; she rubbed Seanix's arm reassuringly. "We came here a month ago; they discovered my only picture of Angie right before then, and thought it would be fun to meet her."

Choking sobs wracked him. "Oh Angie," he moaned. "I tried to convince them she meant nothing to me, but they knew I still loved her, and they made us both pay for that love."

"Seanix…" Quinn whispered but the man continued to speak over her.

"The prophecy is spreading around the vampire community like wildfire. Whoever finds you is going to have a lot of power to force those to do their will. They'll have a bargaining chip no one has had these past couple of years."

Another reason why vampires had to be monitored more closely, Julian decided. He'd always hated the prophecies that traveled throughout the vampire community. Someone would have a vision, and some of the others amongst them would run with it until it was almost unrecognizable from its original spoken words, but the general gist would still be there. These prophecies, rare though they were, could get the vampires riled up and cause a lot of chaos.

There had been one issued by a fledgling Seer, four hundred years ago, who had proclaimed the humans would wipe out the vampire race within the year. Many vampires hadn't believed it was possible, but the ones who did worked themselves into a frenzy and created turmoil amongst the community. They became more careless in their kills, more relentless in their pursuit of humans and in doing so they had threatened to expose all vampires.

The Elders had eventually managed to stamp it out and had killed the Seer who issued the prophecy. It had been doubtful she'd ever had the vision to begin with, and was believed she'd had a bone to pick with the human race.

Whoever had received this vision had seen enough to reveal at least part of Quinn's ability, and the momentum behind the prophecy was growing amongst the community he'd excommunicated himself from. A community he may have to infiltrate again in order to keep Quinn safe.

He believed in what they'd been doing these past couple of years. However, they'd been more focused on trying to find more Hunters and Guardians and get them to safety so they could be trained. Instead of being trained to kill every vampire they came across like they had in the past, they were now learning to differentiate between those vampires who were killers and those who weren't.

They'd mistakenly assumed this would be enough protection, but there weren't enough Hunters and Guardians left in the world, and it would take more time for them to rebuild their population than it would for the vampires to rebuild theirs.

Someone had to put a stop to it; he just wasn't sure how to go about doing so without getting them all killed.

"Do you know the exact wording of this prophecy?" Julian inquired in a gruff voice.

Seanix's eyes rolled toward him; Julian saw the growing insanity within their depths. "A vampire, not born of vampire blood, will burn like the sun the life from anyone she touches. If used correctly, she will become our greatest ally, our savior."

Quinn shuddered beside him. Julian rested his hand reassuringly on her arm, but he could still feel the tremors running through her. Seanix's gaze fell to the body Quinn had sucked the life from. "He may not be a pile of ashes, but I'd say the life was burned from him."

"They're certain it's a female?" Julian inquired.

"Yes," Seanix answered.

"Shit!" he hissed.

"Shit is right," Seanix said. "They're a bunch of brutal bastards. It's a stupid prophecy. How could you not be born of our blood, Quinn?" The maniacal laughter escaping him echoed through the spacious building and more blood spurted from his mouth.

"Seanix, please stop," Quinn urged. "We'll take you to see Angie, but you'll have to be calmer when we do."

Julian bristled over her words, his fangs pricked as he turned to look at her. This man couldn't be allowed to live; he'd already stated he would do whatever it took to get to Angie, including handing Quinn over.

He would do whatever it took to keep Quinn safe, including killing Seanix, and if it made her mad at him then so be it.

"She's dead, Quinn." Julian froze at Seanix's sober words. "They killed her."

"No, she's at the bar…" Quinn's voice trailed off, her mouth parted as she seemed to realize that the gunfire could have easily pierced through the wall and into the bathroom. "She went in the bathroom." She spun toward Julian. "She's fine!"

Julian grabbed hold of her hand when her eyes took on the feral look of an animal backed into a corner. Red began to seep into her irises as tears pooled in her eyes. "Easy," he coaxed as his fingers stroked over the back of her hand.

"No, she's not fine," Seanix murmured. "She's dead. I felt it when she left me."

"Seanix, I'm so sorry. We'll get you out of here…"

"No," he whispered. "There's nothing left for me. Please don't make me leave here, please don't make me live anymore."

"Seanix…"

"Angie was his mate, Quinn. They may not have had the chance to solidify the bond, but it was still there," Julian said kindly in realization. His hand wrapped more firmly around hers as he tried to make her understand. "The vampires here must have suspected something along those lines too and used it to torment him. There's no life for him anymore, not without her." A tear slid down her face as her head bowed.

"Let me go to sleep Quinn, please," Seanix begged.

She brushed back a strand of his filthy brown hair and tucked it behind his ear. "She loved you so much, Seanix. She was lost without you."

"I was lost without her too," he murmured. Quinn tenderly wiped away the tears rolling down his face, cleaning it of the dirt caked to his cheeks. "I want to sleep."

"You will," she promised. Julian expected her to step away and leave him to deal with it. He moved forward, but she turned toward him instead. "Do you mind?" Confused by the question, he frowned at her. Then he looked at their entwined hands as she lifted them off the ground. "I don't have enough energy left in me to do this on my own."

His eyes flew back to hers. "You don't have to do this. I'll take care of it."

"No, it should be me. I'm his friend. I owe him this, but I need your help to do it."

"Whatever you need," he answered honestly.

She brushed aside another strand of Seanix's hair before resting her hand on his cheek. "If you don't fight it won't hurt." Seanix nodded and curled into a ball. "Sleep now; you'll see Angie again soon."

A prickling began in Julian's hand. It wasn't unpleasant, but he could feel her drawing on his life force to pull the soul from Seanix. Seanix's eyes closed, his mouth parted as a look of peace came over his face. "Tired," he murmured.

"I know," she whispered as her fingers slid over his cheek. "It's almost over."

A smile curved Seanix's mouth making him appear almost childlike. The tingling sensation in Julian's hand began to ease; warmth spread through his fingers and up his arm. He realized the life that had been taken from him was now being returned.

Seanix's body didn't shrivel up like the others, but he felt it when the life within the vampire slipped away. His power swelled within him as the force of Seanix's life coursed through his veins charging him like liquid lightning. The force inside him made him stronger, but he couldn't think about that as Quinn's heartbroken gaze met his.

Leaning forward, he encircled his hand around her head and pulled her against his chest. No more tears spilled from her, but her arms wrapped around his back as she clung to him. The others shuffled out of the room while he rocked her back and forth within his arms. He didn't care what he had to do, who he had to kill, he would do whatever it took to keep her safe, forever.

CHAPTER 21

Red and blue lights flashed off of the glass littering the ground like some kind of macabre funhouse from Hell. It made Quinn's eyes throb and her head pound. She wrapped her arms around herself as she stared at Clint's bar.

Pieces of wood had been torn from the front by the force of the bullets that had pierced the building. Glass and wood crunched under foot as police officers rushed about. An ambulance was parked off to the side but the backdoors remained closed and no medical equipment had been taken out. Its silent presence here made her feel even more hollow and deflated than she had before.

"Quinn!" She lifted her head at her shouted name.

Her eyes searched the people gathered solemnly behind the yellow tape set up as a boundary around the bar. She didn't actually see Clint coming toward her, but more the people he shoved out of his way as he made his way through the crowd. He was three people away from her when she finally spotted his squat figure.

She didn't have time to speak before he threw his arms around her and engulfed her in a bear hug forceful enough to crack her knotted back. "Dear God girl, we had no idea where you were! Are you ok?"

"What happened?" she squeaked out when he dropped her on her feet again.

"Someone…" Clint's brown eyes filled with tears; he hastily wiped them away. "Someone shot up the bar."

"What? Why?" She felt like the lowest form of life lying to friend, and the worst actress in the world, but he couldn't know she'd actually been inside when the bar had been shot up.

"I don't know," he said with a sad shake of his head.

Hawtie was crying openly when she stepped up behind Clint and threw her arms around Quinn. "We were so afraid you were inside!" she wailed.

Quinn swallowed before issuing the lie they'd come up with while she and Julian had been ridding themselves of their bloodstained clothes at her place, after disposing of all the bodies in the abandoned building. The vampire's bodies would disappear at sunset, the others they had buried in a mass grave with only a stone to mark it. She hated leaving those innocent women and children like that, but they couldn't allow their bodies to be discovered.

"Angie let me leave early so we could go out," she said with a wave of her hand toward Julian, Melissa, Chris, and Zach. Behind him, she could see Luther and Lou pretending to stroll over from the motel, seemingly drawn on by curiosity.

"At least there was one blessing tonight!" Hawtie declared as she enveloped Quinn in a hug again.

"Where's Angie?" she forced herself to ask around the lump wedged in her throat.

Hawtie's breasts heaved as tears streamed down her face. "Oh, Quinn, it's just awful!" she wailed.

"Let her go, Hawtie," Clint said kindly. "You're scaring her." Hawtie released her but kept hold of her hand in a vice like grip that bruised her bones. Clint clasped hold of her shoulders and began to speak. "I'm sorry Quinn, but she was inside when they started shooting. She didn't survive."

Even though she'd already known this news, tears spilled from her eyes and her shoulders heaved as a sob escaped her. Her lying skills may be questionable, but her sorrow was real.

Julian stepped forward, pulled her away from Clint and into his arms again. Quinn held onto him as she watched the police move in and out of the building. Hawtie glanced down at Clint when he took hold of her hand and turned to face the building again. More tears fell when Angie's body was finally placed on a gurney and wheeled outside.

Looking to shut out the world, she buried her face in Julian's chest. She wasn't allowed to stay hidden there for long before the police came to speak with them. More lies spilled from her mouth, she answered their questions but thankfully they seemed to believe the lies. They stared questioningly at Julian; he responded to the few questions they had for him with unflinching ease.

With the sun about to break on the horizon, they were finally allowed to leave with the promise they wouldn't go anywhere for a couple of weeks in case the police had any more questions for them. Exhaustion made her eyes heavy and grainy. Her muscles felt like lead when she finally crawled into bed that morning.

As the week wore on, she realized her original exhaustion was nothing compared to what she felt throughout the following days. The killers hunting her town had been taken care of, but there were more questions to endure from the cops, Angie's wake to attend, and Clint's bar to clean and rebuild when they were finally allowed to go inside the building again. She kept trying to pick up the scattered pieces of her life, but none of them fit together right anymore.

She'd lost the closest friend she'd had since Betsy died. She'd believed she'd closed off the piece of herself susceptible to grief over the years, she'd been wrong. This wasn't the same kind of grief that had crippled her after the loss of her family, but she missed her friend. She missed Angie's eager chatter, easygoing ways and perky smile.

The only heartening thought was that maybe Angie and Seanix were finally together again. After the events of that horrible night, she understood Angie's melancholy and erratic behavior better after Seanix disappeared, thanks to Julian's explanation of mates. Angie and Seanix had been human when they'd first met, but they'd been soul mates. Seanix's feelings for her had been enhanced by his change into one of the undead.

The bar wasn't the same without Angie, and it would never be the same again. In those early days after Angie's death, she wondered if Clint would reopen at all. They all walked around in a haze of melancholy, barely speaking as they tried to put the place back together. She didn't know who had been the one to clean up Angie's blood, and she didn't ask.

On the day of Angie's funeral, she sat in her window and listened to the vehicles driving by on the street below. She would have given anything to be able to attend, but bursting into flames in front of everyone wasn't exactly an option.

With the pathetic excuse of, she didn't do funerals to Clint and Hawtie, she'd ungracefully bowed out of going. She'd sent flowers, like that would somehow make it any better considering Angie had no family left in town. The disappointment on Clint and Hawtie's faces had been obvious when she'd refused to go. She hated it, but there was nothing she could do about it.

Starting into the third week, Clint decided to reopen the doors of the bar. He did have bills to pay after all, and the place had been in his family for over fifty years. Quinn had been certain she'd never be able to make it through her first shift, but somehow she persevered.

One thing she'd learned from the death of her family was that no matter how badly she desired the world to stop, if only for a minute to acknowledge her misery, it never did. The world had an insistent way of continuing on without any knowledge of the small piece that had been lost, forever.

People also had a way of continuing on when they didn't think they could, simply because they had to. She'd lost another friend, she was grieving again, but she fell back into her routine.

During the whole awful time, Julian's steadfast presence was the only thing getting her through. He stayed by her side, but never made another move toward her. She didn't know if she was thankful for this or disappointed. The last thing she wanted was to come to care for him even more, only to lose him like she did everyone else, but she missed his touch and his kisses.

She hadn't believed it would ever be possible, but she even missed his banter and arrogant attitude.

She didn't understand what had brought about this change in him, and she didn't ask. Instead, she continued on almost robotically as they all talked about the threat against her and the peril of the vampires grouping together and becoming more powerful.

To her, it was the same threat she'd been living with her whole life. She had to keep who she was a secret, that information and situation was nothing new. Luther and Julian were far more concerned about it than she thought necessary.

On her first night off since Angie's death and Clint's reopening, she lounged on the couch while munching on peanut butter cups and watching Dexter. She'd assumed the blood and gore of the show would turn her off after what had happened in the abandoned building, but she found him rather likeable, for a serial killer.

A knock on her door caused her to groan. The last thing she felt like doing was moving her ass from this couch, but as another knock sounded, she realized she didn't have a choice. She shoved the rest of her peanut butter cup into her mouth and chomped on it as she approached the door.

"Who is it?" she asked around a mouthful of food.

"It's Julian."

"Why didn't you just use your key?" she grumbled.

"Open the door."

"Pain in my ass," she mumbled as she threw the locks on the door and pulled it open.

Julian leaned against her doorway with his arms folded over his broad chest. His blond hair had been brushed back to emphasize the chiseled planes of his face. Arctic blue eyes gleamed as they slid over her from head to toe. He looked stunning in a midnight blue t-shirt that hugged his broad chest and the bulging muscles of his biceps. The jeans he wore fit him well and emphasized his taut ass.

"Come on, Dewdrop, get dressed."

She glanced down at her favorite, faded red t-shirt and black yoga pants. This was about as dressed as she planned to get for the evening. "I am dressed."

"Put on something you'll wear out."

"It's not red carpet material, but I have no shame in rocking it around town," she retorted.

He smiled as he stood away from her doorframe. "How about you stop being difficult and put on something without holes in it." She opened her mouth to protest; he rested his hands on her shoulders, cutting her off. "Please. For me."

Her lips compressed but she knew she couldn't argue with that. "Ok, but do you mind telling me what this is all about?"

"After you get dressed, I promise."

He gave her a little nudge toward her bedroom door. She shot him a disgruntled look over her shoulder as she walked into her room. Digging through her closet, she had no idea what she was going to put on. He'd looked as deadly as the seven sins standing in her doorway; she didn't own anything close to matching that.

Finally, she settled on her favorite pair of jeans and a black cowl neck sweater that made her eyes stand out. A small chuckle escaped her as she realized it was the first time she'd thought about her eyes standing out in six years. She brushed her hair hastily and returned to the living room. He still stood casually in her doorway, but his eyes lit up when he spotted her.

She couldn't help but feel pleased as his gaze raked her from head to toe, and the cocky smile she'd missed over the past few weeks slid into place. She'd told herself she was glad he'd backed off of her; she didn't need any more hurt in her life, but she realized now she'd been lying to herself.

"Come," he said.

She took hold of the hand he extended to her. He locked the apartment before turning away and leading her down the hallway. Her confusion deepened when instead of going downstairs, he went up the stairs at the end of the hall. They climbed past the third floor hall and up to the door leading to the roof.

"What's going on?" she inquired.

"You'll see."

He opened the door to the roof and held it open for her to walk out ahead of him. About twenty feet away was a blanket with two small candles sitting in the middle of it. The small flames of the candles danced and flickered in the air. Beside the blanket, an already open bottle of champagne was chilling in a bucket of ice.

Her brow furrowed as she turned toward him. "What is this?"

"This," he said with a gesture toward the blanket. "Is our first date."

Her mouth dropped open. "What?"

"Before everything happened you stated we hadn't been on a date yet. It's time to remedy that."

She would have laughed if she hadn't been so amazed. "And this is your idea of a first date?" she teased.

"In case you haven't noticed this is a pretty small town, you don't even have a movie theatre. Unless you'd like to return to the movie theatre gaming hall?"

"No."

"I didn't think you'd want to spend the night hanging out at Clint's or Hawtie's."

"Not at all."

"And since neither of us eat food, I didn't see the point in trying to find some fancy restaurant. I will take you to a movie tonight, if you'd prefer?"

"You'll sit through a movie?"

"I love the movies." He cocked his head to the side and gave her a devilish grin. "You have to find new things to enjoy when you've been alive for as long as I have."

"I suppose you do," she replied with a laugh.

"Would you prefer to go to the movies?"

Her gaze drifted back to the blanket; she smiled as she shook her head. "No. This is perfect for my first date."

"*Your* first date?" he inquired with a quirk of his eyebrow.

"I dated a boy in high school for a few months, he was really nice, but we didn't go on *dates* so to speak. We hung out at our friend's houses, drove around in his car, or went on group outings to places like the movies and bowling."

"Well then," he said as he held his arm out to her. She chuckled as she slid her arm through his, and he led her to the blanket. "This can be *both* of our first dates."

She almost tripped over her feet when she turned toward him. "You've never been on a date before?" she blurted in disbelief.

He laughed as he settled her onto the blanket. "Not *technically*. Most of the time I spent with my exes had little to do with dating."

The bluntness of his words left her momentarily speechless, or perhaps it wasn't the bluntness, but the unexpected burst of jealousy that tore through her and shook her frame. The idea of him with another woman made her want to claw someone's eyes out.

"I don't want to know," she muttered.

"There are far better things to talk about." He poured her a glass of champagne and handed it to her. "Besides, that's more like tenth date talk, so we can discuss it then."

"You think there will be a tenth date?" she inquired as she sipped at her champagne.

His eyes pinned her to the spot. "I *know* there will be." The heat his gaze aroused in her caused her toes to curl. She had to look away from him in order to gather her scattered thoughts. Staring across the rooftop, she focused on the endless stars dancing in the night sky. The moon lit the sand, causing it to shimmer like a lake in the darkness. "I'm hoping this will lead to many firsts for us."

"Get your mind out of the gutter," she scolded.

"When it comes to you, it's almost always in the gutter, Dewdrop."

She couldn't stop the faint blush sliding up her neck and into her cheeks. "Why have you been so quiet lately then?"

"I'm an ass ninety-nine percent of the time, but even I know when to back off and allow someone to grieve."

"I don't agree with the first part of that statement, but thank you," she murmured.

"You would have a month ago."

"You're right."

He placed a kiss on her forehead. "There isn't anything I wouldn't do for you."

An ache began in the area of her heart as she leaned into him. "They're going to come for me."

"And we'll be ready for them."

"I can't take anymore death, everyone I care about dies. I don't want to lose you too."

He drank down the rest of his champagne and refilled his glass. "I'm more difficult to kill than a cockroach on steroids and a thousand times faster. You won't lose me."

"You can't know that."

"Yes, I can. No one will get to you, or anyone else, while I'm here. And I have *no* intention of going anywhere, ever."

The promise within his words caused her to gulp as she swirled the liquid in her glass. She finished it off and handed it back to him to refill for her.

"What did Seanix mean by a vampire, not born of vampire blood?" she asked. "I was born from a vampire so wouldn't that technically mean I was born of vampire blood."

"No. You weren't entirely human, but you were born more human than vampire. When you made the change, vampire blood didn't turn you, not in the way it has *always* turned someone. Face it Dewdrop, you're something special."

"Is that a good thing or a bad thing?"

"Oh, believe me, it's a very good thing." The way he purred the words caused her body to tense and her lips to tingle with the urge to kiss him. "Now, enough of the depressing talk. This is our first date, and I intend to try and take advantage of you."

A burst of laughter escaped her. "I never thought it possible, but I missed this about you."

"Do you want me to go and get the lotion?"

"That sounds more like a hundredth date kind of thing," she teased.

"Guess we're going to have at least three dates a day then." He placed his glass down and held his arms out to her. "Come here."

She went eagerly to him. He enfolded her within his powerful embrace when she curled up against his chest. Serenity slid through her as she stared out at the town and desert. The monsters who had been hiding amongst their community and killing innocents were dead, but there were still bigger dangers out there. Coming for her.

Maybe she should feel fear about what was out there, but she found it impossible to do so in his arms. This kind of a relationship was the last thing she'd ever wanted in her life, but as his lips nuzzled her temple and her heart swelled, she came to realize she was falling in love with this man.

The words were on the tip of her tongue to utter, she found herself unable to speak them. Still raw from Angie's death, she couldn't expose herself in such a way right now. If he didn't say it back, her already bruised heart would be trampled.

"Quinn," he murmured against her ear.

"Hmm?"

"I'm not going to let anything hurt you. I'll do everything it takes to keep you safe."

She rested her hand upon his cheek when she turned toward him. This small bit of peace wouldn't last, not for them, but for now the town was safe and they had each other. It was more than she'd ever hoped for in her shattered life.

"I know."

***

Julian searched her striking eyes. He didn't think she completely understood what he was saying to her, but she would. There wasn't anything he wouldn't do to keep her out of danger.

He'd promised himself two years ago he'd never allow the monster within to take control of him again, but he would joyfully give in to his evil nature again in order to keep her alive. He was fully prepared to do so; he just hoped everyone else was prepared for it when the time came. If anyone could handle it, Quinn could.

She wasn't malicious, but she understood sometimes they had to do things they didn't want to; she'd proven that when she'd put Seanix out of his misery. She may not completely approve of it, but she accepted his more malevolent nature; she'd shown that when she hadn't turned away from him after watching him take such pleasure in killing Drew. He had to make sure he didn't go so far as to push her away in the end, but he would do that too if it meant keeping her on this earth.

Until then, he was going to enjoy every peaceful minute he could get with this woman. They wouldn't get too many more quiet moments together. Brushing back a strand of her chocolate hair, he cupped her cheek and pulled her closer to him. He was beginning to suspect she may mean far more to him than he'd ever realized, but he wasn't ready to delve into the possibility of her being his mate, not yet.

Her eyes closed as he tilted her head back and kissed her until she went limp in his arms and his control was beginning to unravel. He'd like nothing more than to lay her down on the blanket and lose himself in her, but she was still shaken from Angie's death, and he knew she wasn't ready for it. Reluctantly, he broke off the kiss, pulled her into his lap and cradled her within his arms. They didn't speak as they watched the stars and listened to the sounds of the night.

The candles had burned out, dawn was approaching when her eyes drifted closed, and she fell asleep still curled within his arms. He stared down at the lashes brushing against her cheeks and the scars marring her porcelain skin.

Hard fought battle wounds, he thought as he brushed his fingers over them.

"I love you, Quinn," he murmured.

It didn't matter that she didn't hear him, what mattered was he'd finally admitted it to himself. What mattered was he'd meant the words and that this woman could be *his*. For the first time in his lengthy life he was in love with someone he could give his heart to, and who was actually capable of loving him back.

No matter how hard she tried to hide it, he knew she cared for him too. He didn't need his ability to know that. All he needed was the knowledge that with everything she knew about him, and had witnessed, she still trusted him enough to kiss him, touch him and to have fallen asleep right now.

His fingers paused on her lips. He bent his head to kiss her again before rising fluidly to his feet. Walking over to the stairs, he carried her inside as the sun's rays started to rise on a new day. One he hoped remained peaceful, but he knew with each new day the threat against her loomed ever closer. When that day came, he would be standing beside this woman, and he would be prepared for it.

The End

Look for Book 2 in the Fire & Ice Series coming soon!

If you haven't read it yet, you can also get more of Julian in The Kindred Series.

Where to find the Author

Mailing list for Erica Stevens and Brenda K. Davies Updates:
http://visitor.r20.constantcontact.com/d.jsp?llr=unrjpk
sab&p=oi&m=1119190566324&sit=4ixqcchjb&f=eb6
260af-2711-4728-9722-9b3031d00681

Facebook page: www.facebook.com/ericastevens679

Facebook friend request:
www.facebook.com/erica.stevens.7543

Book Club:
www.facebook.com/groups/545587248917267/

Website: https://ericastevensauthor.com/home.html

Blog: http://ericasteven.blogspot.com/

Twitter: @EricaStevensGCP

About the Author

My name is not really Erica Stevens, it is a pen name that I chose in memory of two amazing friends lost too soon, I do however live in Mass with my wonderful husband and our puppy Loki. I have a large and crazy family that I fit in well with. I am thankful every day for the love and laughter they have brought to my life. I have always loved to write and am an avid reader.

58073588R00158

Made in the USA
Lexington, KY
02 December 2016